UNDISPUTED

BESTSELLING AUTHORS

AIMEE NICOLE WALKER
NICHOLAS BELLA

OTHER BOOKS BY AIMEE NICOLE WALKER

Only You

The Fated Hearts Series

Curl Up and Dye Mysteries

OTHER BOOKS BY NICHOLAS BELLA

Cobra: The Gay Vigilante Series

The New Haven Series

Demon Gate Series

DEDICATION

To Carly Stuurman,
For believing in us!

CHAPTER ONE

Animacio De Niro

WE DANCED AROUND THE OCTAGON SHAPED ARENA, CIRCLING each other like two wild animals. My eyes remained locked with his as I sized him up. He was a decent enough rival, even getting in a few blows, but I was more than prepared for this fight. Quite frankly, I felt certain he was outmatched. We inched closer and closer, and the roar of the enthusiastic crowd hit a new peak that was almost deafening. You could practically taste the energy the audience was giving off; I, for damn sure, could feel it pulsating though my body, charging me up for this bout.

The mat was already stained with the blood of the fighters who had taken to the ring before us, and both my opponent and I added a few more drops to it. My nose was bleeding, but not broken. His was broken and the cut over his eye was going to need at least several stitches. Both of our fists were up as we kept our legs ready for action.

The referee moved around us but stayed out of harm's way, which was wise on his part. My opponent's punches lacked the precision I strived for. One more reason why he wasn't ready to take me on.

I smirked as the bead of sweat dripped down his temple. He knew he was in over his head. Right about now, I bet Rocco was regretting stepping in the ring with me. If he didn't already, I was going to make sure he regretted it by the end of the match. There was no way in hell I was about to give up my championship belt, especially since I'd just won the damn thing. He came at me, lunging with a sloppy punch, but I dodged it and put some more space between us. He was getting tired and would be making more mistakes like that one. My chest heaved with anticipation as I looked at Rocco, who was panting from exhaustion.

He charged me, which was exactly what I wanted him to do. My defensive and offensive game was tight and I knew how to capitalize on the slipups of my opponents. I used his momentum, locking him in a hold, then flipped him over until I was on top. He held up his arms, blocking his face from my blows, but I wasn't letting up. I hit his side, and when he went to protect his flank, I gave him a right hook to his temple, then followed that up with a body blow to his ribs.

"Arg!" he grunted as one of his ribs broke from the impact of my fist striking its target.

Again, I aimed for his sore ribs, hitting them with another blow. He lowered his guard on his face in order to protect his ribs and that was when I switched it up, giving a short jab to his nose. He grabbed my left arm, twisting it in an attempt to put me in a hold and gain the advantage, but I turned in the same direction, keeping my place on top of him. I raised up, kneeing him in his injured ribs twice, really giving them a bruising.

He was weakening, tired and sore from the blows I had dealt out like candy on Halloween. I had plenty to share with Rocco and, by the pained look in his eyes, I knew he wasn't about to last much longer. I used my free hand to jab at his ribs again and when he left himself open to protect them, I gave him another sharp jab to his face and that blow knocked him the hell out. I followed it up with two more blows before the referee pulled me off his ass.

I stood up, growling like a beast in my adrenaline-fueled state. I was so hyped! The referee checked my opponent over, then declared him KO'd. I raised my hands in victory as I jumped around the ring, soaking in the praises from a well-entertained crowd. Everyone loved a winner and I loved winning. I spit out my mouthpiece so I could roar to the crowd as I continued to thrust my arms in the air victoriously. Championship defended by sheer badassness. Mission accomplished.

My head coach entered the arena along with my sparring team, and they rushed me, wrapping their arms around me as I continued to celebrate. I hugged them as we cheered and gave my coach a kiss on his temple, because lord knew he was part of the reason why I was standing there victorious. The other part was my sheer will to want to be on top. The flashing lights of the cameras were almost blinding, but I knew better how not to focus on the lights, only the crowd as they stood up in their seats, cheering and applauding. Of course, there were some assholes booing, too. Dumb fucks shouldn't have betted against me.

I made sure to absorb all the praise like a sponge before I finally took my ass to the locker room where some of the other guys shook my hand and gave me forced congratulations. Every last one of them in my division wanted to be where I was… on top with the belt around my waist. Fucking shark tank full of opportunistic jocks.

"Congrats, man, great fucking match," Tony Maddock said as he patted me on my back.

"Thanks, man," I replied with a smirk. Tony lost his chance to get the belt from then Champion, Richie "The Bulldog" Swartz, three months ago. No doubt, his eyes were still focused on obtaining the gold, so his praise was bullshit in my eyes. He probably watched it thinking he could take me the entire time. The sport of Mixed Martial Arts was a dog-eat-dog competition and everyone was fighting for the bone.

"Man, that shit was awesome! You annihilated his ass," Colt Danners said, slapping me on the back.

"I did, didn't I?" I smiled as I thought about the blow I had landed that knocked my opponent out. It was extra sweet because Rocco talked a lot of shit in the weeks leading up to our match, saying I was too young and inexperienced to take him on. Well, that motherfucker ain't got shit to say now.

I took off my gloves and shorts, locking them up with my belt, then made my way into the showers. The water felt so good on my skin, washing away all the sweat and blood from my body, making me feel refreshed. I finished bathing and walked out with a towel around my waist. I knew the press was waiting like a pack of carnivorous dogs to talk to me. I fucking hated the press, damn vultures. I slipped on a pair of black jeans, my boots, and my white v-neck t-shirt.

No sooner had I laced up my boots when the dressing room doors opened and my head coach and manager, Barry Vincennes, walked over, slapping me on the back. "Damn good match, Macio."

I smiled. "Thanks." I hugged him again and saw my publicist walking into the room.

"Are you ready for the post-fight conference?" Rupert asked me.

I really hated those fucking things, but it was part of my job, so I nodded. "Yeah, let's get this shit over with."

"Good. Remember, if you feel yourself getting agitated, just give shorter answers. Be honest, that's the best you can do," Rupert said, giving me pointers.

"Sure," I said.

We walked to the area where the conference was being held. As soon as I walked into the room, cameras flashed their lights, causing me to blink a little as the photogs captured their images of me looking sexy and grand with my championship belt tossed over my shoulder. I sat down and removed my belt, placing it on the table beside me. I rested my hands on the table, lacing my fingers together. The pose I gave meant I was ready for their insipid questions.

"Macio, how does it feel to win tonight's match?" one of the reporters asked.

A stupid fucking question. *How do you think I feel, dumbass?* That was what I wanted to say. However, my publicist, Rupert, would have had a fucking fit. He'd been trying to clean up my image a bit so I could get more endorsements. So, I went the diplomatic route... well, as diplomatic as I could be.

"It feels great," I replied, keeping my answers short and sweet, since I was already agitated. I'd rather be heading back to my hotel right then instead of sitting there fulfilling this obligation.

"Mr. De Niro, was there any point in your match tonight where you thought you might not win?" another asked.

I snorted. "No."

I'd been told that my short answers infuriated the media, but I could care less. Fuck them. Of course, Rupert cringed whenever someone shoved a microphone in my face because he never knew what I was going to say at the spur of the moment. I once told a reporter who'd had the nerve to ask about my sex life to go fuck herself. Rupert and Barry both told me that was unwise. I hated having to watch what I said, but business was business.

"Mr. De Niro, what do you say to people who think you're too young to hold the title?" one of them asked.

I smirked. "Remind me again, who's the champion?" I shot back. To that remark, there were some chuckles and murmuring. People, especially the other fighters, tended to give me shit because I was twenty-four and cocky. As far as I was concerned, I'd earned the right to be.

"Mr. De Niro, is there anyone in the circuit you think can be your equal?" came another silly ass question from a reporter with a nose too big for his face.

"No," I said, without needing to think about it. Some might say I was a smug son of a bitch and I needed to be brought down a peg or two, but I say, fuck them. I worked my ass off to get where I was and I'd already beat my way through the competition. So, no, I had no equal. I knew it, and all the fighters in the dressing room knew it, too.

"Mr. De Niro, will you attempt to lower your weight so you can compete in a lower class?"

I shook my head. "I hate cutting weight. Where I am now is where I want to be. I don't have any intentions of seeking a championship belt in a lower weight class. That's a stupid fucking question."

"Okay, what about a higher class? Super heavyweight?" was the second part to his question.

I shrugged one shoulder. "Like I said, right now, I'm happy where I'm at." I wasn't opposed to competing in the heavyweight division, but right now, I was content.

"Are you going to celebrate your victory with anyone special?" A female reporter asked.

I rolled my eyes. "It won't be you," I snapped. Out of the corner of my eye, I saw Rupert giving me the cut-off signal in his attempt to put out a fire I just started, because my last comment got the room buzzing, so I nodded. "No more questions, please. I'm tired and just want to relax."

I hated doing interviews, no matter the venue. Of course, it came with the job, so I dealt with it. I picked up my belt and made my way out of the room even as the vultures continued squawking for more answers to their bullshit, stupid-ass questions. Of course, there were more vultures outside, but I walked past them as I made my way to the waiting limousine.

"Fucking hate reporters," I grumbled as I settled into the comfortable leather seat.

"Yeah, I know you do, but you handled yourself well... for the most part," Rupert said with a chuckle.

"Why can't they ever ask intelligent questions? It's all about looking for shit they can make a scandal out of," I complained, rolling my eyes.

"Well, saying you don't have any competition in the circuit sure gave them what they were looking for," Barry stated.

I scoffed. "It's the truth."

"Still, bring it down a notch, buddy," Barry said. "Hubris has been the downfall of many who thought they stood above it."

I tossed him a look and he gave me that stern stare I still got from my father when he was disappointed in me. It meant Barry was serious and not just giving me advice I could give or take. He wanted me to take this advice.

"Fine, Barry… I'll try to be more humble. I see feelings need to be spared and all," I shot back.

"Smart ass." Barry shook his head. "Don't party too hard tonight, buddy. You've got early training tomorrow. 6 a.m., I mean it."

I nodded. I was used to early training days, even when I partied hard the night before. I could always make it and kick ass. "I'll be there."

"Good."

"Speaking of reporters and interviews, you have one tomorrow afternoon," Rupert added.

I frowned. "With who?"

"Ringside Magazine. They want to do an editorial on the man who's the youngest MMA champion in Extreme Titan Combat history."

"Ugh, I don't want to do any in-depth interviews. I don't like how they always want to pry," I fussed.

"You've been putting this off long enough, Macio. Now, I've managed to filter through the many requests we've received to one that you would be prudent to accept," Rupert said.

"Ringside Magazine is *the* number one media outlet in the world of sports. You get an editorial with them and you can see your fame skyrocket," Barry said.

I looked out of the window at all the lights from the strip. Las Vegas was truly a city that never slept, but it came to life at night.

Whores, drunkards, thieves, gamblers, tourists, you name it... they were walking the streets. But that wasn't what was on my mind. I loved being champion. I most certainly loved the money that came along with being not only one of the best fighters in the country, but also the champion. My endorsement game was on point and looking pretty as fuck.

Michaelson's Sports were even talking about making a pair of gloves with my name on them. They wanted me on the design team and I'd be getting some of the profits too. When I heard that, I told Rupert to jump on the deal. Far be it from me to turn down good money. So yeah, I liked the big bucks and the adoration of the crowd. What I didn't like was the fame. The extra scrutiny and bitch ass paparazzi hanging out in trees, behind garbage cans and bushes, trying to get snapshots of me. That, I could live without.

"I'm not looking to be more famous, Rupert," I said.

"If you want more endorsements, you need to put yourself out there, Champ. You're bad shit in the arena, we all know that, but one day you're going to need to retire and you don't want to be broke when that day comes," Rupert stated. "I mean, have you seen what happens to many MMA fighters? Injuries alone could put you out of work, then what? Capitalize while you can."

I turned back to him and huffed. "Fine. What time is this fucking interview and who's the interviewer?"

"Two in the afternoon, and the interviewer is Aiden James," Rupert replied.

"Time is good. It'll be after my training."

"During, buddy. I'm going to work the shit out of you tomorrow," Barry said.

I groaned. "Really, Barry? I'm starting at six in the morning."

"And you'll be ending when I say so. You want to keep that belt around your waist? Well, you need to stay on top of your game," Barry said.

I laughed and nodded. I loved the training, hated the

weight-watching. Sometimes you just wanted that fucking juicy-ass triple cheese burger with the applewood-smoked bacon. God, I wanted that burger so bad, but Barry had me on a heartless strict diet and regiment. I was going to be sore as fuck by tomorrow night, for sure.

"Getting back to what I was saying, the most significant aspect about this interview is the interviewer," Rupert interjected.

"What's so significant about him?" I asked.

"Are you kidding? You need to read more, Macio. Aiden James is one of the top reporters in the business. He gets the stories most of those vultures would sell their souls for. Everyone he's done an interview with has been at the top of their game, and with the exposure they received from his editorials, it's boosted them into huge endorsement rackets, even movie and book deals."

Rupert was seeing nothing but dollar signs right then. More money for me meant more money for him. Being popular meant a loss in privacy… and I valued my fucking privacy.

"Don't think I want to do any movie or book deals," I said.

Rupert snorted. "Don't squash it yet, but keep your options open. First things first, do the interview. I'll swing by tomorrow around one to do a mock interview with you just to make sure you're feeling comfortable."

I chuckled. "More like you want to make sure I don't get out of line with him."

Rupert laughed. "Yeah, well, you're right. This is a step in the right direction."

I saw the lights of my hotel approaching and I was relieved to soon be free of this conversation. "Sure, Rupert."

"Don't worry, we have a little something something for you in your room. Something to take the edge off and celebrate with," Barry said.

I looked at him and smiled. "Well now, that's more like it." I hugged both men as I climbed out of the limo. Of course, the paparazzi were there, mixed in with the other media reporters. Everyone wanted a piece of me and they tossed questions at me like women tossed their panties; and just like how I did with them, I kept walking, ignoring the blitz. I entered my hotel, which blessedly didn't allow them to follow, and made my way to the elevator.

I had the penthouse suite, twenty-five hundred a night. Pricey as fuck, but worth it for the luxury and the privacy it provided. I slid my key card in the slot, opened the door, and entered. My suite was beautiful, if I may say so. Dining room, living room, two bedrooms, with one being the master. Two baths and a private Jacuzzi on the balcony. There was also a gorgeous pool table, and two fifty-inch screen TVs in both bedrooms and a seventy-five-inch TV in the living room. Perfect size for watching the replay of tonight's fight.

I tossed my card on the dining room table as I walked towards the master bedroom. I stopped dead in my tracks when I opened the door and laid my eyes on the very naked man lounging on my bed with a bow on his right ass cheek.

"Welcome home, Champ," he purred with lips I was looking forward to seeing wrapped around my cock.

I smiled and tossed my jacket onto the chair by the window. Barry and Rupert always looked out for me, and I appreciated that. Lord knows, busting a few loads was exactly what I needed after the night I'd had. I pulled my shirt over my head, tossing it without a care, and approached the bed. The guy crawled over to me, rising on his knees as he wrapped his arms around my neck. He was cute; brown hair, gray eyes, and a swimmer's build, so I knew he worked out. He had a nice-looking ass, too. I couldn't wait to plow it.

"I saw the fight. You looked so sexy taking down Rocco Sanders. I've been so excited for you to get back here so I could suck the cock of the champion," he said, grinning.

I smirked. "Yeah, I bet. I hope you ate your Wheaties this morning, because I'm about to wear your ass out."

He looked at my muscular, tattooed chest and his grin grew wider. "I love a man with tats and a nipple piercing."

I smiled. "You do, eh? Well, why don't you show me how much you love my tats by licking each one."

"I'll do whatever you want, baby. You've got me for the next three hours."

Good, because I was going to need every second. Time to have a little fun.

I woke up in an empty bed, something I was used to. The escort sated my needs and left after four hours. He gave me one hour free because I fucked his brains out like the stallion I was. I rolled over and looked at my alarm clock, only to see I woke up with five minutes to spare before the alarm would go off. Well, I could sit back and claim those pitiful minutes or just get my ass out of bed.

Ahhhh, fuck it. I shut the alarm off and climbed out of the bed, making my way to the bathroom. Fifteen minutes later, I was toweling off and slipping on a pair of sweats and a hoodie. I tied my sneakers up, then headed out the door with my duffle bag. My motorcycle was parked right where I'd left it, but unfortunately, I was greeted by some son of a bitch with a camera.

"Pretty brief interview you gave at the conference, Macio. Care to elaborate on your amazing victory?" he asked.

I ignored him as I tossed my duffle bag over my back and climbed onto my hog, starting the engine. "Go fuck yourself," I snapped, then took off. It was assholes like him that made me want to keep what little privacy I had. Last thing I needed was some paparazzi bitch snapping pics of me kissing a dude. That kind of shit didn't go over too well in the testosterone-laden world of professional MMA fighting. It was one of the reasons I steered clear of relationships. I couldn't afford to be in one, especially not when I was on top of my game like I was now.

I made it to the gym where I'd been training for my fight for the past week and parked my hog. As soon as I entered the damn gym,

Barry was on me, telling me to drop and give him twenty.

"Damn, Barry. Don't I get a warm up?" I asked, setting down my duffle bag.

"This is your warm up. Get those muscles pumping, then we'll do some stretches. Go on, knock 'em out," Barry commanded like a good drill sergeant.

I didn't bother to argue any longer and just dropped to the floor, knocking out the twenty push-ups. Yeah, this was about to be a very long day.

I was sweating like a pig on a spit by the time Rupert came in to give me some pointers on my upcoming interview with What's-His-Face. Barry told me to take a break, so I guzzled down what seemed like a gallon of Gatorade.

"You're late," I said to Rupert when he took a seat next to mine.

"Yeah, I know… traffic was a bitch. He'll be here in less than ten minutes, remember to keep your cool."

"I hope he doesn't ask me any stupid fucking questions," I said, taking another sip of my drink.

"Be smart about this, Macio. If you want to become one of the highest paid fighters in not only ETC history, but in MMA history, you'll need to market yourself. Appeal to the crowds, make yourself a commodity the company will back. The more popular you are, the more money you'll make and the bigger an asset you'll become. You're young, buddy, but you have to start learning how to play your cards right. This is Vegas, baby, and big game players run this shit," Rupert explained.

As much as I didn't want my privacy violated, I knew I couldn't be squared away for life and be a hermit at the same time. He was right. "Yeah, I got you. I'll play nice."

He nodded and released a sigh of what I thought was relief.

"Good, because that's him right behind you."

I turned to see some preppy looking guy in a light blue, button down shirt and tan khakis with brown loafers. He was approaching me with a walk that was full of confidence. I guess if you could wear those shoes, you had to have some balls on you. Still, as far as reporters went, he wasn't what I was expecting. As a matter of fact, he was kind of hot. He was shorter than I was and had a nice swimmer's build from what I could tell under his dork clothes. Brown hair, blue eyes that held me in their gaze as he drew closer, and his lips… yeah… I loved his lips. They had a place in this world and would be better suited around my cock. As much as I dreaded interviews, I was starting to look forward to this one.

CHAPTER TWO

Aiden James

IT WAS THE BIGGEST INTERVIEW OF MY CAREER AND I WAS A HOT fucking mess. I might've looked calm, cool, and collected on the outside, but on the inside, I shook like a Chihuahua. Animacio De Niro was known for hating the media and gave one-on-one interviews to no one; in fact, I believed I was his first. My heartrate accelerated to a ridiculous level at the thought of being his first *anything*.

The man was sheer perfection in my mind with his tall, muscular body, black-as-night hair, and dark brown eyes. The intimidating scowl that was practically a permanent fixture on his face didn't take away from his looks; it enhanced them. He reminded me of a gladiator when he took to the ring – ruthless, bloodthirsty, and sexy as fuck. Watching him move around the ring with sweat and blood glistening on his skin was much better than watching gay porn. And that growl… I didn't know how many times I had heard that growl in my mind while jerking off.

Crushing on straight men wasn't my thing and I usually made it a rule to not file them away in my spank bank memory because it was pointless. It took me many years to get to the point where I walked tall and proud as a gay man, instead of hiding who I was. I refused to waste time on guys who would never return my feelings. Macio was the one exception to my rule.

The smell of sweat and hot male bodies hit me hard the minute I stepped into the gym. *Nirvana.* I refused to close my eyes and breathe it in because I wanted to be taken seriously. After my "coming out" article went live the prior month, I anticipated being excluded from a lot of interviews, especially in the testosterone-laden world of MMA fighting. Sure, I had received some rejections to my interview requests, but not as many as I had expected. I almost didn't send the email to Animacio's publicist, but I decided no risk meant no reward.

I knew I had been well and truly rewarded when Macio's dark eyes locked on mine and I realized I would get to spend thirty minutes with his attention focused solely on me. Fuck, he was the sexiest man alive. He was the kind of guy who, with one look, made you want to drop down to your knees and worship his cock. Yeah, I decided not to try that with him unless I wanted to lose all my teeth. I saved that fantasy for later when I was alone. *Don't pop wood in the gym. Don't pop wood in the gym.* They were sage words to live by.

"Ah, Mr. James," the publicist, Rupert, said. "It's nice to meet you in person." The man extended his hand to me and offered a warm smile that didn't quite mask his nervousness. Why was he nervous? Did he think I'd say or do something to offend Macio or was he concerned that Macio would grunt out his typical one or two word replies? I had plenty of experience working with athletes that I had dubbed the Three R's – reticent, reluctant, and resentful. I was confident I could get Macio to open up to me.

"It's good to meet you too, Rupert." I turned and looked into the darkest brown eyes I'd ever seen. I thought they were beautiful in pictures and on television, but I hadn't been prepared for their intensity in person. "Thank you for honoring me with this interview, Mr. De Niro." His response was a slight nod and a grunt.

"We'll be using Barry's office for the interview," Rupert told Macio. The stern look Rupert gave Macio almost made me laugh. It couldn't be more obvious that Macio was being forced to do the interview, which didn't bode well for me.

I followed behind the two men, telling myself not to stare at Macio's tight ass or imagine the way his muscular thighs would feel between mine. I reminded myself I was there to interview the king of the Three R's. *Focus, dumbass, and not on his physical attributes.*

"Here we are," Rupert said. "It's a little messy, but it will afford us the privacy we need." *A little messy?* It looked like a bomb had gone off inside the ten by fifteen room.

"Uh, yeah, this is great." Beggars couldn't be choosers and I took what I could get.

Macio took a seat in one of the chairs facing the desk while Rupert stood in the corner. My options were the chair next to Macio or Barry's chair behind the desk. I chose Barry's chair out of self-preservation.

I began unpacking my messenger bag and set the contents on top of Barry's disaster for a desk. It was a good damn thing I wasn't a germophobe or the interview would've been over before it started.

"What's that?" Macio asked. The deep, gravelly timbre of his voice sent my pulse racing and my dirty mind spinning. *Damn, what must his voice sound like when he was aroused?* Macio picked up my small recorder from the desk and held it up in his hand. "What are you planning to do with this?"

I didn't appreciate his confrontational tone of voice or the way he narrowed his eyes in suspicion. "I record my interviews and play them back when I write my articles. I assure you that it's a normal practice, Macio."

"Mr. De Niro," he corrected. "You haven't earned the right or respect to use my first name, let alone my nickname." I saw Rupert rub

UNDISPUTED

a hand over his face as he released a frustrated sigh.

Okay, so the interview got off to a horrible start. "My apologies." I used a contrite tone, one I didn't feel, to get the interview back on track. "Mr. De Niro, sir." I ignored the scowl *Mr. De Niro* sent me and pulled up my phone to look at the questions I had saved in my notes.

"No pictures."

I looked up from my phone, then turned it around so he could see I was looking at my notes and not getting ready to snap his picture. Damn, but the dude was paranoid. "Rupert has already provided an approved image to use with the article," I replied patiently. "Are you ready?" I nodded at the recording device in his hand. "You can be in charge of the recorder if it makes you more comfortable. If I ask or say something you don't like, then you can shut it off and we can discuss it before we turn it back on and resume the interview."

"Fair enough," Macio replied reluctantly. He pushed the record button and set it on the desk in front of him.

I planned on starting with easier questions to make him comfortable. "How'd you come by the nickname 'The Hitman'?"

"They line them up, I take them out," he said flatly.

I looked at him to see if he was going to expand on his answer and continued when it was obvious he had no intention of doing so. "At what age did you start fighting competitively?"

Macio leaned forward and shut off the recorder. *Already?* "Why is that relevant? All that matters is that I'm the best fighter in the world. That's all people need to know."

"Macio, we talked about this." Rupert's tone of voice sounded fatherly and affectionate. "Aiden isn't your enemy. He voluntarily submitted his list of interview questions to me so that we'd know he wasn't looking to do some sleazy exposé on you. If he asks a single question that wasn't on the list, then I'll shut this interview down myself."

"You did that?" he asked me. "Why?"

"I've interviewed many high-profile athletes since joining Ringside Magazine. Many of them were extremely private individuals and were reluctant to sit down with me. Submitting the questions beforehand made them feel more comfortable." I was surprised to learn that Rupert hadn't shared the list with Macio prior to the interview. My warm, friendly smile was met with skepticism. "Look, the world would like to know more about you, but that doesn't mean you need to slit your wrists and bleed for them. Just give them a brief glimpse into your life; a glimpse that you control. That's the opportunity I'm giving you."

"They'll just want to know more," Macio countered.

"If you're lucky," Rupert said from the corner. "Can you just give the guy a chance, kid?"

Macio's answer was to push play on my recorder. "I started fighting on the MMA circuit when I turned eighteen."

"But you were fighting prior to that?" I asked.

"I started fighting when I was a skinny elementary school kid who was tired of getting picked on. An older boy in my neighborhood taught me a few moves so I could defend myself. I got really good at fighting and I liked the way I felt when I won. I wouldn't say that I started trouble just to get into a fight, but I never backed away from it. Coach witnessed one of my fights and saw the potential in me. He gave me a business card and told me to stop by his gym to see him." Macio shrugged. "I guess you could say the rest is history."

I felt a sudden burst of adrenaline rushing through my system and mentally punched a fist into the air. It was a huge fucking deal that he told me something he'd never told another reporter. I decided to reward him with an easy question. "What would Animacio De Niro eat on a diet cheat day, if he could have one?" I detected a slight titling at the corner of his mouth and vowed to see a full-fledged smile by the end of the interview.

"Depends on my mood," he replied. "Today, it would be a medium-rare steak, king crab legs with tons of melted butter, baked potato with butter and sour cream, an endless supply of good bread, and cheesecake for dessert."

"Damn, that sounds good," I heard myself say. I wasn't talking about food; I was imagining melted butter running down Macio's hand and him licking it clean. Macio cleared his throat and I snapped out of my daydream. I jerked my eyes up to meet his and wondered about the change I saw in his gaze. The intensity was still there, but something else was present that I couldn't quite name.

"Next question," Macio said, getting back to business. "I have hours of training left today."

"How long do you train each day?" I asked.

"Until I'm finished," was his surly reply. Rupert let out a deep sigh from the corner and the stubborn fighter turned to face him. It appeared that the two men carried on a silent conversation between them in a matter of seconds. Macio turned back to face me and said, "On non-fight weeks, I can train up to six hours a day. I mix it up between cardio, weights, and sparring. During fight weeks, I focus on technique so I can save my legs for the ring."

I jotted down a few things in my notebook and felt his penetrating stare on me the whole time. I expected him to snatch it out of my hands to see what was written, but he didn't. "What kind of music does 'The Hitman' listen to prior to a fight or while training to get him pumped up?"

"Metal music. No light and fluffy bullshit."

"Not a Belieber, huh?" I wasn't sure where that remark came from and wished I could take it back the moment it slipped out.

Macio shut off the recorder forcefully. "Believer of what?" he asked in confusion.

"Belieber," I repeated, putting an emphasis on the second b. "It means a Justin Bieber fan."

Macio looked at Rupert for help and only received a shrug, then he turned back to face me. "Who the fuck is that?"

I was shocked he didn't know who Justin Bieber was. *He must live at the damn gym.* "He's a hip hop singer. The exact opposite of a metal band," I explained. "It was a joke; a very poor one."

He turned the recorder back on. "Next question." His voice had gone from irritated to downright disgusted in a flash.

"What are your plans after you retire from fighting?" I asked.

"Ask me that when I announce I'm retiring." He looked at Rupert once more and asked, "You approved these questions?"

"There's nothing wrong with them," Rupert replied.

"I'm twenty-fucking-four years old. Retirement isn't even a blip on my radar yet." Macio turned back to me. "Next."

"What are your hobbies?"

"I don't have hobbies. Fighting is my life," he said tersely.

"And when you're not fighting?" I prodded.

"Training."

"Okay." I could see that line of questioning wasn't going anywhere at all. "Are you in a relationship with anyone?" That question wasn't on the approved list and I expected Rupert to call me out, but he didn't. It was met with a death glare from Macio, however, so I wisely decided to move on and steer clear of that topic. "Batman or Superman?" A smile spread slowly across his face and I nearly jumped up out of the chair to do a victory dance.

"Superman," he said incredulously. "Batman doesn't have any super powers beyond a super large balance in his checkbook." He looked at me suspiciously and asked, "Are you one of those bat freaks?"

"I'm a journalist," I said, as if that explained everything. "Team Superman all the way."

Our eyes held, and for once, I caught a glimpse of the real man behind the façade, but it was gone so fast, I thought I had imagined it. I was about to ask another question, but Barry appeared in the doorway with an expression that meant business.

"Playtime is over, kid."

"This has been more like torture than playtime," Macio told his coach.

I tried not to take his comment personally as I shut off the recorder and began putting my stuff back in my messenger bag. I knew coming in that he hated interviews, so what the hell had I expected? It felt like I was pulling teeth when I tried to get answers out of him, so it probably had felt like a bad trip to the dentist to him.

Rupert came over and slapped me on my back as I rose to my feet. "Don't take Macio personally, Aiden."

I felt Macio's eyes on me and looked down at him. "No offense taken."

"I've been a fan of your work for a long time," Rupert said, pulling my attention back to him. "I thought your coming out article was brave and well-written."

"Thank you, Rupert." I didn't know the man, but for some reason, his kind words meant a lot to me.

Macio stood up from his chair. "You're gay?"

I couldn't tell if his tone was one of disgust or surprise, nor could I decipher his thoughts when our eyes met again. I found myself standing taller in his presence, even though I had no reason to cower. I loved who I was and the journey I took to get to the point where I could say that about myself. "I am." I held his gaze, daring him to say something homophobic or cruel. Animacio De Niro could totally kick my ass, but I'd be damned if I backed down to anyone ever again.

As if he had just realized that all eyes were on him, he extended his right hand across the desk to me. "It was nice meeting you, Aiden."

I accepted his offer and hoped like hell he didn't see the tremor that rippled through my body when his skin touched mine. "It's Mr. James," I corrected. "You haven't earned the right or respect to use my first name."

The shocked look on his face put a little extra sway in my hips as I walked my happy ass out of there. I had been told on many occasions that I loved to have the last word, and it was mostly true. I hoped like hell they weren't the last words I ever spoke to Macio.

CHAPTER THREE

Macio

THAT LITTLE SEXY MOTHERFUCKER WALKED HIS ASS OUT OF Barry's office like he owned the place. The fact that he'd tossed my own words back in my face wasn't lost on me. Hell, in fact, I respected him for it. I was used to a lot of guys talking shit at me, none have been able to back it up since the sixth grade. But there was something about Aiden—I mean, Mr. James, which sparked my interest in more than just his comebacks. I mean, I thought he was just some stuffy ass, dorky fucking reporter who wanted to pry into my life. But his questions didn't come off as too prying, except the one question he asked that I never answered.

"Are you dating anyone?" Why did that always seem to matter to people? Shit, I was twenty-four fucking years old. I wasn't looking to be tied down to one person anyway. I was in the prime of my career and I had lots of oats to sow. Still, I was having a hard time focusing on the interview because I couldn't take my eyes off his mouth and his perfect teeth. I wanted to see those sexy, plump lips of his sucking down the length of my shaft, and then I wanted those white teeth of his to give me a little nibble on my head. My cock was hard during the entire interview and I was actually thanking god for the cup I was wearing. It kept my little contender in his place.

But what damn near floored me was the fact that he was gay. I would have pegged him as some preppy straight dude, one of those metrosexuals who probably prided himself on being smarter than jocks. Well, it looked like he was some preppy gay dude that, while smart, I could tell—didn't seem to lord it over me. I took that into consideration. Out of all of the reporters I've had the misfortunate of meeting… he wasn't so bad.

"Stop day dreaming and get your ass in gear. You're sparring with Mike," Barry said.

"Sure," I replied as I adjusted the strap on my gloves, tightening it.

"See, I told you it was going to be painless," Rupert said, coming up behind me as we exited the office.

"You approved the question about who I'm dating? You know I hate that one," I questioned.

He shook his head, holding up his arms. "That one, he snuck in there."

I cocked an eyebrow. "Oh, and what happened to you stopping the interview if that happened? I was kind of pissed about that, Rupert. You were supposed to have my back."

"Jesus Christ, kid, it's a harmless question. Don't be so uptight. I'm your publicist, my job is to make you more marketable. I mean, look at you," he stood back and gestured towards my body, "You're a vision of male masculinity. Men want to be you and women want to be fucked by you. Knowing if you're available or not plays into their fantasy. That makes you more popular. You're young, yes, but tomorrow isn't promised to anyone." He grabbed the back of my head. "Learn how to seize the day. Jump on the opportunities that come your way or risk regretting it. I'm only looking out for you, buddy."

Ah, shit… maybe he was right about that, too. My level of expertise was in the ring. All I wanted to focus on was winning my next fight. I knew very little about the promotional part of the business. "Okay, Rupert. What should I say if I'm asked that question again?"

"Be honest. Tell them you're single and enjoying life," he suggested. "That satisfies everyone's curiosity and leaves you open for the women to fantasize about being your girl one day."

I scoffed. "Yeah, like that's going to ever happen."

He smirked. "They don't need to know that. You're your own brand, my boy. And now is the perfect time to expand on that."

"If you two are done talking business over there, I need to get my buddy in the ring," Barry called from across the gym. He was leaning against the ring and Mike was inside, flexing and warming up for our sparring match.

"Here I come," I said as I jogged over there, sliding under the rope. "I hope you're ready for this ass whooping I'm about to give you," I taunted Mike.

He laughed as he slipped in his mouth guard. "Bring it," he shot back with muffled words.

We danced around each other for a few seconds, sizing each other up, and then I went in and delivered the blows. For me, it wasn't just a sparring match, it was a real one and I had to win. Mike was one of the few trainers that seemed to really get me and he didn't cry like a bitch the way Eddie and Luke did when I got too aggressive.

Barry gave me pointers as I overtook Mike, landing knees and elbows to his pad-protected extremities. I was on fire and seemed to be burning with a lot of pent up energy I thought I would have extinguished last night with the escort. However, meeting Aiden had seemed to stoke the flames inside of me. I wanted to see him again… maybe we could do another interview. Or maybe—no way could I get involved with someone from the media. That just invited trouble.

"Watch out!" Barry screamed right before Mike landed a blow to my jaw.

Mike tried to follow that up, but I got back on my game, grabbing his arm when he went to jab and taking him down in a triangle armbar hold. He tapped out a second later and I let him go. Both of us rose and punched our hands together before giving each other a hug.

"What in the fuck was that all about?" Barry asked. "You completely let your guard down. That's not a mistake I'm expecting to see a champion make."

"It won't happen again," I apologized. No way was I going to admit that my mind had been on the luscious ass of Aiden James as he walked out of Barry's office or how glorious he'd feel beneath me with my cock inside of him, bringing us both to the height of ecstasy.

"It better not happen again," Barry said. "Okay, round two."

Yeah, this was going to be a long day of training.

My body was sore from the kick ass workout Barry had put me through, but sitting in the private sauna in my hotel room gym was relaxing my muscles. I unwrapped my towel, exposing my nakedness to the steam. I thought back to the interview, or more importantly, the interviewer. Shit, why couldn't I get this guy off my mind? It wasn't like he was the first hot guy I'd ever seen. He wasn't even the only guy who I had let get the last word in on me. Of course, with those other guys, I'd let them talk themselves into a hole I would bury them in come fight night.

I couldn't put my finger on why I couldn't get Aiden out of my head. Shit, he wasn't even the first guy I wanted to fuck that was out of my range... Was he out of my range, though? God his mouth was something I was going to see in my dreams. I wanted to kiss him so badly during that interview just to see if his lips were as sweet as they looked. My hand slid down my stomach, sliding over my sweat-slicked abs until my fingers wrapped around my nine inches of solid steel. I started stroking my cock as I imagined my hand being Aiden's mouth.

"Ahhhhh," I moaned as my fingers grazed my Prince Albert piercing. I played with my pierced nipple as I worked myself into a nice little sexual frenzy. Ooooh shit, it felt fantastic. The only thing that would make me feel better was actually being inside Aiden. That little bastard somehow put his claws in me and I didn't know how, or if I even wanted, to take them out.

"Ahhh fuck!" I panted. I was so close. My hips pumped up in time with my hand as my fist beat my shaft hard and fast. My cock grew stiffer and fatter in my hand and my toes curled as the tingling in my balls intensified. "Ahhhhh! Shit!" I belted out as my cum squirted from my slit, landing on the floor. I quaked as I continued to milk my dick until the last drop, then I fell back exhausted, my hands dropping to my sides.

"Jesus," I huffed as I regained some of my strength. I hoped doing that would help me get him out of my mind. If that didn't work, I didn't know what would. I stood up and used the towel to clean my hand off, then I tossed it on the floor, wiping up my cum. Of course, I left the towel on the floor and walked out of the sauna and into my hotel room. The coolness of my room was heaven on my heated flesh and I threw myself on the bed, relishing it. I wasn't sleepy, so I turned on the television. Commercials. I fucking hated commercials. I flipped through the channels and stopped when I saw Aiden's face.

Ah shit, I didn't need this, but I couldn't turn the damn channel. I turned the volume up to hear what he was talking about. He was being interviewed by David Horner on a recorded episode of the Sport's Today talk show about coming out in such a big and controversial way.

"My intention was not to create controversy, but to set myself free. Maybe my story could inspire others in this business to be who they are," Aiden said.

"So, you think athletes are afraid to come out if they're gay?"

David Horner asked.

Aiden seemed to think about it and then he nodded. "I do. The field of sports in general is such a testosterone-laden business where it's believed that only the strongest and manliest of them all is considered a real athlete. It's a very homophobic business, unfortunately."

"What do you say about critics who claim that it's easier for a sports reporter to come out than an athlete, therefore your revelation wasn't much of a risk?"

"Every coming out story has its own level of risk, David. It's never easy to expose yourself to the world and say, 'hey, this is me.' Many have been rejected, left homeless, lost jobs. Those critics have no idea the strength it takes to be true to oneself," Aiden said.

I watched him take on a different kind of challenge and he was knocking out his opponent the way I taken out mine in the ring. Only he was fighting a battle I… I couldn't. I had to stay in the shadows with only a few hours of comfort from men who were paid to spend some time with me. My life, though successful, was empty. I envied Aiden for his courage and his freedom to be brave. The more I watched him on television, the more I wanted to see him again. When we touched hands for that brief moment, it was as if I had felt some kind of connection to him, but I ignored it at the time. I'd had other things on my mind during that exchange.

The more we talked, the more relaxed I became around him. I liked that Superman was his favorite hero too. Maybe that was why I had used his first name when we shook hands goodbye. Truth be told, I was a little upset when Barry ended the interview. I kind of wanted to talk to him some more, but I guess that was Barry's way of saving me from the damn thing. I turned the channel, because looking at Aiden made me desire him more and I hated wanting things I couldn't have.

I found an action flick on one of the premium channels free of commercials and watched that. This was my last night in the hotel. The week before one of my fights, I liked to take myself out of the comfort of my home and spend it someplace unfamiliar. It meant I couldn't get too relaxed even when I stayed in the lap of luxury. It helped me keep my game tight and my mind focused. I liked the Baldwin Hotel for its privacy and the fact that it was only two miles from Barry's gym and four blocks from the arena. But if I wanted to stay wealthy, I wasn't going to spend another night there. My bags were already packed, with the exception of my jogging outfit I was going to wear tomorrow.

As I laid there enjoying the movie, my cell started ringing. With a quick check of the caller ID, I saw that it was my brother. I answered. "Hey, Bro."

"What's up? I caught your match on Pay-Per-View… couldn't you have dragged it out at least two more rounds so I could at least feel like I was getting my money's worth?" he asked with a chuckle.

I smiled. "Maybe if he hadn't talked so much shit leading up to our fight, I might have taken it a little easier on him."

My brother, Rico, snorted. "No, you wouldn't have."

"You're right, I wouldn't have."

We both laughed at that.

"So, I bet you're feeling awfully good today, defending champ," Rico said.

I sighed. "Yeah, the Light Heavyweight belt is still around my waist, so I'm feeling great. If you know Barry, then you know there's no rest for the wicked. Barry worked me to the bone in the gym today… but I enjoyed the training. Felt like I accomplished a lot. How's the wife and kids?"

"Getting on my damn nerves. You want them?"

"Hell no."

He laughed. "Speaking of, when are you going to get a pair of your own?"

"Never. I see how unhappy you are. Why would I ever want to bring that kind of misery and despair onto myself?" I joked.

I loved my sister-in-law, Macy, and niece and nephew, Melanie and Alex. Of course, like the rest of the world, he had no idea I was gay. I didn't have the kind of family that accepted that "kind of shit," as my father, Ignacio, called it. Even when I had crushes on other kids growing up, I never felt comfortable telling them about my feelings. I remembered being confused and too afraid to seek help. It wasn't until I was sixteen that I met another kid who was just like me. He was my first, and my heart broke when his family moved away. But being with him let me know I wasn't going crazy. And that my desires weren't my own, but shared by other males. That was the first time I didn't feel alone. I cherished those times.

My brother finished laughing at my joke. "Fuck you, Macio," he retorted.

"You never answered my question."

"They're good, but they miss their Uncle Macio. When do you plan on coming out here to L.A. to visit us?" he asked.

"I'll try to make some time soon. I'll let you know."

"Cool. Listen, I'm going to let you go. I'm proud of you, little bro."

I smiled. "Thanks. I'll talk to you later."

We didn't do any mushy shit like saying "I love you" because it was implied. I wasn't sure if my brother would still be proud to call me his brother if he knew that I was gay, in spite of the love we had. Sometimes love didn't conquer all… or maybe that kind of love came with too many conditions. Regardless, I never felt comfortable telling him the truth. Again, as I turned off the television to get some sleep, my thoughts drifted back to Aiden. God, why couldn't I get his very sexy and bitable ass out of my mind?

CHAPTER FOUR

Aiden

MY CELLPHONE RINGING WOKE ME UP. I SILENCED THE CALL AND rolled back over, hoping I could fall back to sleep. I had been gone from my home for two weeks straight and had flown into LAX late the night before. All I wanted in the entire fucking world was a solid seven hours of sleep. I loved my job at Ringside Magazine, but hotel hopping got old during a long tip.

Instead of leaving a voicemail, the person called right back, and I knew immediately who it was and what he wanted. "Good morning, Jerry," I said to my editor when I answered the phone.

"When are you going to turn in your interview with Animacio De Niro?" I didn't get a good morning, a hello, or a bend over and grab your ankles. Just straight to the reason for his call. Jerry Wisnowski was a brilliant reporter-turned-editor, but his people skills were lacking.

"Jerry, I already told you I didn't get enough out of him to write a story." I didn't bother disguising my frustration with him. "The coach and publicist only gave me half an hour to interview him and most of that was spent arguing with the guy over why I was asking certain questions." I slowly released a frustrated breath. I had never dealt with such an infuriating athlete since I had been hired by Ringside five years prior. "I think he answered two questions."

I thought our readers would love to know how Macio got started fighting – hell, a lot of people could relate to being bullied. Knowing the reason he liked Batman over Superman was cute and would give personality to the article, but those two things were not nearly enough. I feared I was about to do something I'd never had to do before; I was going to mark the interview off as a failure and accept that I wouldn't be writing an article about my time spent with Macio… Mr. De Niro.

"You're a writer, Aiden. Make it work." There was a flick of a lighter, followed by Jerry inhaling deeply from a cigarette. "I'm giving you one more week to come up with something. Don't let me down after I stuck my neck out for you." The call with Jerry ended as abruptly as it had begun.

I had never heard Jerry get so worked up about an interview. Other staff reporters had run into a wall like I had with Macio and weren't told to make it work. I sure as hell didn't appreciate his parting comment to me, like he'd really gone out on a limb when I wrote my article about being gay and the homophobia that existed in sports. He wanted no part of that article, but was overruled by his boss who didn't mind making a splash.

Hell, I expected an, "I told you so," out of Jerry and was shocked that I didn't get it. Jerry's problem wasn't with me being gay; I had been very open and honest about who I was from the very beginning. He just didn't want chaos in his calm, orderly newsroom. I had spent more years than I cared to remember in the closet and I wasn't going back for anyone. Jerry might've had a prickly nature, but he wasn't an unkind, cruel man. Once the decision was made to run my article, he got behind it and dared anyone to mouth off.

I couldn't figure out where in the hell he was coming from with the Macio interview. I knew it was the interview of the year, but damn. I was wide awake after that call, so I decided I might as well get up and settle in. I had a shit ton of laundry to do after being gone so long. I glanced at the clock and saw that I had slept for six hours and it would have to be enough because I was expected at my mom's house for brunch.

I zombie-walked my way to the shower, rubbing the sleep out of my eyes as I went. I liked my showers as hot as my men and barely used cold water. The heat from the water beating down on my weary body was just what I needed. My dick apparently hadn't received the memo that I was tired because it stood proudly from my body, demanding attention. Ignoring my diva of a dick wouldn't work either; it was either take care of business in the shower or suffer the consequences of discomfort all damned day.

I wrapped my hand around my cock and began stroking with the intention of making it fast, but *he* appeared as soon as I closed my eyes. My fantasies of Macio only got stronger after being only a few feet from him. Later, I'd castrate myself for jerking off with a straight guy in mind, but right then, I needed to come and thoughts of him always made that happen.

In my dreams, Macio had me in every conceivable way – on my hands and knees, beneath him, over him, against the wall… they went on and on. I dialed up my favorite that morning. I was looking down upon a large city through a wall of windows while Macio fucked me from behind. My body shook all over as the fantasy played behind my eyelids, hotter than any porn video I had ever watched. I imagined the way he'd growl in my ear as he possessively took what I so gladly offered.

It felt so real, as if I could feel his bruising grip on me as he thrust deep and long inside me. I unraveled and came all over the tile floor in my shower while fantasy me spurted all over the glass window in front of him. Seeing my spunk all over the window pushed Macio over the edge; he came hard and deep inside me.

My orgasm was so intense, I had to brace myself against the wall of the shower until I caught my breath and my legs were stable enough to support my weight. As it always did, guilt and irritation slipped in and chased away the last residue of pleasure. I berated myself for not finding another suitable fantasy, or better yet, a live person who could give me what I needed.

I just couldn't seem to get Animacio De Niro out of my head.

"My baby." My mom flung her arms around my neck the second I walked through her door. "I've missed you so much. How was your trip? Meet any hot guys?" She looked hopeful when she pulled back and it made me sad that I might have let her down in some way. I knew she hoped to see me settled by then, but it just hadn't happened yet. I never would have guessed I would still be single at nearly thirty years old.

"Not this trip," I replied.

"Well, I know the perfect man is out there for you." She looped her arm through my elbow and we walked into the living room where my two older sisters and their families had gathered.

Jessica was the oldest at thirty-four, and Brittany was the middle James sibling at thirty-two. My father, Matthew, was killed in action during the first Gulf War when I was only four years old. My mother was left to raise three kids on her own. Drucilla James was my very first hero and there was no one I admired more than her.

My sisters jumped up and greeted me like they hadn't seen me in two years rather than the two weeks I had been gone. I shook their husbands' hands and then wrestled with my nieces and nephews until we were called to the table. My mom was an amazing cook and was always trying new recipes. That morning, I was happy to see she had served up my favorites – crispy bacon, fluffy scrambled eggs, and Belgium waffles with a platter full of different toppings that would please everyone. Her kind gesture was a much-needed balm to my battered nerves.

I'd heard many people complain that it took hours to prepare a meal but only minutes to devour it. That was never true in my family. We lingered and talked about the things happening in our lives. Seldom did anyone ever eat just one plate of food and no one ever left my mom's house hungry or without leftovers for the road.

My sisters and their families left before me so they could get prepared for their upcoming work and school weeks. I just wanted a damn minute to catch my breath and spend some one-on-one time with my best gal.

"Tell me what's wrong, Aiden." Mother's intuition never failed to amaze me.

"There's nothing wrong." I tried to deny it, but the look on her face said she wasn't having it. "It's stupid, really, and not worth wasting your time."

She reached over and gave my ear a yank. "Talking to my children is never a waste of time. So, spill."

"This is ridiculous." I laid back against the couch and crossed my arms over my chest. "There's this guy that I like a lot who is unattainable for several reasons. I know that nothing will ever come between us, but I can't get him out of my mind."

"What reasons?" she asked.

"For one thing, he's straight." I released a frustrated groan. "Even if he wasn't, there would be no chance for us. We're too different."

"Don't believe the saying that opposites attract but don't last long." A wistful smile spread across her face. "Your father and I were as different as night and day, but we made one hell of a team. It was hard work," she admitted. "But what worth having isn't?"

"True, but that doesn't change the fact that he's straight and I'm gay."

"Aiden, I've never known you to fret and fantasize over a straight guy. Maybe your radar is broken."

"It's called a gaydar, Mom." I leaned my head back against the couch and laughed harder than I had in weeks.

"Whatever it's called," she said, then paused for me to laugh some more before she continued. "Yours must be broken."

"It's not; believe me." There was no way in hell that Macio was gay. I needed to accept it and move on. "What about you? Let any silver foxes catch you lately?" I asked, changing the subject. I hated that my mom was alone. It was sweet that she felt so devoted to my dad, but I doubted he would've wanted her to spend the rest of her days without love.

"Well… maybe."

I was so surprised because the answer had always been a resounding no whenever I asked her. I immediately forgot about my problems and listened to my mom talk about a handsome, widowed doctor who had come into her gallery looking for art pieces for his new home. I loved the way her cheeks blushed when she talked about him.

I ended up staying longer at her house than I normally did on a Sunday night, so it was late when I checked my email. I was shocked as hell to find that Macio had contacted me. At first, I thought it was a joke, but then realized that no one knew how bad I crushed on the man. My heart raced and I found myself holding my breath when I opened his email.

Mr. James,

I owe you an apology for the way I behaved during our interview. I just didn't want you to think I was a complete jerk.

Mr. De Niro

I must've read those two sentences ten times before I worked up the courage to respond. I agonized over every single word that I wrote.

Mr. De Niro,

I think our interview got off to a rough start, but it was heading in the right direction before we were interrupted. I understand that you are a very private man and I respect that. I just wish we'd had a little bit more time to chat.

Mr. James

I didn't expect to hear back from him, but his response was almost immediate.

Mr. James,

I noticed that our interview hadn't appeared in your magazine and figured you didn't have enough information to write a paragraph, let alone an entire article. Most journalists would've made up a bunch of shit to fill the page. I wanted to thank you for not doing that. It's okay if you call me Macio. You've earned the respect.

Macio

Holy fuck, such a simple statement shouldn't have made me so fucking happy. It changed nothing between us. I was still a gay man lusting after a straight one. Still, reading that I had earned Macio's respect meant the world to me.

Macio,

I wouldn't dream of making up a bunch of shit just to write an article. I'm not that kind of journalist, but I respect your reasons for being wary. It's okay for you to call me Aiden. You've earned the respect.

Aiden

I was certain that it would be the last I heard from him that night or any night. It was nice to get past the awkwardness we both must've felt during his interview, but I didn't expect it to lead to a grand friendship. I guess that was why his final email really rocked my world.

Aiden,

I'll be in L.A. visiting my brother this week. Perhaps we could meet up and finish the interview. I feel bad that you came to Vegas to interview me and left with nothing. It's the least I can do.

Macio

My response to him was short and sweet.

Name the place and time!

CHAPTER FIVE

Macio

THE SMILE THAT SPREAD ACROSS MY FACE WAS NICE AND WIDE when I read the words written in Aiden's email. *Name the place and time.* This wasn't easy for me to do. I just didn't open up well… to anyone, really. But there was something about Aiden that made me feel like I could tell him things and he wouldn't exploit me. The fact that he didn't write some bullshit article was a pretty good indicator that he could be trusted. It also helped that I wanted to fuck him like there was no tomorrow.

Since meeting him, I'd worn my dick out jerking off in the sauna, shower, in bed, even in the locker room, for Christ sakes! He was in my blood, flowing through my being, making me hard with just the slightest thought of his beautiful, warm smile. Or his gorgeous blue eyes with the ridiculously long eyelashes. Ah, shit… there it went again… my dick poking a tent in my sweats. I swore Aiden was like a virus I couldn't get rid of and he ran a fever through me with barely the mention of his name. I had to have him.

First things first, get the second interview. My fingers trembled over my keyboard as I prepared to type in a response. I wanted our meeting to be as private as possible. I had no idea if he lived in a house or an apartment building, but I didn't want to meet in a place with nosey neighbors. My hotel room would be best. What Aiden didn't know was that I was already in L.A. I'd taken a gamble that he'd be willing to do another interview since our first attempt was an epic failure. Not even my brother knew I was in town yet.

Rico was my excuse to escape. It wasn't easy to break away from Barry and Rupert, who were both pulling me in two different directions. Barry had worked my body hard with strength and conditioning training, which I loved. Rupert had been training me on how to conduct a proper interview and still keep myself guarded. Between the two of them, I could take on the world. At least, I felt that way.

So why in the fuck were my fingers trembling so much and I hadn't written a reply? He must be thinking I was going to punk out, but that wasn't me. I just wanted to make sure I formed the right words. There was no take backs on emails sent. Okay, here goes nothing.

I'm already in L.A., my plane flew in this afternoon. I'm staying at the Dorchester hotel. Why don't you meet me here tomorrow evening at five, in the penthouse?

I was only going to be in this hotel for one more night. It was expensive, for one thing, but once I made contact with my brother, he'd insist that I stay in his guest room. Barry gave me five days to visit family and relax... then I was to fly back and train like a gladiator. So, I was going to make the most of this visit. I scooted back, elbows resting on my knees and my hands locked as I waited to see the response from Aiden.

I will be happy to meet you tomorrow evening. And like before, if you aren't comfortable with one of my questions, we can discuss it. I don't want you to feel any pressure to answer anything you don't want to.

-Aiden.

I smiled again, then typed my reply.

I am looking forward to our interview.

-M

I shut off my laptop and walked over to the window, stepping out onto my balcony. L.A. was beautiful at night, not quite as lively as Las Vegas, but it had its own flair, no doubt. My cock was still throbbing in my pants and no amount of breathing in fresh air seemed to be helping. I was going to have to handle this erection personally. I reached down, grabbing my dick and giving it a nice squeeze, and quaked a little from the pleasure. My libido was always in overdrive and I thought the only reason I didn't get more aroused during the day was because of how much I trained.

Six days a week, twice a day between cardio, strength building, Muay Thai, Ju Jitsu, and Akido. My body was a well-oiled machine, but even after all of that, I still had energy to burn. I walked back into my hotel room, closing the balcony doors behind me. Instead of turning on a porno, I picked up one of Ringside's magazines… the one with Aiden on the cover. His coming out story. I'd read it multiple times and jerked off to his pictures at least five times. It was actually my second copy, because I pretty much ruined the first issue with spunk.

I was taking better care of this one and held it away from me as I stroked my cock. I memorized the shape of his mouth and imagined those sexy lips sucking me down whole. My muscles flexed as I stroked my cock faster and harder. It didn't take long for me to hit that moment and my mouth opened as my back arched. I tossed the magazine aside as my dick fired off its pent-up load all over the carpet, my thighs, and my hand. I quaked hard as I relished the pleasure of another release.

With the last drop oozing from my slit, I let go of my cock and just laid there on the sofa, spent… but not completely satisfied. No, I wanted the real thing, damn it… and I always went for what I wanted with extreme aggression and a take no prisoners attitude. That was why I was the undisputed champion. Oh yeah, I was really looking forward to our interview now. Ahhhh, Aiden…

Being away on vacation didn't mean I wasn't going to work out. I'd utilized the hotel gym for a few hours, working up a nice sweat, and I felt great afterward. Lunch was Tilapia, ribeye, and broccoli; after burning all those calories, I needed to refuel with a lot of protein and electrolytes. I called my brother and told him I was coming to L.A. tomorrow to visit him and the family. He, of course, was ecstatic and insisted that I stay with him in his guestroom, which I knew he would do. He also said he could pick me up from the airport. But since I was already in L.A., I told him not to trouble himself that much. That I'd take a cab. There was some debate on the necessity of a cab when he could just pick me up. It took reminding him of how much he hated the traffic at the airport to get him to give in. So, it was settled.

I looked at my watch, Aiden would be here in less than ten minutes. I was nervous, not going to lie. This was the first interview I'd ever had without Barry or Rupert there to guide me or even bail me out of it. Just one on one, like it was in the ring. I was dressed in what I normally wore when I was chilling. I felt it was best to keep the mood comfortable. So, black t-shirt and gray sweat pants it was. No socks or shoes. Being a MMA fighter, I was used to being barefoot a lot. I also did a quick breath check, all was good on that front.

I had already let the hotel reception personnel know that I was expecting a guest, and for them to simply give the reporter, Aiden James, my room info. The less hassle we had to go through, the better. I had also ordered a bit of room service in the form of a fruit platter and sangria, to which I was now munching on an apple slice as I waited. My heart began pounding the moment I heard a knock on my door.

I got up and walked over to it, peeping through the hole. It was Aiden. Okay, deep breath. I opened the door. "Hi," I said, smiling. Damn, he was fine as hell, even dressed in a gray button down shirt with a black and gray sweater vest and black slacks. Still with the loafers. He had his bag with him that I figured had all of his tools of the trade.

He smiled up at me. "Hello, Macio," he said, and his voice was as soothing as I'd remembered.

"Come in, please." I stepped out of the way to give him room to enter. I also took advantage of the view and checked out his ass again. Oh yeah, nice and plump, just the way I loved them. "Ah, you can make yourself comfortable."

"Thank you, I will," he said as he looked around my hotel. "Nice room."

"Thanks, I like the view," I said.

He turned and looked out of the balcony window and nodded. "It is a great view." He turned back to me. "So, where do you feel comfortable doing it?"

"What?" I asked.

"The interview."

"Oh, yeah. Of course. Umm, right here in the living room is good." My mind went blank… or rather, straight to the gutter when he said, "*Doing it.*" Oh, right, he was here for an interview. I motioned to the sofa and chair, letting him chose which one he wanted.

He settled down on the chair and began pulling out his recorder and his notebook. I sat on the sofa, drawing one leg up and resting my arm on my knee as I watched him. He seemed a bit more anxious this time around than the last time. It was the total opposite of our first meeting. I was feeling antsier and he looked to be in control of his emotions. Now there was a reversal, I sensed it and I wondered if he did, too.

"I took the liberty of ordering some snacks and Sangria. You're more than welcome to some," I offered, hoping to make him feel more relaxed.

He looked at the fruit and wine and smiled. "Thank you." He reached over, plucking a strawberry from the tray, and my eyes were glued to his lips as he took a bite out of the berry. When his tongue darted out to lap up the juices from the fruit, I felt my dick stir in my pants. It was fortunate that I had decided to put on my cup before he arrived. "It's very good," he said, paying compliments to the fruit.

"Yeah, it looked like it was good," I flirted, and he looked up at me with a blank, yet curious expression. I should probably dial back my lust. "So, I'm ready when you are."

"Right. Very good." He finished off the berry, wiped his fingers clean, and then picked up his recorder. "Would you like to be in control of this again?"

I nodded and took the device from him.

"Okay, are there any questions that you answered in our first interview that you'd like to elaborate on?"

I thought back to some of the questions he'd asked and decided to be a little more forthcoming with my replies. "Sure."

"Good. I'll go over them and then move on to the ones unasked. Is that all right with you?" Aiden asked.

I nodded. "Sure."

Again, he looked surprised. I guess I couldn't blame him for being that way. I was way more relaxed and open to him now than I had been when we'd first met two weeks ago. But a lot had happened since then. A lot of lusting and fact-finding and did I mention lusting? Yeah… I wasn't the same man I was then. I pushed play on the recorder and he fired away.

"How'd you come by the nickname 'The Hitman'?"

I smirked. "Because I eliminate my opponents with extreme prejudice. The promotion lines them up and I take them out. That part is still true."

Aiden smirked, then looked down at his notepad. "Many have

wondered, if you live in Vegas, why do you stay at a hotel?" He looked back up at me with those beautiful blue eyes.

"I like to stay at a hotel that is near both the arena and the gym where we all have to train a week before the event. I also like to be taken out of my comfort zone by being somewhere unfamiliar to me. It's all about convenience and getting into the right mindset to fight," I replied. I liked the little cute smile he gave me before he looked at his notepad again.

"What are some of your favorite musicians?" Aiden asked.

"I like all kinds, really. Well, except for that one guy you mentioned. I actually heard one of his songs… not my thing. I love Queen, Led Zeppelin, Korn. I like music that keeps my blood pumping when I'm working out."

Again, Aiden was looking confused, so I was curious.

"Is there something wrong?" I asked.

He looked at me with those big blue eyes. "Wrong? No… I'm just… well, to be honest, Macio, I'm just surprised by how open you're being." He held his hand up. "Not that I don't appreciate it, I do. It's just different from our first meeting. I felt like I was pulling teeth and I really don't like putting anyone in a position they aren't comfortable with."

When he said he was being honest, he meant it. I liked that he didn't try to lie and pretend that there was something else going on.

"I was uncomfortable in the first interview. I'd never done one before, and I wasn't sure what type of reporter you were. Most are scum and will sell their soul or their momma's soul for a story. They pry and exploit for their own gain. But I see you're not like that, so now you get the real Macio," I said.

He smiled and my dick stirred again. "I'm very happy you're at ease with me now, Macio."

I winked and I swore I saw him blush. "I didn't stop the recorder, but I'd like that stricken from the interview."

"Oh, yes, of course. Sorry. Don't worry, that won't be in our interview. Just the answers to my pre-approved questions," Aiden assured me, and I believed him. "What are your hobbies?"

"I was very honest on that one. With the amount of training I do, I don't have much time in my life for hobbies. But I do enjoy reading mysteries, paranormal, and horror."

"Not much for romance?"

"Can't say that I've ever experienced it."

"How sad. So, I take it there's no one special in your life?"

That was the question I had refused to answer before and I paused the recorder, which brought on a worried expression on Aiden's face.

"I'm not completely comfortable replying to this question, but I'll do my best, okay?"

His worry seemed to fade when he realized I was going to soldier on. I just needed a moment to figure out how I was going to reply. I hit the record button again once my thoughts were arranged.

"Currently, I'm single. Because of my busy schedule, there isn't much time in my life for romance or relationships. But if I ever meet that lucky girl, I hope she could love a man with only a few hours to spare in their day," I said. I'd practiced that question with Rupert and I thought I nailed it. Of course, one of the reasons why I wasn't comfortable with that question was because it was the only lie I'd told thus far. I wasn't looking for a woman, but the world couldn't know that.

Aiden nodded. "I'm sure she will," he said. If I didn't know any better, I might have detected a bit of regret, or was it jealousy, in his tone. Now, this I wanted to explore. "Did you have anyone you look up to in the MMA world? Any role models?"

I nodded. "Yeah, Kirk Winchester was an amazing fighter before he went into retirement. My coach, Barry Vincennes, had an amazing fight record before an injury shelved him. I look up to them and take my lessons from them, too. Then there's Bruce Lee, Jet Li, Jackie Chan, Donny Yen, Muhammed Ali, all amazing fighters. I could name more, but those are my favorites."

Aiden continued to ask me several more questions and they were all pretty basic, nothing too personal that would cross my lines of comfort. All in all, it was a great interview and I actually enjoyed it. However, I think I enjoyed my time with him more. I didn't want him to leave, and I put my hand on his when he reached for his recorder.

"Why don't you stay?" I asked.

His perfectly shaped brows wrinkled in confusion again as he looked at me. "Stay? I don't understand."

I licked my lips. "I think you do," I said as I lightly stroked his hand with my finger. He looked down at our hands touching, then back up to me with an even more confused expression on his face. Jesus, for a fucking reporter, he wasn't catching the clues I was tossing. I guessed I was going to have to go big or not at all.

"I don't have any more questions," he said innocently, and I swore that was the cutest fucking response.

My cock was so hard by now, it was pushing up on my cup. "I have to be honest, Aiden. One of the reasons I wanted to do this interview again is because I can't stop thinking about you."

"Huh?"

You would have thought I was speaking another language by the confused expression on his very handsome face. "I can't get you out of my head." I reached up, running my thumb over his delectable bottom lip. "The shape of your mouth. I keep imagining what it would feel like pressed against mine or wrapped around my cock."

He pulled back, eyes bulging and his mouth dropping open… which only added to my imagery. "But, but you're straight?" he gasped in shock.

I shook my head. "I've never been straight. In fact, that's the only question on your list I didn't answer truthfully to."

"Holy shit!"

I couldn't take it anymore. I grabbed him by the back of his head, pulling him forward, and planted my mouth on his. At first, he was stiff, but that vanished quickly as he leaned into me. When our tongues touched, it was like an electrical storm went off between us. God, I'd wanted to taste him so much and finally, I had him. He wrapped his arms around my shoulders and I reached down, grabbing a handful of his luscious ass.

He moaned as our tongues mingled and I was the one to break our kiss, only to plant softer kisses along his jaw as I made my way to his neck. "I want you so badly," I growled against his heated flesh.

"Oh my god, I want you too," he confessed, to my delight. I stood up, bringing him with me, and reached under his thighs, lifting him up with ease. He wrapped his legs around my waist and held on as we kissed our way to my bedroom. Once inside, I tossed him on the bed and smiled down at him. His own cock was poking a tent in his nicely pressed slacks, and boy, was it a beautiful sight. I took off my shirt and I saw his eyes glaze over as he gazed at my flesh. I made sure to flex some muscles for his viewing pleasure, then proceeded to pull my pants and jock off.

While I was doing that, he pulled his sweater vest over his head and started unbuttoning his shirt. Now that I was fully naked, I started in on his pants, giving him a helping hand. When he was as nude as I was, I stood back, drinking in his beauty. He was everything I looked for, only better. I could no longer contain my lust and was on him again, kissing and licking his chest. I sucked on his nipples as he moaned in pleasure. My hard on rubbed his thighs and I purred from the light friction. Soon, I would be inside of him. I couldn't wait. But first things first, I wanted to taste every inch of him.

"Oh my god!" Aiden panted as I dipped lower, licking and kissing his abs as I made my way towards his pulsating cock. "Holy shit," he cried out as I took him into my mouth. I reached up with my hands, playing with his nipples as I sucked on his cock. He grabbed my hands, keeping them pressed to his body as he squirmed beneath me. I savored his tasty precum as it leaked into my hungry mouth. It was as sweet as I'd imagined and I couldn't get enough of it.

My head bobbed over his crotch as I brought him to the edge. His flesh grew harder in my mouth and I knew he was about to blow.

I slid my hands to his hips, grasping him as he pumped fiercely into my mouth. It was as if he were beyond control and I loved that he was giving himself to me completely. He yelled in ecstasy as he came hard, bucking wildly as he filled my mouth with his jizz. I swallowed and sucked until he was fully drained. Aiden fell back on the bed, panting and quaking.

His well-toned chest heaved as he struggled to catch his breath, but I didn't give him much time. I flipped him over, parted those sexy buns of his, and dived in. He moaned and trembled as I tongued and lapped at his wrinkled hole. By how hard it was for me to stick my tongue inside of him, I could tell he was nice and tight. Perfect for my cock, which he would be experiencing momentarily. He was squirming again and moaning in pleasure, and the sexy sounds he was making only fueled my desire for him.

"Arrrrg," I growled as I pulled back. "I want you so fucking badly." I climbed onto the bed, pressing my chest to his back. I licked the side of his face until I reached his mouth and then I shoved my tongue inside of him in a possessive kiss. He was purring under me and I knew he wanted me inside of him just as much as I wanted to be inside of him.

I pulled back. "You want my cock?" I teased as I stroked myself between his ass cheeks.

"Yes!" Aiden panted breathlessly and without reservation.

"How badly do you wanted it?" I prodded, both literally and figuratively. By now, my precum was slicking the insides of his cheeks as my cock begin to journey closer to his hole.

"Fuck me, please. Fuck me so hard! I want to walk out of here limping!" Aiden flirted.

Well shit, that was all a man like me needed to hear. With him having said that, I couldn't hold back any longer. I had to have him. I sat back, snatching open my nightstand drawer, and grabbed the lube. I squirted a nice amount on my palm, then slathered my cock up with it and smeared some on Aiden's hole. Next, I aimed my dick and started to push in slowly, letting him get adjusted to my thick, nine inches with my pierced head. He quaked and moaned as I slid in deeper until my balls hit his cheeks.

"Ahhhh yeah, ooooohhhh, fuck," Aiden moaned and I trembled as I was inside of him. Never had I shared such intimacy with another man since my teenage years with Zachery, my first. Even that couldn't compare to what I was feeling now. I pumped my hips slowly at first, letting Aiden feel my flow, and he sighed and started begging for me to go faster and harder.

"Fuck yeah," I growled and grabbed his hips, pulling him to his knees. He raised up on his hands, bracing himself on the bed as I rode him hard. The bed shook with how hard I was fucking him and he loved every thrust. I looked in the mirror and smiled when I saw how rigid his cock was, bobbing up and down with each pump of my hips. God, he felt great! I'd never been so satisfied fucking anyone before. I was like a thirsty man being given a drink of water after days of going without. This was perfection.

I reached under him, wrapping my arms around his smaller frame, and pulled him back against my chest as I pounded his ass. His sexy mouth was open as he gasped for air. I growled in my lust, which really seemed to turn him on even more. His cock was drooling pre-cum like a leaky faucet and his nipples were hard against my arm as I held him to me. I turned his face to mine, claiming his mouth again, and he surrendered.

I was so close to shooting and I could tell he was too. I reached down, grabbing his cock, and started stroking. He was moaning and grunting as I worked him to his orgasm. I loved the way he held onto my ass as I fucked him. We were one as I brought us both to the pinnacle of ecstasy. He was the first to come, shooting thick, creamy strings of liquid pearl across my sheets as he cried out in pleasure.

"Yeah… fucking shoot that sexy load," I growled in his ear. "Ahhhh, arrrrggg fuuuck!" I was about to blow my load. I held him harder as my hips worked their magic, and then it happened. I roared and grunted as my balls tingled, then bellowed the moment the first jet of spunk flew from my cock, filling his ass. I pumped against him with relentless abandon as I milked my cock inside of him. He gripped my thighs as I pumped away until I was spent.

I pushed him back onto the bed and kissed him lightly on his shoulder and neck. "Was that everything you hoped it would be?" I asked as I slowly pulled my cock from his ass.

He chuckled and nodded. "Everything and more."

I rolled over onto my back and smiled. "Yeah, for me too."

Fucking Aiden was better than anything my imagination had conjured up, and all I knew at that very moment was that I wanted more of him. This one taste wasn't nearly enough to quench my appetite. But for now, I gathered him up in my arms, which was something I never did with any of the escorts I'd fucked in the past. I held him close to me, relishing how he felt beside me. I loved when he wrapped his arms around my torso and rested his head on my bicep. We were both feeling major relief and sheer exhaustion, him more than me. I maybe could muster enough energy for another round, but this one had been so amazing, all I wanted was to drift blissfully off into dreamland, so that was what we did.

CHAPTER SIX

Aiden

I'D BEEN HAVING THE SEXIEST DREAM OF MACIO DE NIRO AND never wanted to wake up from it. We were together in a fancy suite and he'd just fucked the hell out of me, and then let me cuddle. The dream was more vivid and intense than my previous ones and I wasn't quite sure what to contribute it to, not that I was upset.

I could feel consciousness trying to pull me out of my dreamland with Macio and I fought it. I wasn't ready to let go of the way his strong body felt against mine as he moved forcefully inside me, or the deep growls against my ear as he made me his; and I never wanted to let go of the hungry way he kissed me as if he couldn't get enough of me. I'd hold onto the way it felt when he spilled inside me until the day I died.

I became aware of the chilly, air-conditioned room and tried to burrow deeper beneath the covers to prevent reality from penetrating my dreams of Macio. The next thing that penetrated my foggy brain was how hard my dick was where it was pinned between my stomach and the mattress beneath me. I was so hard and horny, I felt the stickiness of precum against my skin.

I had resigned myself to rolling over and jerking off to the last vestiges of the dream when I felt the slightest touch of a finger trailing up and down my spine. My eyes popped open in alarm and panic started to roll through me when I couldn't see where I was or even who I was with in the pitch-black room. My head was turned away from my bedpartner and I wasn't in a hurry to face him. My god, who the hell had I picked up when frustrations over Macio got to be too much?

I slowly became aware of other things as I laid there silently, hoping that the person touching me thought I was still sleeping. There was a tenderness in my leg muscles, raw spots on my knees, and my asshole ached like it had been fucked by a champ more than once. I spread my legs slightly to get more comfortable, which my bed buddy took as an invitation to tease the crack of my ass with the same finger that had bumped along my spine.

I felt the heat of his body before I felt his bare flesh press against my side. His dick was equally as hard and leaking where it pressed against my hip. His dick wasn't the only rock hard thing about my new friend either, I felt his hard-muscled chest and abdomen along my side. I was starting to get past my wariness and ready to pat myself on the back for the hotness I hooked up with when my lust-fogged brain picked up on a frightening detail; I had dried cum between my thighs.

"Fuck!" I rolled to my side and sat up. Oh my God! I'd had unprotected sex with a motherfucking stranger. I rubbed my fists over my eyes to try and rub out the remaining sleep from them. *Why the fuck did I feel so exhausted? Did this douchebag drug me?* I never had unprotected sex. Ever. "What have I done?" I felt the man in the bed roll away from me and I heard a lamp snap on. I continued to cover my eyes like a coward rather than face what I'd done. Then I heard a chuckle rumbling deep in the guy's chest and my heartrate accelerated even more when I recognized it. I uncovered my eyes and turned slowly to look at him.

Macio. He smiled at me and it all came rushing back to me like movie clips. I saw the interview that was laden with a new tension I later realized was sexual when he confessed to wanting me. Kisses that were so fucking hot, they'd permanently be seared into my soul. The hard fucking I begged for followed by a nap where I cuddled into his side. When we woke a few hours later, I rolled him to his back and rode him like a bronco until we were both shouting and coming. I had tried to leave then, but he tugged me back onto the bed. Cuddling after sex was something I never would've associated with Macio, but I realized I could quickly become addicted to the tight way he held me against his body.

The next time I had woken up, Macio was staring at my lips as he traced them with his finger. I kissed his finger and his gaze slid up to mine. My breath hitched in my throat at what I saw there. I had never seen anyone look at me with so much want and need. It felt like the shields he erected around him were down and I got a glimpse of the real man. I saw the raw longing for a life he felt he couldn't have and it physically hurt me to look into his eyes. I did the only thing I could think of to replace the emotion in his eyes to one I could better handle.

I slid down his body and took his cock into my mouth and worshiped him the way he deserved. If we were only going to have one night, then I'd make it one he would never forget. I wanted to be the best he ever had and worked his cock like a seasoned pro while stroking my own erection until we had both come.

"What's wrong, Aiden?" Macio's voice pulled me back to the present. He placed one of his big hands on the back of my neck and began to massage the tensed muscles there. I'd never look at his hands the same. The world saw fists that could destroy his opponents, and while

I still saw them that way, I also saw hands that touched me with so much tenderness, I wondered how I'd be able to move on from him.

"We didn't use protection last night, Macio. That's something I've never done before and it has me rattled."

"I get tested every three months as part of ETC's medical requirements," he said soothingly. "I promise you, it's okay." He shook his head slightly in disbelief before he confessed, "I've never had unprotected sex either. I've never wanted to be raw inside someone until you."

"I get tested every six months, Macio. I can show you the results of my latest test…"

"Shhh." He covered my lips with his finger. "I trust you, Aiden."

"Why?" It was so much easier for me to trust him because I knew about ETC's rigid medical testing, which would be expected in a blood sport. Macio didn't know jack about me though.

Macio shrugged and said, "I just do. Lord knows you could destroy my career with one word, but I know you won't. If you tell me that you get tested and practice safe sex habits, then I believe that too." A fierce scowl formed on his face and his next words dispelled any fantasy I had that what we shared would be repeated. "But don't trust any other guy with your body this way, Aiden."

It was foolish to entertain the thought that something real could happen between us, even if only for a minute. Macio and I lived in different worlds; I lived in the open while he stayed in the closet. Lives were shattered and destroyed when those two worlds collided and I refused to do it ever again. I shook off the melancholy that had begun to creep in. "I promise you that I won't. I'd like the same guarantee from you." I wasn't foolish enough to believe that Macio had been a virgin before we met nor did I think he'd be celibate for the rest of his life. I squelched those thoughts immediately because they hurt way more than they should.

"That's a promise I can easily make." Macio leaned forward and pressed his lips softly against mine, as if he was sealing his promise with a kiss. "Can you stick around for a while longer and have breakfast with me? I'll order room service and we can eat in bed." Even though there was spunk all over the bed, I couldn't imagine any place I'd rather eat breakfast than in bed beside Macio.

"It sounds wonderful."

I left Macio to order our food and went to take a shower. I hated to wash the smell of him off my skin, but I desperately wanted to shake off the exhaustion that was pulling at my eyelids. I came alive when he joined me beneath the spray of hot water. I got immense pleasure when Macio washed my hair with his shampoo, then my body with his shower gel, because I would still leave his hotel room smelling like him. I returned the favor, of course, and by the time I had finished, we were both hard as steel again.

Macio slid his hard dick between my ass cheeks and teased my puckered hole with the broad head. "Can you take me again, Aiden?"

"Yes," I hissed between my lips.

Macio slicked his cock with the lube he kept on the shelf next to his shower gel and pushed inside me with one hard thrust. Even though he'd already had me twice, the sheer size of him still took me by surprise. He allowed me to adjust to him and then set out on a fast pace. For as long as I lived, I'd never forget the sounds of our wet skin slapping together or the tight way he held my body to his, as if he never wanted to let me go.

The kiss we shared after we were spent was equal parts hot and sweet. I was doing my damnedest to keep things in perspective and not allow myself to get carried away with fantasies that would never come true. I knew I needed to gain an upper hand in the situation for my own fucking sanity. Lounging around in the bed while sharing breakfast would only make things harder when it was time for me to leave.

I dressed in the master suite while Marco went to answer the knock at the door. I knew he wouldn't like my decision, but I knew he'd accept it without too much fuss. I expected him to come through the bedroom door with a cart full of covered dishes, but instead, I heard voices coming from the living room of the suite. My heart plummeted when I cracked the bedroom door enough to hear what was being said.

"Uh, what are you doing here in L.A., Rupert?" I heard Macio ask.

"I'm out here meeting with Michaelson's to hammer out the final details for your gloves and figured I'd drop by. You've not been yourself lately and I was worried about you. We need your focus to be on your training and nowhere else."

"I'm fine, Rupert. I just wanted a short break to spend time with my brother and his family," Macio replied.

"Kid, I know you're not being completely honest with me." Rupert's fatherly tone irritated me and I couldn't be sure why. I understood that he was Macio's publicist, but that didn't make him his keeper. I didn't know how Macio kept from choking on the short leash they had him on. "You came out here for more than a family visit or else you'd be staying at Rico's house like you always do."

"How'd you know I wasn't?" Macio asked irritably.

"I called his house this morning and he told me you weren't arriving until later in the day. Of course, I knew you'd already been out here for a few days, but I didn't tell him that. You're entitled to your privacy." I bit back a laugh at that comment. He could have privacy, but not from Rupert and Barry.

"Yes, privacy," Macio said to Rupert. "That means from you too, Rupert." I punched the air with my fist. "I just needed a few days. I promise I'll be stronger than ever when I get back."

Rupert was silent for several long moments, then he finally said, "You're right, Macio. I apologize for intruding. I just needed to see for myself that you were doing okay. Have you had breakfast yet? Let me treat you."

"I, uh…"

"Come on," Rupert cajoled, "surely you have thirty minutes to spare for me."

"Okay," Macio agreed. "Why don't you go downstairs and get us a table at the restaurant while I get dressed?"

"Deal," Rupert agreed. "I'll see you down there."

I went into the living room as soon as I heard the door shut. Macio's look of disappointment made me feel better about the riotous emotions coursing through me. I commanded my brain to memorize everything about him in that moment because he wasn't Macio the fighter, he was Macio the man standing in front of me wrapped in a terrycloth robe with wet hair from our joint shower.

He crooked his finger in my belt loop and pulled me to him. "This wasn't what I wanted, Aiden. I wasn't ready to say goodbye yet."

"Me either," I answered honestly. "But we both knew it was going to happen, so maybe it's better to get it over with; sort of like ripping off a Band-Aid."

"Maybe." He didn't sound convinced. "Thank you for a wonderful evening, Aiden. It was more incredible than in my filthiest fantasies."

"Yeah?" Hearing he fantasized about me did funny things to my insides and weakened my resolve to leave his hotel room. "For me too, Macio. I'll never forgot this night for as long as I live." Even though he said he trusted me, I needed to make sure he knew how much I respected him. "I would never tarnish what we shared by betraying your trust and going public with our night. Not that anyone would believe me," I added with a smirk.

"I know you wouldn't." Macio looked at his feet for a long time, then returned his eyes to mine. "If things were different..."

I stopped his words with a kiss. I didn't want to hear false promises that would never come to fruition; it would ruin the memories as surely as anything. I wasn't foolish enough to believe he'd change for me and I would never ask him to, just as I knew I would never love in secrecy again.

I stepped back once our kiss ended. "I wish you nothing but the best." I felt him watching me as I gathered my stuff and put it in my messenger bag. I turned to face him once I was done. "Goodbye, Macio."

"Goodbye, Aiden."

I was overwhelmed with emotion when I left his room and stepped onto the elevator. I knew the score, but that didn't stop me from feeling destroyed. I castigated myself for being foolish the entire ride down to the ground floor. I knew I'd pick myself up by my loafers and soldier on, but also knew it would be a while before it happened.

I stepped out of the elevator once the doors opened and came face to face with Rupert, who wore a sly grin on his face. "Uh…"

Rupert grabbed me lightly by the elbow and pulled me aside to ensure privacy from prying ears. "Save it, kid. Neither of you can lie for shit." He narrowed his eyes at me menacingly and said, "If you even think about going public…"

"I wouldn't." I shook my head vehemently. "I'd never do something like that."

Rupert studied me for several long moments before he nodded his head. "I don't know why, but I believe you." Then he leaned in so his mouth was almost pressed against my ear. "I will destroy you if you do."

The venom in his voice caused the hair on the back of my neck to stand up. I had only seen a jovial, fatherly side to Rupert before and decided it was much preferred over his mob-like side.

I pulled back from him and looked him in the eye. "I'll never give you cause." I walked away from him without a backwards glance. I hoped that my confident posture disguised the way my knees knocked together from fear that nothing in my life would ever be the same again.

CHAPTER SEVEN

Macio

FUCK RUPERT'S COCK BLOCKING ASS! I HAD EVERY INTENTION OF eating breakfast with Aiden, and I wasn't happy that he interrupted my plans. I wanted to tell him that I had plans to eat with my brother, but something told me he might have wanted to tag along. It wasn't like he didn't know my family. Still, fuck him for ruining my would-be breakfast with Aiden. Not only that, but now I had a room service bill on my hands and food that might not get eaten.

I slipped on a pair of black boxer-briefs and then my Michaelson jogging suit. Because they were my sponsor, I really couldn't wear any other competitor's clothing. However, for what they were paying me, I didn't complain. According to Rupert, the more popular I became, the more money I would make. So, I was just going to go with the flow. The interview I did with Aiden should help in that regard.

My heart skipped several beats as I thought about Aiden and I

looked at the rumpled sheets on the bed with a longing I hadn't felt…
ever. I knew it was a one-time thing. A fantasy fulfilled, but I couldn't
help feel that familiar loneliness I felt whenever I had to look forward
to another night alone, only this time it was more intense. I really
didn't care too much when those escorts left. A fun time was had,
money exchanged hands, and that was that.

However, with Aiden, it was all so different. Being inside of him
was the most intense sexual and emotional experience I'd ever felt
and I wanted it to go on forever. When we woke up hours later and he
pushed me back on the bed and rode me hard, I knew what real pleasure was. He didn't have sex with me for money and what he felt was
real. God, it was all so real! There was something in his expression
that spoke volumes to me and I came hard just from looking at him.

Aiden, Aiden, Aiden… having sex with him was everything I
had hoped it would be and a million times more. He blew my mind
when I blew my cock. I'd jerked off countless times thinking about his
lips wrapped around my dick and when he slid down the length of my
body and took me into his mouth, I nearly exploded. It was the best
fucking blow job I'd ever gotten and my dick was hard just thinking
about it.

"Man, fuck Rupert!" I snarled as I shoved my feet into my
Michaelson sneakers. The only other competitor that was bigger than
Michaelson was Nike, so I was looking forward to working with them.
Though I liked Nike's clothes and shoes better, they hadn't offered me
a two-million-dollar endorsement deal.

I snatched up my key card and headed down to the ground level to meet up with Rupert in the hotel restaurant. I couldn't make it
through the lobby without having to stop for some of my fans and
sign autographs. When I first started fighting for the ETC, I didn't
like having to do it. I felt like strangers were intruding on my time.
But Bobby told me that my fans were my real bread and butter and I
needed to show them proper respect. When he put it that way, I began
to understand.

So here I was, stomach growling for some grub, but it did feel good to put smiles on people's faces. They were asking me a bunch of questions about my last fight and it was almost like I was back at the post-fight conference, only a little better.

"I just try to keep my body conditioned and I watch what my opponents do carefully while in the ring. I capitalize on their mistakes and then make them my bitches," I said to the approving laughter of my adoring fans.

"You're the best fucking fighter in the ETC!" a middle aged fan with a bald head said.

"Thank you," I replied, then handed him back his napkin that he wanted me to sign. "Listen, I'm heading out to eat, gotta keep this body healthy and well-fueled."

"Oh yeah, shit... sorry to hold you up, man. Yeah, go eat. Can't wait to see you in the ring at the next championship bout," another man said. He'd already gotten his autograph.

I smiled and nodded, then walked away after saying my friendly goodbye. Rupert was sitting at a table eating an English muffin and I joined him just as the waiter stepped up ready to take our orders. I just ordered the same shit I had with room service, which I told them to just leave in my room. Rupert ordered his typical breakfast of eggs, bacon, and pancakes with a side of fruit.

"Very good, Sirs, I'll be back with your orders soon," the waiter said, then walked away.

I saw a big glass of OJ and knew it was for me, since it was on my side of the table. Another liberty Rupert took today. I took a few swallows and set it down. "So, how's the deal coming along with Michaelson's Sports?" I asked.

"Well, I have the meeting today to go over the final details. Once we work it all out, I'll be contacting you to give your seal of approval. If you like the deal, we go with it. If not... well... there is the chance that we could lose the deal. I don't want to scare you with that information, but I do need for you to know that is a possibility," he said.

"Well, you know what I can work with, what I like. I have faith that you will get me a great deal," I said. Business wasn't my strong suit. I didn't trust easily, but I trusted Rupert.

He nodded. "You know I will, kid." He took a sip of his coffee, then cleared his throat. "I, umm, ran into that reporter, Aiden James, in the lobby. Is there anything you want to tell me?"

Oh shit, I was hoping the two didn't run into each other, just to avoid this conversation. But I guess it couldn't be avoided, especially after the Ringside article comes out. I wondered if Rupert was pissed that I didn't tell him I was going to do the interview. I just didn't want him tagging along, like he would have done, and ruin my night like he'd ruined my morning.

"Yeah, I had, ah, contacted him. I thought about what you said and felt that giving Ringside that interview was a move in the right direction. So since I was out here visiting my brother, I figured I'd kill two birds with one stone," I said, telling him eighty percent of the truth.

"Well, that's what I'm here for, kid. To handle those kinds of things for you," he said, and he was also giving me a look like he didn't fully believe me.

"I know. I just thought I'd handle this on my own."

"Must have been a long interview to go overnight," he commented.

Shit, he knew. "So?"

"'So?'" He leaned in close so he could whisper, "Fucking escorts trained in the art of secrecy is one thing. Fucking a reporter working for *the* most read magazine in the world of sports is another. Have you lost your mind?"

I leaned over closer to him. "No, I haven't. Besides, I trust Aiden. He won't say anything."

Rupert sat back with a frown on his face. "Let's hope you're right."

I knew I was right. That level of betrayal just wasn't in Aiden.

I felt it with all of my heart. At least Rupert dropped it for now and began telling me about two more interviews he had set up for me that I needed to attend. I went along with his plan and ate my hearty breakfast of steak-rare, eggs with cheese, and grits, along with a bowl of fruit. When we finished, he went to his meeting and I signed out of the hotel.

My brother was very excited to see me and so were his wife and children. Especially my niece and nephew who thought that Uncle Macio was the coolest person in the world because he could beat up anyone. I hugged everyone, flashed muscles for the kiddies, and even lifted them both on each arm as they cackled and kicked their little feet in joy and amazement. After all of that initial excitement, I put my belongings away and caught up with my brother by the pool as he was grilling steaks.

I reached into the cooler, grabbing a beer, and popped the cap before bringing it to my lips for a nice chug. "So, how's life treating you?" I asked Rico.

He grinned. "Not nearly as good as it's treating you. I heard about the endorsement deal you've got going on."

I frowned. "How in the fuck do you even know about that? I haven't gone public with that deal yet."

"Shit gets leaked, you know how it is. Someone who probably works for Michaelson's Sports gave a few tidbits of info for some cold hard cash. That's how rumors get started," Rico said, then he flipped the steaks over.

Rumors indeed. Although the deal that was in question wasn't a rumor, but that was what I hated about the business of being famous. Everyone wanted a piece of you. I confirmed what I knew with my brother and he whistled.

"Holy shit, that's bank right there if all goes well. I wish you the best, little bro," he said, patting me on my back "Damn, it's like hitting solid steel."

I flexed my muscles and smiled. "Hard work to get these bad

boys," I said, pumping my biceps. My brother wasn't the fitness freak I was, but he wasn't slacking, either. His body was more of someone who was naturally athletic. He loved playing baseball and soccer, hated the gym. So that was where his muscles came from.

We killed time talking about the past and all of the silly shit we did as kids. When his children came out to join us, we had to clean up our language, especially with the warning glare his wife gave us. Finally, the food was done, and we all sat down to eat and talk some more. I really enjoyed myself. I spend so much time training, little moments like these were a welcome reprieve. I was going to enjoy the next three days, that was for sure.

"You're late, you know I don't like that," Barry snapped as soon as I stepped into the gym.

"I know," was my response. "I'm sorry."

"It's unprofessional," Barry complained.

"I know," I barked. I wasn't in the mood to hear that shit.

"Get your fucking head in the game, buddy. Suit up," Barry ordered, and I nodded as I made my way to the locker room to get dressed.

I had two more weeks before I had to defend my championship belt, so I totally got why he was pissed. Now was not the time to start slacking on my training, but I'd been unfocused as of late. It'd been a month since I'd had sex with Aiden and I just couldn't get him out of my system. Maybe because it wasn't just sex. I had "just sex" with those fucking escorts. With Aiden, it was passion, admiration, and full on fucking lust.

God, I wanted him more and more every damn day. I went to bed thinking about him, every curve and smooth line of his body was seared into my memory bank. I wanted to run my fingers over his flesh as I licked every inch of him. The way I felt about him, I didn't even know if I had the words to express. It was like Aiden was flowing through my bloodstream, like he'd become a part of me. I closed my eyes and saw his face looking back at me, and the longing I felt for him was not only painful, but unbearable.

That was how Aiden made me feel. I thought once we had sex, I'd be okay, but my feelings for him had only increased over the past month, burrowing deeper and taking root inside my very soul. It used to be, the only thing that mattered to me was winning and this was the only time I felt like I was losing.

I had refused to send him emails, thinking that breaking ties was for the best. No way could I just be his friend or professional when all I wanted to do was feel his gorgeous body beneath me again. I just wasn't doing good trying to keep my distance from Aiden. I finally broke down and created an anonymous Facebook account under the name Tyler Johnson. I had friended him a week ago and was still waiting for him to accept the damn request.

As for the interview, I did with Ringside magazine, it was a huge success, to both Barry and especially Rupert's surprise. It got me more exposure and even more fans. I had my professional social media accounts, which were used to increase and promote my brand. I noticed a huge increase in followers and friend requests after that interview went live, which was a good thing. Other interviewers jumped on the opportunity to get their turn with me, since I seemed to be open to the idea.

Of course, I left that for Rupert to filter through. He knew what was best and which interview would get me the maximum exposure in a positive way. Also, he knew which ones would be trying to pry too much into my personal life. I wanted to keep it purely on my business in the ring with only a few personal tidbits. The two interviews I did with MMA Elite Fighters and Sports World National did just that, so I enjoyed those interviews. Although, none compared to the experience I'd had with Aiden.

Before I went back out there, I checked my Facebook updates.

Yes! It was about fucking time. Now we could be in contact on the sly. I sent him a PM, telling him who I was and giving him a winky face emoticon. Now I waited to see what his response would be. I hoped he didn't unfriend me. That would be a fucking blow to not only my ego, but also my feelings. Well, time would tell. For now, I had to train or risk Barry's wrath.

CHAPTER EIGHT

Aiden

TRIED TO PUT MACIO OUT OF MY MIND AFTER I LEFT THE
Dorchester Hotel. I threw myself into my work and spent a vast
majority of it in the United Kingdom, interviewing popular rugby
and soccer players. I was surrounded by gorgeous men with incredible
accents and not a single twitch of interest from my dick for any of
them. It wasn't that my dick was broken, either, because he fired on all
cylinders when thoughts turned to Macio, which was too frequently
for my comfort.

There were times when I thought I had gotten past what we had
shared. I had even convinced myself that I had dreamed up the intensity between us. I wanted it to be the sex of the century, so therefore it
was. Then I would see an article written about him or his picture and I
remembered all over again the deep connection we had that went way
beyond sex. I would close my eyes and relive the night in HD color,

causing my misery to return tenfold.

When I returned to L. A. after nearly three weeks of absence, I worked to improve my personal life. It turned out to be hard work because I didn't want to go out to dinner or clubbing with friends, I would much rather have spent my time recalling all the things that Macio had made me feel during our one night together. As miserable as I felt since leaving Macio behind, I was proud of myself for disguising it in front of my friends, family, and coworkers.

I went out when invited, I engaged in the conversations around me, and I even danced with beautiful men at the clubs. I just never took any of them home. I didn't think my lack of fucking would garner much attention since I was never one to pick up a bunch of strangers, so I didn't think it was that big of a deal when I ignored the dark-haired hottie at the opposite end of the bar who was trying to catch my eye.

"You need to get over him," my best friend from high school said into my ear. "Whoever *he* is."

There was no one on the planet I trusted more than Seth Anderson, but I wouldn't even tell him about Macio. "I don't know what you're talking about, Sethy." I used the dreaded nickname his mother gave him to annoy him so maybe he'd get distracted.

"Nice try with the nickname thing." Seth rolled his eyes and marched on. "You can't fool me, Aiden. I've known you for too long. The casual observer might chalk up your behavior as aloof or simply not interested in that sex-on-a-stick at the bar, but there's something else at play here."

"There really isn't, Seth." I pushed aside all thought of Macio and turned to face my friend. "I'm simply tired after a long trip abroad. I need a few days to rest up and then I have to write and submit the interview articles."

"I'm not doubting any of that," he replied. "What I don't understand is why your resting up can't include a good, hard tumble with that guy." He nodded his head in the direction of the guy once more.

"I know you're not one to hook up with random guys, but it seems to have been a long dry spell since you ended that disaster of a relationship with Geoff McGuire. Would it kill you to get laid?"

I groaned out loud at the mention of Geoff. Jesus, what had I been thinking? Okay, beyond the fact that he was incredibly sexy with a hot, strong body and a face to match. I admired his intelligence and his wicked sense of humor too. I really thought he was the one until I realized just how deep in the closet he was.

I meant, closets were a lot like people, and had many layers. The first layer in your closet were the clothes you currently wore, and behind them were the out of season clothes that you'd wear when the weather changed. From there on, it got a bit sketchy with the clothes you hadn't worn in ten years or more. You told yourself, and anyone who'd listen, that you'd wear that item "you just couldn't live without" once you lost those final ten pounds. Even further behind those treasures of days gone by was your great-great grandmother's moth-eaten wedding dress that you couldn't say how it got there. It would be right around there that you'd find Geoff hiding.

It took me longer than it should have to realize what was going on when I never met his friends or family and he referred to me as his "good friend" if we ran into his coworkers while out. It hurt me deeper than I cared to remember and Seth bringing it up only added to my misery of missing a man I could never have. *God, what the fuck was my problem with these guys?*

"Can you really blame me?" I asked Seth. "Something like that really fucks with your mind."

"No, man, I get that," Seth replied sympathetically. "I just don't like seeing you unhappy."

"I'm not unhappy." *Liar.*

"Look, I didn't invite you here to bust your balls." Seth nudged my shoulder playfully. "I wanted to have some dinner and a few drinks with my best friend. I'll ignore the lack of sparkle in your blue eyes and pretend that everything is wonderful so we can have a good time." Seth held up his glass of beer and I tapped mine to his.

The pager lit up and vibrated against the bar, indicating that our table was ready. I followed Seth to the hostess station where he exchanged the pager for the cute guy's phone number. Seth sent me a wry smile over his shoulder as we followed the host to our table as if to say, "That's how you do it."

His shenanigans helped me temporarily forget about my problems and I was able to kick back and enjoy a delicious meal with my best friend. I devoured my perfectly seasoned and grilled steak while catching up with Seth. We hadn't seen one another in nearly two months, so the conversation flowed easily between us. I was grateful I had agreed to dinner with him rather than stay home and mope.

Seth got up to use the restroom while we waited for our waiter to return the leather folders with our credit cards inside them. I decided to check my email and saw that I had an unread message on Messenger. I clicked open the app and saw it was a message from Tyler Johnson, whose Facebook friend request I had recently accepted. I saw a preview of the message and it stole my breath.

It's M. I set up this page so we could chat and no one would know.

M, as in Macio? I was just about to reply and find out, but Seth returned to the table. I slid my phone into my pocket and smiled at Seth. I knew that my actions made me look like a guilty teenager caught doing something forbidden. The idea of secretly messaging Macio felt naughty and forbidden. Seth's shrewd gaze told me he hadn't missed it, but luckily, he let it go.

My heart raced during the entire trip home as I rolled over everything I wanted to say to Macio, if it was him. I wouldn't be tricked easily. But as I pulled into my driveway, a thought hit me between the eyes hard enough to hurt. How was chatting with Macio under a false account any different than sneaking around with Geoff? The sobering thought stiffened my resolve to move on with my life. I knew I should unfriend Tyler Johnson, aka "M," and delete his message, but I decided to sleep on it instead of acting rashly.

My tenacity faded as the sun came up the next morning after a sleepless night. I opened Messenger and read the complete message.

It's M. I set up this page so we could chat and no one would know. I miss you, Aiden. Things haven't felt right since you walked out of my room at the Dorchester. I hope you'll reply, but I'll understand if you don't.

I had to be careful because he would be training that time of day and I had to consider that someone might see a preview of my response pop up on his phone if it was left in the open. Still, it felt cruel to leave him hanging another minute longer. I kept my response simple, honest, and safe. *It was good hearing from you. I look forward to catching up.*

That morning in the shower was the first time that using Macio's brand of shampoo and shower gel didn't make me sad. I had purchased it from the store on the way home from the hotel in a spur of the moment reaction to missing him. I thought that smelling like him might give me a bit of comfort while I nursed my disappointed heart. All it did was make me relive our night together every time I used it. I knew it was pathetic and I needed to stop, but I couldn't bring myself to throw it away.

I knew it would be several hours before he'd be able to respond to me, so I decided to listen to the recording and review my interview notes so I could start working on my article rather than take the day off like I'd planned. I suspected I would check my phone every five seconds if I didn't stay busy.

I dove into my project and completely lost track of time. My only reference to the time passing was the number of cups of coffee I drank. I was up to cup number five by the time my phone lit up with a message from Macio. I checked the time and was shocked to see it was just a little past lunchtime. *Hi.*

That was it; one word. Yet, it spoke volumes to me. I felt a strong sense of doubt, and even vulnerability, in those two letters. It made my heart hurt in my chest. My reply was as honest as I could be. *I've missed you too.*

Nothing came for a few minutes and I thought maybe he had to go back to training. I set my phone back down to work again, then his next message came through. *Who is Seth Anderson?*

It took me a minute to register his question, because of all the things I expected him to ask, that wasn't one of them. Maybe *how are you*, or *what have you been up to*, but not who I had dinner with the previous night. I remembered seeing the tag notification from the post that Seth made the night before that included a selfie, which meant that Macio had been looking through my page. *He's my best friend from high school.*

Macio's reply was immediate. *Just friends?*

I didn't owe Macio anything, but I wanted to give him everything. I was in very dangerous territory with him because I knew he was going to be hell on my heart. I couldn't see a way that anything real could happen between us, but that didn't slow me down, let alone stop me. *Just friends. I wouldn't lie to you.*

I have no right to ask, he fired back.

No, but I want you to have the right. Fuck! I wished I could take it back, even if it was the truth. Hell, I wanted Macio to have a lot of rights. I felt the need to inject some humor to relax the conversation. *Hey, I let you come in my ass. That grants you some rights. ;)*

Do you know how uncomfortable it is to have a hard-on beneath a cup?

I couldn't help but laugh at his question, then I found myself groaning when an image of me removing the offensive cup from his body popped up in my mind. That image wasn't the only thing popping up on my body. *Can't say that I do. Sorry.*

I'm only sorry that you're not here to help me deal with it. God, Aiden, I need to see you.

Macio's raw honesty moved me deeply. Only the strongest of emotions or pure desperation would make a strong, private man like him say those things to me. I could play it cool, but games weren't my thing. *I'm covering your next match in Vegas.*

I swore I could feel his intensity through the phone when he replied. *I will have you – all of you. Repeatedly. This time there will be no interruptions to our breakfast.*

His words caused goose bumps to pop up all over my body. Starting something with him might turn out to be the biggest mistake of my life, but I'd be damned if I went the rest of my life second-guessing what could've been with him. *Don't you threaten me with a good time!*

Break time is over. Promise me you'll meet me after my fight.

Promise. It was one I easily made. *Message me when you can.*

It was his turn to make a promise and he was true to his word every day for the two weeks leading up to his next fight. I let him take the lead because he was the one with the crazy schedule. We chatted with one another about anything and everything. I felt myself falling deeper and deeper for him with every conversation we had. I learned that Macio had a niece and a nephew he was crazy about. We talked about how we were both raised by single parents and marveled at how differently our surviving parents handled their grief and sorrow.

My mom took comfort in her children while Macio's father found his in a bottle of cheap liquor. I had an entirely new respect for my mom as a single parent and for Rico and Macio for practically raising themselves. He told me about the homophobic things his dad would say in front of him and Rico and I understood that it was more than losing his career that worried him. Even though his father wasn't much of a parent, he was the only one Macio had.

So, what happens when I push the little phone icon thingy? Macio asked the night before his fight, the night before I laid eyes on him once more.

Then you get to hear my voice. It wasn't more than ten seconds before he called me through the app.

"Aiden." Just the sound of my name in his gravely, growly voice had me hard as a spike instantly.

"Oh my," I said. "That's the same voice you use when you're coming inside me."

Macio growled through the phone. "You know I can't have sex tonight. I have to save my legs."

I wanted to say, "To hell with it," but fighting was his life and I'd never do anything to jeopardize his career. "Yeah, but I don't." That didn't mean I wouldn't tease him though. "I have every intention of jerking off tonight. The question is, do you want to participate and help me along or is that too much for you?"

"You better shout my fucking name loud enough for my neighbors to hear it in Vegas," Macio replied. "One of these days, I want to watch you stroking your cock while thinking about me."

"Macio."

My need to touch him and taste him grew every day until I thought I would die from it. Phone sex wasn't going to satisfy me completely, but it was enough to get me through one more fucking day. I released my aching dick from my pants and began to stroke it. I hadn't been that hard since the night we spent together. It felt like I had just been going through the motions every time I took my dick in my own hand.

"There won't be a single inch of your body that doesn't know my mouth tomorrow night, Aiden."

I jerked my dick faster and faster while Macio filled my ear with the dirty things he planned to do to me. When I came, I made sure I shouted his name as loud as I could. "Macio!"

"That's what I'm talking about, baby." Macio's voice soothed me and helped me come down off my high. "You're all mine tomorrow night."

I was already his.

CHAPTER NINE

Macio

IDEN AND I SAID OUR GOODBYES, AND HAVING TO END THE conversation was one of the hardest things I've had to do in a while. Fuck, why did I have to have phone sex with him the night before my fight? My cock was raging like a pissed off teenager behind a senior citizen in line with coupons and I was just as anxious. Every time I saw a message from him, my breath got caught in my throat. It was like time stood still and he was all I could think about. I had to be careful where and when I read his messages, too. One time, Barry caught me and that prompted a twenty-minute conversation about how I needed to keep my mind focused on my career and not some guy I was fucking.

I told Barry he had nothing to worry about, but he knew there was something different about me; I really couldn't hide it. But at least he didn't pry too much. I was still on point in the ring, so I guessed he didn't deem this new thing I had going on as a serious problem. As long as I increased my social standing and my brand, Rupert seemed happy.

Ahhhh man, what was I going to do about this hard-on I foolishly let Aiden seduce me into? Fucking tease. I was going to fuck him through the bed tomorrow night, I knew that much. I reached down, grabbing my big boy, and gave him a little squeeze.

"Mmmm, shit," I moaned. This was no good. I needed to work that energy off.

I climbed out of my bed and did a few jumping jacks and then some push-ups. After I worked up a nice sweat, I took a cold shower, which felt fantastic. I climbed back in bed, and using the On Demand feature on my TV, turned to the World Entertainment Wrestling channel to watch one of their events, which I enjoyed. Where a lot of theirs was scripted, the beef we had in the ETC was real. We talked shit, we had to back it up. There were no heels or faces, just two fighters duking it out and the best one won. No fixed matches, unless you had a blind, dumb, or dirty referee.

I thought about my opponent for tomorrow, Derek McConnor, fucking blowhard. He thought he could intimidate me at the weigh-in, flashing his puny muscles and breathing his stinking fucking breath in my face. I just stood my ground and stared him down like he wasn't shit. I'd prove McConnor wasn't shit in the ring, too. I had worked too fucking hard to do anything less. And I hated having to cut weight to be able to defend my title. If there was one thing about my career I detested, it was cutting fucking weight, but that was why my diet was so strict.

It was also one of the reasons I wasn't so sure I wanted to balance the line between my current light heavyweight class and the heavyweight one. One pound over, and I'd lose my chance to fight in the light heavyweight division. I was comfortable where I was, for now. Rupert wanted me to strive for both, but for him, he was just seeing more dollar signs with all the promotion and endorsement that would be coming my way being able to hold two belts if I could make it happen.

I trusted Rupert, but fighting was my expertise and you could only put the body through so much. I sat back and enjoyed the wrestling show, then turned off the television to go to sleep. Contrary to what people thought, I slept pretty damn well the night before a fight, which only helped me stay focused in the ring better. I smiled before I drifted off to sleep, imagining the banging I was going to give Aiden's sexy ass tomorrow night in my hotel room. Yes, indeed.

I woke up charged and ready to take on the world. I hit the gym for some quick sparring, not too much; I didn't want to wear myself out, just wanted to get my blood pumping. I had a great meal loaded with protein and the day went by pretty fast. There was always a lot of fanfare the night of the fight. Pre and post-fight conferences where they hyped the fighters and got people even more excited about the upcoming matches. I was guessing there were going to be tons of pay-per-view purchases like usual.

Barry was chatting with the cut doctor, which gave me a little bit of free time to message Aiden.

Are you here? I sent the message, smiling at my screen as I waited for his response.

I wouldn't miss your fight for the world, he sent back.

My smile widened when I saw those words appear. My heart skipped a few beats and my dick reared its ugly head, but I ignored it. My fingers blazed over the screen as I typed my reply.

This fight's for you, baby. I'm going to kick this guy's ass and wipe the mat with him.

You better.

Speaking of things we better do, you better not be wearing any underwear, unless you want me ripping them off of you, I typed. I could just see him blushing and grinning at the message. God, he was so sexy! But more than just his physical beauty attracted me to him. He was gorgeous inside and out. It was so easy to talk to him, even through texts. Over the past few weeks, I felt closer to Aiden, more than I did with my own brother. I told him things I couldn't tell anyone else, not even Barry or Rupert. Yeah, we definitely had something special going on and I was going to see it through all the way.

Maybe I do want you to rip off my underwear, Aiden replied. *Maybe I'll even wear some edible ones so you can eat them off me.*

Ahhh fuck… the things he did to me! My dick jerked beneath my cup and I knew it was looking to play. I laughed at the thought of me eating off his underwear. The calories alone would be hazardous to my health, let alone the flavor. I was not a fan of edible undies.

Spare me the edibles, baby. I have to watch my figure, I replied.

And what a great figure it is to watch. All right, then, no edibles, but I will be wearing underwear. I want you to rip them off me.

Fine then, have it your way. I smiled as I thought about how much fun I was going to have after the fight.

"Hey buddy, time for the pre-fight conference. You ready?" Barry asked me.

I hurried up and typed the letters TTYL and slipped my cell into my pocket, then stood up. "Yeah, let's do this."

I went to the conference and did the poses they want us to do, facing off with our fists raised. Once again, Derek was flapping his big fucking mouth off about how I wasn't shit and how he was going to make me his bitch.

"I'm going to beat the fuck out of you, bitch," he said as he nudged his forehead against mine.

I shoved him back and he charged forward. The president of the promotion, our coaches, and security got between us, pulling us further apart as the media went into a frenzy. Cameras were flashing like crazy as the crowd erupted in excitement. This was a highly-anticipated match, as Derek had surprised everyone by defeating Garret Silva in the match to see who'd challenge me. Garret had been on a winning streak at the time, and the fan favorite, so it was a huge upset.

I let Barry and my corner crew lead me back to the dressing room so I could get prepared for the fight. I couldn't help but wonder if Aiden was in the crowd of media pundits, flashing their cameras or camera phones. I bet he was, and I felt sure he was looking damn good, too.

"Hey, are you focused?" Barry asked me, slapping my cheek lightly.

I nodded. "I've just got my head in the match, Barry. Thinking about how I'm going to tear down my opponent," I said, which was a total lie. I was thinking about how I was going to rip off Aiden's underwear and then wondering which kind he would be wearing. Boxers or Briefs? Or would he totally blow my mind and be wearing a jock or thong?

Barry smiled. "Good. That's where you head should be. Now, re-member what we talked about. Keep your distance from this guy, he's got a longer reach than you and he's a fucking cheater. If he goes to gouge your eye, that's when you counter with the arm bar, don't let up until he submits. You need to be prepared for him to cheat."

"I am," I said. I'd break his fucking arm if he tried that shit. I'd seen guys bleeding bad and losing their eyesight because of that ille-gal maneuver. I was going to be on my guard with Derek.

Barry laughed as he tied up my hands with the commission standing by, watching to make sure we weren't going to be cheating on our end. We then put on the gloves provided by ETC, as I couldn't fight with my own. All to keep things fair and standard. I had two more company endorsements on my shorts now. Michaelson's Sports was the first, and now I had American Franks and Texbest Beef. That meant more money for me and my team.

"You ready to kick this motherfucker's ass, kid?" Barry asked me.

"Fuck yeah." I made my way out of the dressing room, towards the octagon-shaped ring. My opponent was already waiting and bouncing around, throwing punches like that was going to unravel me. I took off my robe and stepped into the ring. We both approached the referee and stood glaring at each other as he went over the rules. When the bell sounded, I became The Hitman.

We circled each other for a second before we collided, fist and legs being blocked and countered. I had studied all of Derek's fights and knew his weaknesses, and when he charged me, throwing a right hook, he lowered his guard and I took a chance, side-stepping and leaping with a knee to his chin. The blow knocked Derek dizzy as his head snapped back, and that was when I was on him, following up my successful blow with a barrage of punches he tried to block until I tackled him, taking him down and giving him more punches until I landed another good blow that rendered him loopy as fuck.

Before I could throw in another right hook to truly put his lights out, the referee yanked me off of him, shoving me back, and then turned to check on Derek. After a few seconds, he declared him KO'd and I raised my hands in victory as my corner rushed into the ring, congratulating me.

"Fuck, that was forty-two seconds, kid!" Barry exclaimed as he beamed from ear-to-ear.

Well, damn, that was a record for me! I wrapped my arms around him, hugging him and my trainers. Every win I got meant they were all doing something right. I wanted to celebrate, but not in the way they wanted me to. Lots of requests to go out drinking, but I turned them down. Said I just needed to decompress. There was only one person on my mind right then. I couldn't wait to get done with the post-fight conference where I saw Aiden in the crowd, smiling back at me.

I was curious what he was going to ask when he raised his hand. I nodded at him and he stood up. "So, now that you've successfully defended your title again, how do you plan on celebrating tonight?"

Ahhh, the little slick bastard. He knew how I planned to cele-brate. It was our special secret and my cock stirred in my pants as I thought about how I planned on spending my night. "I'm a chill kind of guy. The only thing I want to do now is eat something tasty and suck down a nice protein drink." It was the boldest thing I've said publicly and that was only because the true meaning of my words would hold relevance to Aiden and no one else. To the other sharks in the room, they'd just think I was going home to eat a big dinner or even dessert and drink one of our sports drinks. That was what I hoped they'd think, anyway.

I answered a few more questions, then I stood up when Rupert came to save me. He knew my limit was ten questions. That was good enough, especially since I was being more media-friendly and actually answering their questions. As long as they weren't too intrusive. For instance, one bastard had the nerve to ask me about my sex life when I was walking to the stage at the weigh-in; I just ignored him. Now that I was done with the conference, I slipped out of the arena, climbing into the limo with Barry and Rupert.

This time, Rupert and I were going to the same hotel, Barry was going home. We only rented the limo for fight night. Rupert was all about arriving in style like a champion. Me, I could care less. My hog was good enough, but whatever. As long as I got back to my hotel room quickly, I was fine with the transportation. They were talking to me and I was nodding, but the only thing on my mind was Aiden and finally being able to be with him again after all these weeks.

It had been a brand new kind of torture for me to be thinking about him and not being able to have him. I could almost taste him on my tongue and couldn't wait to lick every inch of his perfect, sexy body.

"Hey, kid, are you listening to me?" Rupert asked.

I turned to him. "Um, sorry. Just coming down from an adrenaline high."

"We need to capitalize on this win, kid."

I held my hand up. "Rupe, I get you're ready to dive into the next venture, but let me have tonight be a business-free zone, okay?"

He smiled and nodded. "Sure. I get it. Sometimes I get so excited for your success and I want to be a part of it. I just want to see you soar, Macio." He put his hand on my knee, patting me. He gave my knee a little squeeze before removing his hand and sitting back. It was an odd exchange, but maybe he just felt emotional because of how the night had gone.

"Thanks, Rupert. I really appreciate you," I said. I wanted him to know that I cared about him and respected his position.

"I'm surprised you didn't want any escorts tonight," Barry said.

Rupert frowned and looked at me. "You didn't?"

Damn Barry, I wished he hadn't brought that up.

I shook my head. "Not tonight. Just want to rest," I lied.

"Well, whatever my boy needs to unwind. But you let me know if you're feeling randy," Barry said.

I smiled and nodded. "Don't worry, you'll be the first person I call." I hadn't wanted to fuck an escort since the night Aiden and I had sex. It was odd. That was supposed to be a one night stand and I was supposed to move on, but I just didn't want meaningless sex any more. I needed to feel that connection again and I had only had those feelings with Aiden. Being inside of him calmed the beast inside of me. He made me feel like I was more than just a fighter.

The limo pulled up to my favorite hotel, and both Rupert and I climbed out after saying our goodbyes to Barry. Rupert helped me maneuver my way through the crowd that had gathered in the lobby to congratulate me on my win. I was polite, but relieved when we were finally on the elevator.

"Exciting night, eh?" Rupert said.

"Yeah… can't wait to relax."

"Well, make sure you do," Rupert said right before the doors opened on his floor and he walked off.

Once I got to my room, I set my belt down on the dining room table and sat down in one of the chairs as I waited for Aiden. I texted him.

My cock is hard and I'm waiting.

Open the door, he texted back.

I felt a surge of excitement flow through me and I literally jumped up when I read his reply. I jogged over to the door, opening it, and there he stood, hot as fuck. I grabbed him by the back of his neck and pulled him into my room and closed the door, locking it. Once I had him in my arms, I pushed him against the door, kissing him with all the hunger and desperation I'd been feeling.

"Fuck, I've missed you so damn much," I managed to say between kisses.

"I missed you too," Aiden echoed as he wrapped his arms around me and the fire that burned between us flared into an inferno. I let him pull my t-shirt over my head, which forced me to break our kiss for a second, then I was back on him. He tasted so sweet as I ravaged him with my mouth. I leaned down, kissing his chin and neck. I ripped his shirt open, sending buttons flying in all directions. We were both breathing heavy as we made out. I kissed, licked, and sucked my way down his torso, paying special attention to both of his perky nipples.

I loved the moans he was making as I licked over every one of his abs until I was at his crotch. I undid his pants, pulling them down, and he stepped out of them. He was wearing a hot pair of briefs that I ripped off him just like I'd promised. Aiden yelped and laughed when I did and I looked up at him, his face was all flushed as he smiled down at me. Again, my heart started pounding fiercely in my chest. I wanted him so damn badly and not just his body.

I took Aiden into my mouth, wanting to give him as much pleasure as I could. I sucked him down whole, savoring the delicious flavor of his precum. I loved how he ran his fingers through my hair and the little tugs he gave me as I bobbed over his cock. I licked my tongue all over his shaft, then pulled back.

"Turn around, I want to eat something tasty," I said.

"You're so fucking silly," Aiden said, grinning.

I laughed and growled when he turned around, giving me a view of his plump buns. I bit them both and he giggled, which was the cutest sound I'd ever heard. I licked and kissed his cheeks, then parted them for the real dish. Aiden moaned in pleasure as I rimmed him, and I wanted him weak in the knees with ecstasy. I ran my hands up and down his back and ass as I ate him out. It was like I couldn't keep my hands off him. It had been too long since I'd had him in my arms.

God, the sounds he was making were going straight to my dick and I couldn't wait any longer. I had to be inside of him, to feel his heat encompass me. I stood up, turning Aiden around, and then scooped him up in my arms. He wrapped his around my shoulders and I hastily pulled my pants down to my thighs. This was going to be raw and hard. I spit in my palm and slicked my cock up, then kissed Aiden again. We both moaned with longing as I slid inside of him.

"Ahhh god, yes!" Aiden cried out.

I grabbed a handful of his hair, then pulled his head back as I pumped my cock into him with all of the ferocious passion I felt. I growled as I kissed him all over his face and neck, as if I could devour him with my desire. He kissed me back, matching my lust with his own, damn near bringing me to my knees. That was just how much power he had over me, just the scent of his cologne sent me reeling. I also noticed that he used the same shampoo and shower gel that I did, and that turned me on even more.

"Fuck, Argghh, god… I need you, Aiden!" I growled as I thrusted into him, driving my pierced cock over his prostate.

"Yes… oh god, yes! I want you inside of me forever," Aiden panted, and that was all I needed to hear to set me off.

"Ahhhhh, I'm cumming," I moaned.

"Oohh yes, cum inside me. Baby, I'm so close. Ooh god, I'm cumming with you," Aiden groaned.

I felt my balls tingling, sending pleasure coursing through my body with an intensity that rivaled any orgasm I'd ever had with anyone else. We both grunted and moaned as our bodies released. I loved feeling him spill all over my chest and stomach, knowing it was me that brought him to such heights of pleasure. We quaked against each other and my legs grew so weak, I slumped to the floor, taking Aiden with me.

We both leaned against the door, panting, our limbs tangled and sweaty. This moment was so perfect, I didn't want to move, and I didn't think Aiden did either. We just sat there, basking in the glorious post-coital bliss that fantastic sex always brought on. I'd never felt so close to anyone in my life. I wanted to hold on to Aiden and never let him go. What did this mean, these feelings that gripped my heart and soul? What did it mean for us?

CHAPTER TEN

Aiden

THE HEAT GENERATED FROM OUR TWO BODIES WOKE ME UP. I opened my eyes and discovered we were in the exact same position we'd fallen asleep in. We were snuggled together on our sides, facing one another with not even an inch of space between our bodies. Macio had thrown his leg over my thigh as if he feared I might try to escape him. Fat fucking chance of that.

My body started to wake up along with my brain, but I ignored the fullness in my balls and the insistence of my erection to mate. Macio had to be exhausted after all the hype and buildup to the fight, not that the actual fight lasted very long. Hell, Macio spent more energy fucking me than he had in the ring. My man laid that fucker out in less than a minute. *My man?*

Was that true? Was Macio my man? I wanted it to be true a lot more than I should, because as much as I cared about him, I felt that only devastating heartache was waiting for me when whatever we had going on ended. I wasn't foolish to believe that Macio and I would have some sappy-ass happily ever after together; I gave up on fairy-tales a long time ago. Was I willing to endure the pain later to enjoy the clandestine meeting and secret chats on Messenger? How long before I started to resent that I couldn't be seen with him in public?

Those questions were all valid, but they evaporated from my mind the second Macio's grip on me tightened and my name slipped between his lips on a sigh. God, he was worth it – we were worth it. I resolved myself to hang onto him with everything I had and to fight for what we shared. No one made me feel more alive than he did. It wasn't all about the sex, either. As incredible as we were physically, it was the emotional connection I didn't want to live without. When we talked, it felt like I had known him all my life. I had to struggle to recall that we'd only known one another for a short period. I trusted him in ways that I never had with anyone else.

Even more amazing was the trust he placed in me. It humbled me and nearly moved me to tears on more than one occasion. Macio was the one with everything to lose, yet he wanted me. I would even be so bold as to say that he needed me at times. Even strong, fierce men needed a safe place to lay their heads and unburden their souls. I was that safe place for Macio and I vowed to always be.

My dick was no longer willing to be ignored and my greedy ass wanted to be filled. Macio began to stir when I kissed and licked his neck. My normally growly beast was almost purring as I slid lower to flick my tongue over his pierced nipple. I learned just how much Macio liked it when he fisted a hand in my hair and held my head to his chest.

Once he lifted his heavy leg off me, I rolled him to his back. I was dying to feel his power beneath me and couldn't wait much longer. "I need to feel you inside me." I had a lot of memories to burn into my brain because I didn't know how long it would be until I would see him again. I didn't care if I had to crawl out of that room, I would take him into my body until neither of us had anything left to give.

I saw his intense eyes glittering in the dark and they were my beacon of hope I held onto when my brain tried a last-ditch effort to convince me to leave before I got in too deep. *Mmmm, deep.* I slid down Macio's lubed cock until I took him all the way inside me. I felt his power and strength vibrating through his body beneath my parted thighs and wondered if it was the same thrill Macio got when he rode his motorcycle.

I ignored my body's urge to hurry; instead, I took my sweet time riding up and down his cock. I knew we only had a few hours left and I wanted to give Macio a truly special memory to take home with him – one I hoped he pulled out when our separation got to be too hard. I felt his desperation in the way he gripped my hips and tried to get me to fuck him faster, but instead, I soothed his inner beast with long, wet kisses.

I tugged his nipples to drive him wild. He raised his head and sucked the skin above my heart hard enough to leave a mark. Knowing that I'd wear him on my skin for days snapped my control and I gave into Macio and my body's urge to fuck hard. My cock slapped against my abdomen as I bounced furiously up and down until I came across his chest. Macio gripped my hips and pulled me down hard onto his erection a few more times before he filled my ass with his seed.

I collapsed onto his chest once we were both spent. Macio trailed his fingers up and down my spine, as he was prone to do. The sweet gesture would normally lull me back to sleep, but he was thinking so hard I could almost hear it. I propped myself up and peered down at him in the darkness. "What's worrying you so much?"

"Your ass is going to be sore tomorrow," he said.

I flicked his chin playfully. "Yes, it will be, but that isn't what's on your mind. Tell me." I brushed his hair off his forehead and felt the evidence of his worry in the v-shaped furrow above his brow. "Is it us?"

"No," was his rapid-fire response. He held me tighter to his chest, as if he thought I would somehow disappear. His actions told me much more than his words. He had the same doubts that crossed my mind when I first woke up. I wanted to assure him that everything would be okay, but I knew he'd have to come to terms with them himself.

I became aware of just how sore and tense my body was after two rounds of thorough lovemaking with Macio. *Whoa! Lovemaking? Where had that come from?* I realized it was true. There was a totally different vibe between us since the first time we'd had sex. We had moved on from fucking. "I think I'm going to take advantage of that killer jacuzzi tub in your bathroom to ease some of this soreness. Care to join me?" I asked.

"As if I could just rollover and go back to sleep with you naked and wet so close by." Macio gave my ass a hard swat and then released me. "No bubbles though."

I rolled off him and got to my feet. "Dang it. I wanted to blow bubbles at you."

"I got something for you to blow," Macio told me.

"Later." I tossed the words over my shoulder on my way to the bathroom. I felt his large presence in the room with me even though he didn't say anything while I got the bath ready. I turned and faced him when the tub was half full. Macio was leaning in the doorway, wearing a satisfied grin. "Like the view?"

"It's my favorite."

"Seen many?" I regretted the words as soon as they left my mouth. I worried I would ruin the easy vibe of the moment.

Macio shrugged, then straightened to his full height. "Enough." How? When did he find time and who did he trust enough to keep his secret? He walked to me as proud and sleek as a panther. The hot kiss he gave me completely obliterated my thoughts. "We can talk or we can soak naked in the tub," he told me.

We ended up doing both. I laid in the circle of Macio's arms and let the hot water soothe my muscles and the insecurities that had popped up just minutes before. "Thank you for a wonderful night," I told him.

Macio was silent for several long moments. "Was it enough?" I knew he wasn't talking about the sex. "It's all I can offer you, Aiden."

If it had been anyone but him, I would've said no. "Yes. I understand the predicament you're in, Macio. I know you're not trying to hurt me in any way. I'm amazed that you want me as much as you do and humbled that you trust me."

"I do trust you." He kissed my temple and rubbed his hands up and down my arms.

"We need to be very careful, Macio." I turned so I could look into his eyes. "That photographer from Dirty Laundry has it in for you. He's convinced you're hiding something and he's bound and determined to bring it to light."

"Why me?" I could tell by his tone just how confused he was that people wanted to know more about him.

"For some, your privacy makes them more curious than if you were more open. They see you as hiding secrets rather than just wanting to separate your personal life from your professional one. Some will see you as a challenge they want to triumph. Regardless of the reason, Troy Danvers is dangerous." I cupped his face. "If this is what you want…"

"I do." Macio's voice was firm and resolute, as was his grip on my heart.

"Then we need to be especially careful," I told him. "I won't do anything to hurt you or your career, Macio."

"Hey," he said softly, "why don't you let me worry about that." He tugged me back down so I rested against his chest. "I don't want to waste our precious time together talking about that dickbag photographer. He hasn't found anything about me up to this point, and I'm not worried about that changing."

I couldn't help but wonder again how Macio was getting his needs met until I came along. Then I felt his large hand between my legs and I forgot to worry. "Macio." I melted against him and felt his dick hardening against my body.

"I need to see you come apart for me one more time." The deep timbre of his voice in my ear ratcheted up my desire.

If asked, I would've said that I had nothing left to give, but Macio proved me wrong. He worked my cock with one hand and teased my hole with the other until I emptied my balls once more. Macio rose to his feet and I turned and got on my knees.

Macio traced my lips with his thumb. "Do you have any idea how often I think about these lips and the pleasure they give me?" I shook my head. Macio cupped my chin and pressed his dick to my lips. I opened my mouth and sucked him in. Macio hissed with pleasure before he said, "More than what's healthy."

There were no more words, only satisfied grunts as I worked to pleasure him. I savored the way he gripped my hair and owned my mouth. Never had someone's pleasure been so important to me. Every growl, moan, and groan that emanated from Macio's throat spurred me on until he came while shouting my name. The adoring look in his eyes was all the reward I needed.

We toweled off and got back in the bed. I pushed away the melancholy that tried to invade my happiness and snuggled closer into Macio's side. His heartbeat thumped away solidly beneath my ear, reminding me that he was real – what we shared was real. It would have to be enough.

"You want to give room service another shot?" Macio asked me after we woke again. He laughed when my growling stomach answered for me. "I take that as a yes. Same thing you ordered last time?"

I was flattered that he remembered. "Sure."

We both got dressed while we waited for room service to arrive. Macio came up behind me, wrapped his strong arms around me, and pressed his nose to my neck. "I love that you smell like me now."

I hoped he was referring to me using his stuff in the bathtub because I was too embarrassed to tell him I had purchased the same shampoo and body wash as him. I stayed in the bedroom when Macio went to answer the knock at the door. I was thrilled that history hadn't repeated itself and it was the hotel staff at the door and not Rupert again.

I looked at the overwhelming amount of food on Macio's plate and grinned. He had a rare steak, an egg white omelet with vegetables and cheese, fruit, and hash browns. "Refueling," he said between bites. "The morning after a fight is my favorite because I can add some extra calories into my meal."

I caught him eyeing my French toast a few times, and made a big production out of eating it. I brought the fork slowly up to my face, then closed my eyes and moaned loudly once the bite was in my mouth. When I reopened my eyes, I saw a new look of longing in his dark gaze. I felt the sticky residue of syrup on my lips and licked it with my tongue. "Want a taste?" I asked him.

"Yeah, I do." Macio said. He laid his fork down, reached for me, and slid his tongue inside my mouth for a French kiss instead of a bite of French toast. "All of the taste but without the calories," Macio said after he broke our kiss.

I sat there staring into his eyes, wondering once again just how I had arrived at that moment with him. What was it about me that attracted a man like Macio and made him want to take risks to be with me? Out of all the men he could have, why me?

"So, that's why you didn't want an escort last night."

Macio and I jerked apart and turned to look at Rupert, who'd let himself in. Macio and I were so wrapped up in one another, we didn't even hear the door open. My heart sunk when Rupert's words penetrated the shock at seeing him there. I pushed my hurt away because I knew that Macio wasn't a virgin when we met and I had no claims on his past. Besides, we had more pressing matters to contend with at the moment. My heart sunk when I saw the angry scowl on Rupert's face and wondered what consequences our night would have for Macio.

"My evenings are none of your business," Macio said firmly. "What Aiden and I have…"

"Could destroy your career," Rupert finished for him. "Do you know what you're risking?"

"Maybe I should clear on out of here and let you guys talk." I started to stand up, but Macio placed his hand on my arm to stop me.

Macio's chin went up and his spine stiffened. "Rupert, you're my publicist, not my keeper. My personal life is my own – not the fans', not Barry's, and certainly not yours."

"Kid, I only want what's best for you." Rupert tempered his voice so that he once again sounded like a concerned father.

"Aiden is what's best for me, Rupert." His confident words were a balm to my frazzled nerves.

Rupert let out a resigned sigh before he offered Macio a tentative smile. "Okay, Macio. If he makes you happy, then I'll do everything in my power to make sure you get to spend time with him." Rupert then looked at me. "I look forward to getting to know the only man to penetrate Macio's walls."

Macio's phone rang beside his plate. "I need to take this." Macio rose to his feet and was half way to the bedroom before he answered. "Hey, Rico. What did you think about my fight?"

There was an odd expression on Rupert's face as he watched Macio walk away. I couldn't quite put a name to the emotion I saw there. Rupert turned and looked at me once Macio shut himself inside the bedroom. "How much will it take for you to go away?"

His question shocked me at first, but then anger set in. Did this dumbass think I was just another guy he could pay off? I wasn't interested in Macio's money. I only wanted the man. I told myself to be patient because I was sure Rupert had seen many ugly things in the business and knew nothing about me. I told myself that he'd trust me once he did.

"I won't hurt him, Rupert. I don't want his money. I don't want to hurt his career. I only want him." I was as honest as I could be and hoped it would thaw some of the tension between us. "Neither of us meant for it to happen. We both thought it was a one-time thing, but it developed into something more significant."

"I want to believe you, Aiden, because I do want to see my boy happy." Something in the way he said "my boy" troubled me. "I don't think you're what Macio needs right now. You're both a distraction and a ticking time bomb for his career." Rupert sneered at me and added, "But I'm not worried. You'll be nothing more than a distant memory before long. Macio will fuck you out of his system, then go back to putting all of his energy in his training."

His words broke my heart, but I'd be damned if I let him know it. Rupert didn't know fuck about our relationship or what we were coming to mean to one another. There was no way I'd let him run me off. "I guess we'll just have to see, won't we?"

Rupert opened his mouth to answer my challenge, but Macio walked back into the room.

"What did I miss?" Macio dropped a kiss on my forehead before he sat back down across from me.

"Nothing," Rupert said. "I was just getting to know Aiden a little bit." He offered Macio a saccharine-sweet smile before he turned his focus back on me. His countenance shifted from ally to enemy in a heartbeat. His eyes just dared me to open my mouth and tell Macio what he'd said.

I ignored him and focused my attention on the gorgeous man I wanted to share my life with. If Rupert thought he could scare me off, then he had another thing coming. I'd figure out what to do about him later, in the meantime, I sent him a look that said he could kiss my lily-white ass.

CHAPTER ELEVEN

Macio

THERE WAS A CHILL TO THE ROOM WHEN I WALKED BACK IN, something had transpired between Aiden and Rupert, but neither man said anything when I asked. So, all I could do was let it go... for now. I did want to reiterate to Rupert that I wasn't going to give Aiden up, so I made a show of kissing him on his forehead, something Rupert had never seen me do with anyone else. He needed to know I was serious about this relationship.

"Rupert, I appreciate you checking in on me, but I only have a few more hours in this hotel room. I'd like to spend them with Aiden without you hovering," I said.

Rupert's body seemed to grow a little stiff, as if what I'd said insulted him in some way. On one hand, I felt bad. I didn't want to hurt his feelings. He'd been looking out for me, helping my career grow and keeping my secret. On the other hand, who the fuck did he think he was to come barging in on me in my private hotel room? So, he was just going to have to have hurt feelings today.

"It's fine. I'll leave you two alone, but we do need to talk. With last night's win, that garnered you more business ventures, kid. I want to go over them with you today," he said.

I smiled and nodded. "Sounds good. How about later this afternoon?"

"One?"

I had to check out of the hotel at twelve, so yeah, I guessed that was fine. "Sure. I'll call you."

Rupert nodded and gave another concerned look toward Aiden, then left. He may have said that he'd help keep my secret… he really had no choice, but there was something in his expression when he looked at Aiden that told me he didn't approve. I was sure he wasn't going to be the only one not on board with this risky business I had going on. Barry would no doubt voice his objections when I had to tell him. If I wanted to keep my relationship private, then he was going to have to know about it too.

That was a concern for another time. Right now, I was lost in the perfect blues of my sexy boyfriend. *God, boyfriend. Is this really happening?* I had no idea when or if I'd ever be able to use the term of endearment. I actually felt giddy inside, which was an odd emotion for someone like me who could break slabs of bricks with my elbows. That was what Aiden did for me. He smoothed out my rough edges and let me be open. Not even with the escorts I'd fucked in the past had I felt open to be gay. I could truly be myself in every sense of the word around Aiden. The fighter, the lover, and the man.

"Are you okay?" Aiden asked, sliding his hand across the table, covering mine in a comforting gesture.

I turned my hand around, taking his hand in mine. "I'm happy, Aiden. I…" my voice trailed off and I had to find it again in order to finish my thought. "When I'm with you, I feel this sense of freedom that I'd never felt before. You make me happy. I'm not a poet, and sometimes I struggle with saying the right words. All I can do is tell you honestly how I feel. I want you more than I've wanted anyone in my life."

I watched as his throat grew tight as if he were struggling not to cry and that just made me want him more. To know that my words, as simple as they were, meant that much to him made me feel like a billion fucking dollars. I was just glad that I followed my heart and not someone else's advice and pursued him. I didn't want to think about this relationship not working out. Stranger things have happened, and maybe Aiden and I will defy all the odds and maybe we won't. I'd never know if I didn't hold on to him with everything I've got, and my grip was tight.

"I'm happy too, Macio," Aiden said, grinning. "I love that you speak your heart, and that's what you're always going to get from me." He leaned over, I met him halfway, and our lips touched in another hungry kiss.

I pulled back, smiling. "Let's finish our breakfast."

He nodded and we ate our meal. He left before I did, as not to arouse any suspicion. The moment when Aiden left my sight, I felt a pain in my heart at the instant loneliness. I sucked it up because it was something I was going to have to deal with. I pulled myself together, packed up my shit and left the hotel room, checking out. I put my luggage with bag claim and met Rupert in a restaurant three blocks away.

He was sitting in a booth and the host led me to his table where I slid in opposite him. "You know, we could have met in the hotel lobby."

"I'm hungry and the food here is better," Rupert stated.

"I'm not."

His nostrils flared a bit when I said that. "I'm sure you enjoyed your meal this morning," he commented. "You should at least have something to drink."

When the waiter stepped up to our table, I ordered a tall glass of water. He nodded, took Rupert's order, then left. "Okay, so what's going on with this new business you mentioned?"

"Before we get into that, I'm going to have to express my concern for what you're doing," he whispered.

I took a quick look around the place. It wasn't overly crowded, but I didn't feel comfortable discussing my relationship with Aiden in a public place. Rupert should know this. I looked at him. "Now is not the time."

He huffed, then sat back. "Fine. You're right, you're right. But we really do need to discuss this, Macio. I didn't want to get into it at the hotel in front of your guest, but—well, we'll talk," he said.

"Fine, but my decision isn't going to change. Just know that," I warned him.

He held his hands up in surrender. "I'm going to move on for now. I got a call from Jackson Jock Spray and MaxPower energy drink. They both want you as their spokesman. We're talking a combined one-point-four million-dollar endorsement deal, kid."

I sat back in the booth, thinking about what he was telling me. I had to make the right decision on this. I knew from other athletes that not every endorsement deal tossed your way was a good one. I had to protect my brand and not be everyone's whore just because I was the undisputed champ. I had my pride, damn it. And not only that, I didn't want to be pulled from all ends by these companies either. They controlled a huge portion of your life because they were paying you to be their billboard. Which meant I'd have to stop drinking Gatorade and only drink MaxPower.

This was a big deal decision. I couldn't be hasty. "I'm not sure about that, Rupert."

"What is it that you're not sure about, kid?" he asked, eyebrows furrowed.

"I don't want to have too many companies getting a piece of me and dictating my life. I already can't wear Nike. I don't want to give up drinking Gatorade. It has less sugars than MaxPower," I pointed out.

Rupert nodded. "All good things to consider… I get you. Listen, we can turn down the MP endorsement. That's not the one offering the most money anyway. What is your stance on Jackson's Jock products?"

I sighed. "They're good."

"Okay, we can go with them and that's a million-dollar endorsement deal."

I nodded. "Fine. Make sure there's no funny bullshit going on in the fine print. Then I'll sign it," I said, giving him my trust, as he hadn't let me down yet.

Rupert smiled. "You know I'm going to look out for you, kid…" he leaned in, "Even when you don't want me to, because I love ya and only want the best for you."

I smiled and nodded. "Yeah, I know. The feeling is mutual."

The waiter returned with our drinks, bread, and Rupert's salad. I downed the water to kill my thirst, then set the glass down.

"Are you sure you're not hungry?" Rupert asked, taking a bite of his salad.

I shook my head. "I'm good. So, is there anything else—business related—that you wanted to discuss?" I asked.

He smirked. "The other thing I want to discuss is also business related, but it can wait."

"It will wait and be damned," I said, knowing he meant Aiden. I stood up, stretching my legs. "Catch you later."

I didn't wait for him to say anything else to me before I walked off. I went back to the hotel, grabbed my bag, then tossed it over my shoulder and walked to the parking lot. I groaned when I saw that fucking photographer again. What was his bitch ass name? Ahhh, right, Troy-I'm-Going-To-Get-My-Ass-Kicked-For-Being-A-Snooping-Bastard-Danvers. He was taking pictures of me as I walked up to my motorcycle.

"Hey Macio," he said, grinning as he snapped some more photos.

"Isn't there someone else you can fucking annoy, bitch?" I growled.

"Oooh, I love when you talk dirty to me," he said. I snarled at him. "What, you gonna hit me? Go on, I'd love to get paid."

I laughed. "I hit you hard enough, you won't remember who to sue, bitch," I snapped, then started my hog and pulled off, leaving him smirking that arrogant smirk of his that made me want to knock his fucking teeth into the next century.

I really had to be careful around that asshole. He was stalking me more and more these days. I wished he'd leave me the hell alone and find another athlete to obsess over, but I guessed I was it for now. Hopefully, he'd grow bored and move on. Maybe I needed to make him move on. I had an event coming up in a few days for Michaelson's Sports. The big charity party they wanted their new manwhore to attend. I'd go to that and be social and do a few mini interviews… that should help. God, I hated this part of fame, I really did. People should be allowed to have a private life. Well, for now, I was going to focus on training and of course, Aiden. The thought made me smile.

"Hey, Macio, come here for a minute, we need to talk," Barry said, stopping me from entering the ring with my sparring partner. Ahhh, shit… I could only imagine what this was going to be about. I walked over to him. "What's up, Barry?"

"Follow me, Champ," he said as he led me to his office.

Yeah, this wasn't going to be good at all.

"Have a seat." Barry motioned to the chair and I sat down. He opted to lean against the desk. "I've spoken to Rupert and he told me about this thing you have going with that reporter."

I slouched in the chair and sighed. "His name is Aiden and it isn't just some 'thing', Barry."

"It's dangerous, Macio. He could out you."

"Aiden would never do that. If he wanted to, he could have done it after the first time we were together. He didn't."

"Okay, let's say that he really wants to be with you... how are you going to even make this happen? Have you thought about that? You have paparazzi surrounding you at any given moment. All it takes is one mistake for you to be exposed by someone else."

"We've talked about it, we'll just have to be careful," I said.

Barry sighed and shook his head. "Macio, buddy, I know you think you feel something for this guy—"

"Don't talk to me like I'm some kid that doesn't know his own feelings, Barry."

"You may know your own feelings, but I don't think you're fully respecting the delicacy of your situation. You're the champion in *the* most brutal sport in the world. A real man's man blood sport. They aren't going to take kindly to a gay MMA fighter. You'll lose your fan base, sponsors, and the support of the promotion. Have you ever heard of a gay MMA fighter being successful?" he asked me.

I shook my head.

Barry rubbed his eyebrow, which was something he did when he was frustrated. "That's because they aren't. For all we know, there are probably more men in the sport who are gay, but they keep it under wraps."

"That's what I'm going to do," I protested. "It's what I have been doing."

He shook his head. "Fucking an escort to get your rocks off is one thing. They are discreet and they are gone a few hours later. You're trying to have some kind of relationship with this guy. That means a lot of sneaking around, never being free to date in the open. This isn't going to end well, Macio. For you or him. It's best to break it off now before you both get in too deep," Barry said, which was a blow to my heart.

I wasn't blind to the obstacles that surrounded us... I just believed that what we had outweighed the risk, and I still believed that. I had to. Even though Aiden and I had to keep what we had on the down low, I'd never been happier. I loved talking to him for hours every night skyping with him and even our phone sex was hot.

"I hear you, Barry, I do, but—"

"But you're going to continue on with this relationship and risk it all."

"I can't help what I'm feeling for him, Barry."

He threw his hands up. "You're stubborn as fuck, kid."

"About this, I'm going to have to be, yeah."

"Fine. I've expressed my concern."

"You did."

"If you're going to keep trying to have a boyfriend, I guess I have to help you two idiots out so you don't fuck up and get busted," Barry said.

I smiled. "Thanks. Oh, Barry, there is a certain paparazzi bitch that's been stalking me."

"Yeah, I know of the bastard. For some reason, he's made you his object of obsession. Troy Danvers, which is one of the reasons I'm concerned about this relationship. But…" He put his hands up, stopping me from saying anything, "I'll work with you. You say this guy makes you happy, I want you happy. But I think we need to give the media something to talk about. Something that may throw them off your trail. With you seeing Aiden, you need to solidify your straight persona."

"What do you mean?" I asked, slightly confused.

"You have this event coming up tomorrow night. I'll get you a female companion that I want you to be affectionate with for the sake of the cameras…but not too affectionate."

Oh, I wasn't sure about this. "Ahh, I don't like that idea."

"Tough shit, kid. You have the media in your business whether you want them or not. You want to date this reporter, who is openly gay, by the way. That just adds on a whole other dynamic that makes trying to hide your relationship so much more troublesome."

"How is going to this one event with a woman going to help?" I asked.

"Oh, it won't just be this one event. You're going to have to establish a fake relationship with her in order to successfully hide your gay relationship with him."

"She's my beard?"

He nodded. "Exactly."

I frowned. "How much is this going to cost me?"

He laughed. "Knowing Kathy, a nice pair of Manolo Blahniks and you paying for every meal you go out on."

I blinked, slightly confused. Kathy was Barry's daughter, who at one point, had a crush on me back when I first started training with her father. But once I turned her down… three times, she let it go. "Barry, I'm not sure having Kathy do this is a good idea. I mean, she did have a thing for me."

"She's over you, Macio, and she knows that you're gay."

"You told her?"

"She asked me after you turned her down when she was eighteen. I knew she would keep your secret, just like I know now. You need people who can be trusted to help make this work for you," Barry said.

"I feel weird doing this with your daughter," I said, feeling skeptical.

"Listen, kid… if you were straight and ended up dating my daughter, I'd be perfectly fine with it. You're a good man, Macio. Besides, you would just be putting on a show and hanging out as you've done in the past on several occasions. Therefore, the media will be happy that you two have finally come out in your relationship. Star athlete dating the coach's daughter is a fairytale in our world. Look at how the public ate up that wrestler marrying the boss's daughter in the WEW," Barry pointed out. "They loved it."

That was true. Maybe this could work out. "How is she going to feel about it?"

"Hell, it was her idea, but I've already discussed it with her. She wants to help you, Macio. You know that she cares about your happiness. See, I was planning on talking to you today about this Aiden

James. I also knew you would tell me the same thing you told Rupert, so this was my plan B," Barry explained.

Well, that was so Barry. He believed in planning for the future. "Well, if she's okay with the farce, I think we can make it work."

"It's all to protect you, Macio. She's fine with helping you out."

"Thank you, Barry."

He nodded. "Now, go out there and kick some ass."

I smiled and nodded. Seeing how far Barry and his daughter were willing to go to help me and Aiden really meant a lot to me. Barry was a better father to me than my real father ever was. I made sure to make him proud in the training. By the time I was done with a full day's strength and conditioning, I was more than ready to go home and call Aiden. I was immediately excited when he answered the phone.

"Hey lover," he said.

Ooh, I liked that a lot. "Hey, baby. I had a very interesting day today."

"Good or bad?"

"Good." I decided to tell Aiden how my day went and the conversation I'd had with Barry. I wanted him to know about Barry's plan to have me "date" a woman. I didn't want him to find out by watching TV or reading some bullshit mag. "Are you mad?"

"I'm not going to lie, Macio. It's going to be hard for me to see you with someone else, even for a good purpose like this, but I'll deal. Barry is right, if people think you're straight, it will calm down some of those diehard curious fans of yours," Aiden said.

"And make it easier for us to get together," I added.

"I know, and I get it. I just don't want to share you," he said in that honey-coated voice of his that went straight to my dick.

"Mmmmmm, you don't want to share me, baby?" I asked as I slid my hand into my shorts, taking hold of my cock.

"I don't. Your cock is all mine," he said, and I could tell he was doing the same thing I was.

"Turn on Skype," I growled. He did, and I saw his gorgeous face immediately and I smiled. "There's my baby."

"What are you doing?" Aiden asked in a teasing tone.

I smiled, then moaned. "Jerking my cock and thinking about how hard I'm going to fuck your sexy bubble butt. Now, mmmmm, what are *you* doing?"

"Jerking my cock and thinking about how good it's going to feel to have you inside of me, fucking me hard."

I smiled and aimed my phone at my dick so he could see me jerking it, then I brought it back to my face. "Like that?"

He laughed. "Fucking tease!"

"I'm close," I moaned. My toes were curling as my balls started tingling.

"I'm close too. I want us to cum together," Aiden said.

"Fuck yeah… are you riding me, baby?" I asked.

"Yeah, Ahhh, Macio, your cock feels so good inside of me," he said, moaning.

I was imagining him giving me the ride of my life and my hand worked furiously over my shaft. I started breathing harder, my back arching.

"Yeah, cum with me, Macio," Aiden cried out.

"Ahhhhh, fuck yeah!" I shouted as spunk flew from my cock, spilling all over my thighs, stomach, and hand. I was quaking hard as the pleasure rippled through me. The sound of Aiden cumming really set me off and it was almost like he was right here with me. It was actually pretty fucking amazing. I could hear him breathing hard as he was calming down from his orgasm, like I was. I looked at my phone and saw the side of Aiden's face, which was kind of sweaty. "I gave you a workout, eh?"

He laughed and picked up his phone, bringing it to his face. "That felt sooo damn good."

"It really did. That was amazing. I miss you, Aiden. When can we get back together? I feel like I'm dying of thirst whenever you're not with me," I admitted. I wanted to feel him in my arms again. I wanted so damn badly to slide myself inside of him and become one. I wanted to see the look of ecstasy on his face, knowing I was the one giving it to him. I needed him like I needed air. "When can I see you again, baby?"

"Well, I'm going to be in Vegas this weekend covering the Heavyweight championship match between Gaynor and Philips. We can meet up then," Aiden said to my utter excitement.

"Boxing is for pussies unless you're throwing some elbows and knees and feet into the mix," I taunted.

Aidan laughed. "Ahh yeah, MMA fighters and your belief that you're the baddest bad boys in all the land."

"Hell yeah, we are." I laughed. "Come to my home, my property is very private and peaceful. I have high gates and cactuses to keep out nosey fucking paparazzi."

"Oohhh, your home… not some hotel room. This is getting serious, isn't it?"

"As serious as it can be. I can't wait to have you in my arms, to feel your legs wrapped around my waist as I fill you to the brim." I couldn't help but growl at the thought and my dick twitched back to life when I heard Aiden let loose a longing moan.

"After the bout, you better be ready for me, because I'm going to ride you hard and put you away wet," he said.

"You better." We both laughed and gave each other another round of phone sex since we'd worked each other up into another sexual frenzy. Afterward, we talked for hours about every topic we could just to hear each other's voices. Finally, the sun was coming up and we were too tired to go on. We said our goodbyes and I totally crashed.

"You look very handsome," Rupert said, coming up behind me. "Ahhh, let me do it." He took over tying my tie for me since I was having problems. I wasn't used to dressing up and having to wear bowties and shit.

"Thanks, fucking thing was getting on my damn nerves," I complained as I stood still, letting him work his fingers on the tie.

"Yeah, I could tell. Okay, there, all done." He looked me up and down, appraisingly. "Gorgeous," he whispered.

The comment caught me off guard, I didn't think he meant for me to hear it, or maybe he didn't mean to say it vocally. He looked up at me and smirked. "It's nice seeing you in something formal is all I meant. You look very Bond," he said, clearing up my confusion.

"Um, yeah. Well, we both know I look like the guy who is going to kick Bond's ass," I joked.

Rupert laughed and patted me on the back. "True, especially with those killer fists and feet you have. Now, did you memorize the answers to the questions Barry and I gave you this morning?"

"With the short notice, I did my best," I pointed out.

He shrugged. "You're the one hellbent on dating that reporter. Plus, you kept it a secret from us. We're just trying to make sure we can protect you from yourself. Be glad Barry's lovely daughter is willing to be your beard."

I rolled by eyes. "I am. Don't get me wrong, I do appreciate the length you're all going to help me. Anyway, I did memorize them."

Rupert nodded. "Good. Whatever you're not sure of, let Kathy answer. That way you two will look more like a couple, which is what we want the public to believe."

I nodded. "Okay."

"Remember, don't be afraid to be intimate. I know she's a woman, but you can't be shying away from her."

"I know," I said with a bit of annoyance.

"Hey, kid, I'm just going over the pointers. You'll be on your own tonight."

I frowned. "Aren't you coming?"

"I'll be there, yes, of course. The wife and I will be looking pretty and filtering questions. I'll be working the room for you. But you'll be there answering questions on your own. That's why I've been doing all this training with you, so you can handle those sharks," Rupert said.

I smiled. "Yeah, I'm ready."

"Good, because I think the limo is here. I see lights in the driveway."

I walked over to the window, looking out. Sure enough, there was the limo Rupert had rented. He wasn't going to ride with us. He was going with his wife, Lori, who was waiting in the car. He'd only stopped by really quick to check in on me and make sure that I was ready for tonight. Thank goodness he did, because I might not have ever gotten that damn bowtie fixed.

"Okay, let's go." I grabbed the corsage from the refrigerator and met Rupert at the front door. We both walked out, he headed towards his Mercedes and I climbed into the back of the limo and the driver shut the door behind me. "Wow, Kathy, you look amazing!" I exclaimed when I saw Kathy Vincennes sitting across from me in a stunning and very sparkly black dress with spaghetti straps. Her black heels had to be at least four inches high, which would put her at five eleven. A good balance to my six-four. Her silky blonde hair was done up in a fancy bun with curls trickling down. She looked beautiful. If I was straight, I'd be a lucky man. Well, I was a lucky man because she was willing to help me. So, all in all, she was a great friend.

"Thank you, you look really good yourself. So handsome in a tux. You should wear them more often," she said, smiling.

I laughed. "You know I prefer my t-shirt and jeans."

"Or your shorts and gloves."

I winked. "You know me well."

"I do," she said, coming closer so that we were now sitting side by side as the limo drove smoothly to our destination. "Listen, for tonight, we really need to silence all doubts. The more believable we look as a couple, the more people will grow less curious about your sexuality. Right now, you're not dating anyone. You're not seen in any pictures with anyone. You don't go to the wild parties like other MMA fighters do, so you're never photographed with some slut on your arm. I'm sure there's a lot of speculation about you, it's just that no one is mentioning it out loud. But that's why you keep getting asked that question about who you're dating."

"Well, you're all business tonight, ain't cha?"

"I want to help you, Macio. My father loves you, and I do too. We need to make sure we solidify your persona as a hot, straight stud who is spoken for, okay?" Kathy said, smiling.

I nodded. "Yeah, okay."

"Good. Now, let's go over our responses to the questions we are sure to be asked tonight," she said, and that was what we did to make sure we were on the same page.

It didn't take us too long to get to the event being held at the Fredrick's Hotel ballroom. Media was lined up at the door, snapping photos of an actor and his date who had just climbed out of the limo in front of ours. I was nervous, I always was at these kind of events. I could walk into the octagon without one nervous jitter, but put me in a suit and on display? Yeah, I turned into a punk. Our door opened and I climbed out first to a flurry of blinding light from flashing cameras and questions from the reporters who were in attendance. I turned back towards the limo, hand extended, and Kathy slipped her dainty hand into mine as I helped her out of the limo.

More flashing lights and more excitable questions were being directed at us. We stood still for a few moments as our limo drove away. As far as I was concerned, that was enough time for them to get their snapshots of us. I started walking Kathy into the hotel when we were stopped by the reporter who was granted permission to cover the event, at the door.

"Wow, Macio, looking extremely handsome in..." the brunette reporter prodded.

"Ralph Lauren," I supplied, referring to my tux.

"You are dressed to the max. And who do we have here,

hmmmm?" she asked, perking her eyebrows inquisitively.

I smiled like I had practiced and pulled Kathy closer to me. "She's my date for the evening."

"Ooohh, just the evening?" the nosey bitch asked.

This was why I hated doing these things. When Aiden first interviewed me, he was not intrusive like them. Always prying and prodding. Man, I missed him. I wished he was here with me at my side instead of Kathy. But this was my career and I had to play the part.

"Well, we'll see, won't we?" I said, smiling. I turned, looking at Kathy, who kissed my cheek as more cameras flashed.

"I've got to say, I hope it lasts because you two make one sexy, hot couple," the reporter said.

"We do, don't we?" Kathy commented.

I smirked and led Kathy into the hotel. I was glad the reporter didn't try to ask any more questions, probably because another celebrity was climbing out of their luxury sports car.

"Just breathe, you did great," Kathy said as she rubbed my chest and adjusted my tie.

"Thanks. Now to get through this night."

"Don't worry, you'll survive."

I hoped I would. At least, I was selling a new image of my brand. Hopefully now, even that snooping reporter would be satisfied. Regardless, it wasn't going to stop me from seeing Aiden this weekend. My heart skipped beats every time I thought about him and the weekend we were going to share. Bring it on, please. For now, play the part. I'd be glad when this evening was over.

Rupert met up with us and congratulated us on how well we were working the crowd. We mingled and posed for pictures. Finally, I'd put in enough time, so Rupert told me I could leave, which I did. They brought the limo around and Kathy and I climbed in.

"Oh thank God!" she exclaimed. "My feet are killing me."

I caught the hint and reached down, putting her feet on my lap. I removed her heels and started massaging her aching walkers. "Is this better?"

She moaned as she let her eyes close. "Feels great. I think everything went terrific tonight."

"As long as they bought it, I'm happy," I said.

"Oh, they bought it, trust me. You were fantastic, such the attentive boyfriend. Women are going to really be eating you up now. Gay men will just have to be sad you're taken. That's how we want the public to react," she said.

"Well, one gay man won't have to be sad at all," I commented, referring to my baby, Aiden.

"Well, yes… him. He'll be fine," she said with a bit of snark, which made me stop massaging her feet and look at her.

"You don't have a problem with him, do you?" I asked.

She looked at me. "I don't even know him. I've seen him on TV before and he's really cute. If you like him, I guess he's really nice. I just want to make sure he's okay with us," she said.

"Us?" I asked, one eyebrow cocked.

"Yeah, you and I pretending to be a couple."

"Oh, that. Yeah, he's fine with it. I've already told him. We're meeting up this weekend."

"Oh, that's good." She nudged me. "Back to my feet, buddy."

I chuckled, then continued massaging her feet until we arrived at her home. I walked her to her door and she kissed me on the mouth, taking me by surprise. When she pulled back, she winked. "Just in case any photogs are lurking by. You never know." With that, she went inside her home and shut the door.

Wow, this night had been crazy as fuck. I walked back to the limo, climbed in, and called Aiden. I couldn't wait to hear his voice. "Hey baby, I've missed you."

CHAPTER TWELVE

Aiden

I HAD SERIOUS DOUBTS WHEN MACIO TOLD ME BARRY'S IDEA OF having his daughter act as Macio's beard. I chose to keep them to myself rather than voice them because of the excitement I heard in Macio's voice. It was something he felt he needed to do and I had two options available to me: I could support him and see where things took us or I could walk away before I got in too deep. I chose to support him because I just couldn't walk away without giving him - us - everything I had.

It hurt like hell when the photos of Macio and Kathy together first appeared on the internet after their pubic outing. I could honestly say I had never seen a more beautiful couple than the two of them. The media ate them up and referred to them as a modern-day Barbie and Ken. More captivating than their physical appearance was the connection the couple seemed to share. The expression on their faces when they looked at each other was pure adoration. I told myself that it was all an act; Macio was doing it for us and Kathy was being a good friend. It was too bad I couldn't convince my heart.

Still, I knew we had an entire weekend to look forward to when I returned to Vegas for the boxing match. Macio and I planned every little detail of our time together. I had planned on arriving a day early to spend more time with him, but I had to fill in for a sick coworker at a Lakers event. The anticipation of seeing Macio again made the nearly four-hour drive feel like four months. My body hummed with the excitement of being in his arms once more.

My GPS took me right to his security gate. I punched in the code and waited for the ornate iron gates to part and grant me access to my man. I drove slowly down the winding lane until I reached the circular driveway in front of a surprisingly large, two-story stone home. I parked behind a black Mercedes and stared up the large, stone staircase to the elaborate arched doorway to Macio's home. For some reason, I wasn't expecting something quite so grand. As beautiful as it was, it didn't suit the guy I'd fallen in love with.

I grabbed my bags and the toy I'd bought for Macio's Rottweiler pup, Caesar, out of my trunk. Macio was crazy about the dog and I felt like I knew the little guy from all the stories Macio had told me about him and the pictures he sent through Messenger. I didn't want to show up at Caesar's home without a gift, and as far as Caesar's master went, I offered him my most valuable asset – my heart. As cheesy as it sounded, I couldn't think of anything else that would mean more to Macio.

I knew I was wearing a goofy grin on my face when I rang the doorbell, but it faded when Macio didn't come to the door after a few minutes. My second attempt was met with the same results as the first. I twisted the doorknob and discovered that it was unlocked, so I let myself in. I stood in the middle of the white marble foyer feeling out of my depths and a tad bit unwanted. Here I thought Macio was counting down the minutes until I arrived, yet he couldn't be bothered to answer the door when I did.

I heard music coming from somewhere in the back of the house and caught a whiff of sizzling meat. I allowed my nose to guide me through luxuriously decorated rooms until I stood inside a kitchen larger than my apartment. The entire back wall was made of windows that overlooked a sparkling oval pool surrounded by exquisite patio furniture and gorgeous desert landscaping. As lovely as all of that was, it wasn't the reason I stood in stunned stupor in the middle of Macio's kitchen with my heart in my throat.

Feminine laughter rang out over the music as Kathy pressed her scantily clad body against Macio's and held her phone in the air to take a selfie of them. The white bikini she wore to show off her perfect tan left nothing to the imagination. I saw Kathy's lips move, but couldn't hear what she said over the music. Whatever it was, it must've been hilarious because Macio laughed harder than I'd ever seen him. It was a knife to my fucking heart and I nearly turned around and walked right back out of his house. Maybe I would have if Caesar hadn't seen me and started barking.

Macio's head jerked up from whatever he'd been looking at on Kathy's phone and the smile he only gave to me appeared on his face. In contrast, all light and laughter faded from Kathy's face when our eyes met. What the fuck was she even doing there? It was supposed to be *our* weekend together. *Run, Aiden, before it's too late.*

Macio threw open the French patio doors and charged toward me. "There's my baby." He wrapped me up in a bear hug and lifted me off the ground. He held me so tight, I could feel his heart pounding happily in his chest. "God, I've missed you."

Macio captured my mouth in a kiss hot enough to make me forget my name. God, I missed the masterful way he kissed me, the feel of his tongue rasping against mine, and his taste. How did I even contemplate for a second that I could walk away from him and never feel his touch again? I gave over to his dominance and let him back me into the kitchen island.

Macio pulled out of our kiss and pressed his lips to my ear. "I need to have you. It's been too long."

"I need you too. I…"

A low whistle followed by a throaty laugh interrupted my response. Macio groaned and rested his forehead against mine. I blinked in confusion for a few seconds, then I remembered *she* was there. I began to understand a little better why Macio was taking extra precautions in our relationship because our brains short-circuited every time we were near one another.

"She asked if she could meet you when I told her that you were staying with me this weekend." Macio's eyes pleaded with me to understand and I couldn't let him down.

"It's fine. We have the rest of the weekend together." Famous. Fucking. Last. Words.

Macio said he would do the cooking while Kathy and I got to know each other better. Mostly, I listened to Kathy talk about how wonderful she thought Macio was and how close they'd become since they started "dating." She even used air quotes in an attempt at humor, but all I saw was a woman who wanted what I had. I didn't like her, nor did I like the situation we found ourselves in.

Kathy ended up drinking too much wine at dinner and had to stay over. She made it very clear how familiar she was with his home and even bragged about how she was the one who helped him decorate it. She looked damned pleased with herself, but Macio didn't look like a man who loved his home. None of the rooms had any of his character in them until we reached his master bedroom suite. That space was all Macio with a large, wood-carved bed that was as masculine and powerful as the man who slept there each night. The far wall was all windows and it overlooked a desert landscape that was something right out of a magazine. The tension I'd felt since I arrived began to dissipate as soon as Macio came up behind me and wrapped his arms around my chest.

I had once confessed to Macio about my fantasy of him taking me from behind in front of a wall of windows. Reality far surpassed my fantasy when he pressed my hands above my head on a plate of glass after he removed my clothes from my trembling body. The aggressive way he fucked me made my fantasies look like child's play. I didn't bother to temper my reactions to him just because Kathy chose to use the spare bedroom next to his instead of one of the other four that were further away. I shouted with pleasure as my guy rammed his big cock into me over and over like he'd die if we couldn't be connected. The way I moaned and begged only seemed to spur Macio on further until we came loudly together. I sprayed my spunk all over his window while he filled my ass.

We shared a hot shower and another round of lovemaking before we collapsed into a tangled heap in the middle of his bed. I physically ached to have his arms around me when we were apart, to feel his hot breath on the back of my neck and hear him breathing in my ear. I tried to fight off sleep so I could soak it all in, but the two amazing orgasms after a long day pulled me under quickly.

I had high hopes when we woke to find that Kathy had already left. I wished that I felt the same conviction that Kathy wanted to help us – well, Macio, but I couldn't shake the feeling that there was more going on in her head. Macio also seemed to be relieved that she was gone. He no longer had to worry about splitting his attention between the two of us. I knew he was in a precarious position. He didn't want to alienate Kathy by ignoring her because she was putting herself out there for him. He also knew that our moments together were few and far between and he wanted to put all his focus on us.

Our day was spent either in the pool or on the chaise lounge chairs that were wide enough for two. I had brought swim trunks with me, but Macio told me that I wouldn't need them. Splashing and playing around in the pool led to poolside sex where I rode Macio's dick like it might be my last chance.

It was time for me to leave for the boxing match before I knew it. I wished he could come with me, but that would undo everything we had accomplished with Macio's fake relationship with Kathy. I kissed him long and slow before I left and took solace in the fact that I would return to his house that night to sleep in his arms again.

I had hoped the fight would finish early, but unlike Macio's fights, it went the full twelve rounds. I hung around for the conference afterward so I could interview both fighters. I schooled my features into something you'd expect from a professional journalist rather than the lovesick teenager I felt like on the inside.

It was close to midnight by the time I arrived back at Macio's house. I was shocked to see almost every light in the house glowing through the windows and a dozen or more cars parked out front. I checked my phone to see if I'd missed a call or a message from Macio, but I hadn't. He didn't say anything about a party when I left, so I figured it was a spur of the moment decision. As private as Macio was, I suspected that Kathy was behind it.

I entered the house timidly, unsure of how I'd explain my presence to his guests. My laptop was in his bedroom and there was no way I was returning home without it. Turned out, I was worried for nothing; I saw quite a few photographers and reporters milling around. Most the guests were poolside enjoying the desert night air. I wondered where Macio was, but knew I couldn't go looking for him.

I heard Kathy's laughter and turned my head in that direction. She and Macio stood with their arms around each other in a group of people. Kathy had her head leaned against Macio's chest and her petite hand pressed against his abdomen. I watched in horror as she slid her hand lower until it was nearly touching Macio's crotch. He made no attempt to move her hand or politely step aside. Instead, he smiled down adoringly at her upturned face.

"God, look at them," I heard a guy off to my left say. "You just know they can't wait for us all to get the hell out of here so they can fuck."

"They've had their hands all over each other tonight," another guy said. "They disappeared into his bedroom for a good thirty minutes when I first got here. He looked tense and tight when they went inside, but not when they came back out."

"Her lips looked red and swollen when they came back out. I half expected her to wipe his cum from the corners of her mouth."

"Lucky bastard," another man added. "I'd give just about anything to crawl between her thighs."

The rest of the men laughed and agreed with him. My stomach pitched and rolled until I feared I was going to puke right there on the white marble floor. I had to get the fuck out of there before I did something foolish like cry. Luckily, the hallway back to Macio's room was empty and I was able to grab my things and get back out before anyone noticed me.

The gathering was too busy fawning or fantasizing about the newest "it" couple to notice me walking back through the living area with my two bags. I walked out of Macio's home determined never to return. My chest hurt the entire drive home from the pressure of holding in my heartbreak and tears. I wouldn't allow myself to break while on the highway, nor would I answer the dozens of calls Macio made to my cellphone.

He had to have known that I would arrive at his home during the party and didn't care enough to even tell me about it. How long would it have taken to send me a quick message? Was that how I could expect things to go? Any plans that we had together would take a back seat to Kathy's whims? How long was this supposed to go on? What was the end game? That last one was something that Macio could never answer when asked.

My emotions were all over the place and I felt like I'd been battered by a hurricane by the time I pulled into my driveway. My home wasn't nearly as grand as Macio's, but at least I could say it was mine and not some cold showpiece that existed to make others happy. It was my safe place, just like I thought I'd been for Macio.

I collapsed onto my bed and allowed the tears to flow as I replayed the evening over and over in my head. Unfortunately, my brain chose to torture me with images that matched the men's depiction of events. I couldn't get the images of Kathy on her knees with Macio's dick in her mouth out of my mind. I didn't want to see that or envision Macio with her legs over his shoulder as he fucked her, but I couldn't stop it from happening.

The phone calls from Macio never let up and I finally turned off my phone. I cried out my heartbreak until my throat was raw and my eyes burned. I cried until I had nothing left to give, then I drifted off into a restless sleep filled with misery. My pounding head woke me up hours later. I sat up slowly, feeling disoriented, so it took me a while to realize the banging I heard wasn't my headache, but someone at my front door.

Once my brain started functioning, I recalled the disaster from the night before and my heart broke all over again. I didn't have to worry about offending whoever was at my front door with nudity since I never bothered to undress when I arrived home. I could tell by the bright light streaming through the windows that it had to be mid-afternoon. I figured it had to be dumbass Seth trying to annoy the fuck out of me because my family knew I was planning to be out of town until later that evening.

I unlocked the door and yanked it open in preparation to blast Seth for being a rude ass jerk. My mouth fell open when I saw who stood there. "Macio." My voice had been reduced to a dry, raw croak after hours of crying.

"Baby," he cooed when he caught sight of me. I could only imagine how ravaged my face was after my breakdown. Macio moved forward to step inside my house, but I put my hand up to stop him. I shook my head forcefully because I didn't want him there. I knew what needed to happen between us and I didn't want my home to be tarnished by it. "Aiden, please."

I wasn't the only one who was wrecked. Macio looked worse than he did after one of his fights. His eyes looked red and puffy, as if he'd been crying, and his hair was sticking up in every direction from running his hands through it. I suspected that Macio wasn't a man who cried often and I selfishly took comfort that he wasn't taking my anguish lightly.

"I need to hold you," he said. "I've been out of my mind with worry. You never came home last night and…"

"Home." The word was barely recognizable in my gritty voice.

"Stop being stubborn." Macio gently pushed me back, then came inside. He shut the door before he guided me into my kitchen. "Glasses?" He retrieved one from the cabinet I pointed to and then filled it with ice and water from my refrigerator door. "Drink."

I chugged half of the glass and then pressed it against my neck, as if that simple action could soothe the burn and ache of my throat. The ice water helped, but I knew I'd be feeling the physical discomfort of my despair for days. "I came to your house after the fight, Macio. You were too busy with your girlfriend to notice." All the frustration from the previous night roared through my bloodstream and straightened my spine. "You could've warned me."

"I tried…"

"You didn't, Macio. You could've excused yourself to use the restroom and sent me a text. I was nowhere on your list of concerns last night and you let me walk into that fucking disaster." I broke eye contact with him and looked at my feet while I tried to find the right words that would make what I needed to do easier on both of us. I realized there was no easy way and decided to bite the bullet and get it over with. "Macio…"

"Don't, Aiden." His hand reached for my shirt to pull me close like he always did, but then it fell to his side. "I promise you that I fixed it. What happened last night will never happen again. Kathy…"

"Don't mention her name in my house." I knew I was acting childish, but I couldn't get past the things those men said and insinuated at the party last night. "Do you know what the people in your house said about the two of you last night?" Macio shook his head, so I enlightened him. At least he had the decency to wince when I got to the speculation about what went on inside his bedroom for the thirty minutes they were locked away. "You think you're uncomfortable? Try being me. And where exactly did you want me to go while you had your little party? Hide in your bedroom? In your closet?" I was beyond worrying about his feelings at that point. I was furious that he could treat me so callously. "Your closet is pretty fucking big, baby, but it's not big enough for both of us."

Macio flinched and paled. "I'm truly sorry, Aiden. I never meant for any of that to happen. I wanted a quiet evening with you and Caesar and it blew up. Ka..." The look I gave him dared him to finish his sentence. "I'm responsible for what happened. It was my house and I should've said no. It doesn't matter that it was supposed to be over before you came home, I should've known that free drinks would make people linger." *That, plus a chance to stare at the most beautiful couple on the planet.* "It will never happen again. When I tell you that my time is yours, then that's how it will be."

I stepped around him and walked to my patio door. I needed a break from the intensity of his brown eyes that begged me to give us another chance. I wanted to; I wanted that more than I wanted to breathe, but I was afraid. I had been down this road before and the journey wasn't a happy one. I had cared about Geoff, but it was nowhere close to what I felt for Macio – not even in the same stratosphere. As I saw it, I only had one avenue open to me. Honesty.

I turned back to look at Macio and said the only thing I could. "I'm in love with you, Macio." My words caused his eyes to widen and his mouth to fall open. I boldly pressed on because I had nothing to lose by that point. "In such a quick time, I've come to love you more than I have anyone. You have the power to destroy me, in fact, last night pretty much did." I walked to him and set my glass on the counter before I placed my hands on his hips. "I'm not asking for a declaration from you..."

"I love you too," Macio blurted out. I wanted his words to be the glue that pieced my fragmented heart back together again, but I knew it would take more than words. He placed his hands on my neck and pressed his forehead to mine. "So damn much, Aiden. I need you in ways that I've never needed anyone else. Please don't give up on me. I promise you that it'll be different."

I pressed my hand against his cheek and felt the rasp of his scruff against my palm when he leaned into it. "Then show me."

CHAPTER THIRTEEN

Macio

MY HEART WAS POUNDING IN MY CHEST LIKE A PISTON. NEVER IN all of my twenty-four years had I ever felt this way about anyone. Never had I uttered the three words that could make or break a relationship. But I couldn't bear the look of pain in Aiden's face. He was so honest with his emotions, I had to give him the same respect. I had known I'd fallen madly in love with him… probably the first time we'd had sex. The connection between us was strong then, but I just hadn't identified the reason why. I knew now. It was love. The most passionate, heart-gripping, never let you love anyone else again, kind of love.

I knew I'd fucked up, but there were several issues that went wrong last night that Aiden hadn't given me a chance to explain. When I took Kathy into the bedroom, it was to complain about how she went and arranged the press party to promote our relationship without telling me. I was so overwhelmed at that moment, I didn't think of warning Aiden. I was just trying my best to stay in character, even though I was pissed the fuck off the entire time. I was good at hiding my emotions and then letting them loose in the ring.

But this was my private life, there would be no ring to unleash into. Just people who could be hurt. Aiden was the last person in the world I'd ever want to hurt. But once the party continued past its end time, Kathy had convinced me she did the party thing for Aiden and me. With the press being there, Aiden would have an excuse to be there too, and no one would question it. At the time, it made sense… I thought Aiden would come see me and I could explain it to him, but I never saw him again that night.

When the party ended, I noticed he'd left me. His bags were gone and he'd left without even saying a word. I felt like I'd been stabbed in the heart with a knife and the blade had been cruelly twisted to really make me suffer. Every time I tried to call him and he refused to answer me, the knife dug in an inch deeper. I'd never known the heart could feel so broken and, before I knew it, I was crying tears of pain and frustration. If I could just talk to him and explain myself, maybe I could fix this. That was why I didn't hesitate to grab the keys to my bike and drive out to his home.

I didn't know why he'd left, but now I did. I held him in my arms tightly, close to my heart. The same heart that was mending itself back together. I wanted to make sure Aiden knew he was everything to me. I kissed him again and moaned in happiness and pleasure when he kissed me back with as much hunger as I'd kissed him.

I pulled back. "I promise I won't let this thing with Kathy… I know, I know… you don't want me to say her name. But I won't let it get out of hand ever again. I didn't expect her to show up ten minutes before they did. She pretty much thrusted them on me and once the party was underway, I just played the part."

"What did you do when you went into the room with her?" Aiden asked, his big, beautiful blue eyes looking up at me with so much anguish and concern.

"I went off," I said. "I told her that I didn't appreciate her putting this in my lap without my consent or warning. She swore she'd never do it again, that she was just thinking about how much it would help me out, and she apologized for overstepping. We were only in the room for about ten minutes. That half an hour shit is an exaggeration. People love to gossip. She wasn't sucking me off. As if I could ever get it up for a woman," I quipped, hoping to bring a smile to Aiden's lips. It didn't work. I sighed. "I would never cheat on you, baby. I don't even think about any other guys except you."

He looked off to the side and, for the first time, I could see his insecurities. His fear that maybe he wasn't enough, or maybe our relationship was doomed. I wasn't going to settle for any of those doubts.

He shrugged. "I… I worry sometimes when I'm not with you… how you get your needs taken care of."

I leaned against the counter. "I jerk off… a lot. I call you and we phone sex the shit out of each other… which goes back to me jerking off… a lot. Before I met you, baby, my life was empty. I'd fuck some escort with a fake name for a few hours just to burn off the excess energy and he'd be gone. There was no substance… no passion… nothing. I was lonely even when I was inside of them. But then a headstrong reporter came into my life and gave me a bit of sass and my world was flipped upside down."

I saw Aiden's eyes widen and some of that sadness he was feeling started to visibly fade away from his beautiful features. "Go on."

I smiled. "Well, it's a rather boring story," I teased.

"I like those," he replied, wrapping his arms around my waist and leaning his head against my chest. I closed him in my embrace, kissing the top of his head, then continued. He needed to know how much he meant to me now and always. "Well, this reporter who dared to get the last word in on me was on my mind every day. Those lips… that ass… I just had to taste him. So, one day, I set up a meeting and when I finally got a piece of him… I became addicted. I told myself that I couldn't pursue him, but my heart didn't give a shit what one side of my brain was saying. The other half of my brain kept playing the scene of our first time over and over in my head and my heart liked that a lot."

Aiden laughed. "I was the same way."

"I love you, Aiden. I feel like you've become a part of me. I can feel you flowing through me even now and when I'm not with you, it hurts. The only thing that helps get me through the loneliness is knowing that we are here for each other." I lifted his face to mine and kissed him. The kiss started off slow and sensual, then grew to be all-consuming. I turned around, lifting him up and putting him on the counter. We practically tore off each other's shirts as we made out. I sucked his left nipple, teasing and licking it as he ran his fingers through my hair.

"Ahhhh god, I love you, Macio," he purred, and the sound of my name coming from his lips, coupled with those three special words, sent me reeling with desire.

I pulled off his jeans, and as soon as he was naked, I took him into my mouth. He moaned and leaned back against the countertop. By how loud he was, I knew he was relishing my mouth on him. I was going to fuck the living shit out of Aiden so he would never doubt how much I loved him or how important he was to me. I pulled away from his cock because I didn't want him to cum just yet, god knew he was close.

I undid my own pants, letting them fall into a bunch around my ankles. "Got any cooking oil?"

His face was flushed with passion and anticipation as he looked at me, nodding. "There." He pointed to the cabinet behind me. I shuffled over there, opened the door, and removed the peanut oil. I poured a bit in my hand, just enough to get my dick nice and slick, then I shuffled back to Aiden. I lifted him up and he wrapped his legs around my waist, then we both moaned in ecstasy as I slid him down on my cock.

"I'm going to fuck your ass raw, baby. You're going to need a wheelchair by the time I'm done with you," I growled.

"Give me everything you've got," he challenged.

I grinned as I started pounding away. His grip on my shoulders tightened as I jackhammered his ass. I loved watching him panting and moaning; mouth open, gasping for air. I never wanted anyone else to give him this feeling. This was mine and mine alone to experience with him. I kissed him again and stood still while he used my shoulders as leverage as he rode me. Thank god I trained as much as I did. Not only was my strength game on point, but so was my dexterity.

"Yeah, ooh baby, you feel so fucking good to me," I growled, and nipped his chin before claiming his mouth again. We switched up again, with me taking over. I pushed him back on the counter and really drilled his ass as he cried out in pleasure. I jerked his cock until he spilled all over his chest and my fingers. Watching him orgasm set me off and I roared loudly as I unloaded inside of him, filling him with every ounce of my liquid desire. I quaked hard as the last drop left my slit, then I collapsed on top of him, breathing raggedly into his ear as I came down from my climax. His chest was heaving against mine as we both basked in the afterglow of amazing sex.

"This… this is what I want with you, Aiden," I said, finally. I lifted myself up and braced my hands on the counter so I could look down at him. "I don't want you to feel jealous of anyone. Not Kathy, not any escorts—who I no longer deal with, by the way. No one will come between us."

He looked up at me and I saw the tears flowing again. "Thank you, Macio. I really needed to hear that."

"So why are you crying?" I asked, confused.

"Because I'm happy."

I smiled. "Oh, good. I'm happy too. We're going to make this work."

I pulled out of him and I was nice and slick. I took him to his bedroom where we made love several more times before sleep took us. I couldn't stay the full day, because I had an interview to do the next day and needed to get back to Las Vegas in time for it. Not to mention some hardcore training. Still, I wanted to share as much time as I could with Aiden. After we ate dinner, he gave me a little goodbye bj and I was indeed a happy camper as I rode back home.

It'd been a month since Aiden and I had proclaimed our love for each other, and I couldn't be more contented. The media continued to eat up the relationship I had with Kathy. As far as I was concerned, as long as they were satisfied with that, I could spend my time with Aiden without people being too curious. I was sitting in a restaurant at the moment, Kathy had excused herself to go to the lady's room. This was something I had to do to keep up appearances. I pulled out my cell and texted Aiden.

Hey baby, what are you doing?

Writing this article on Boris Giles. What are you doing?

Before I typed that I was out with Kathy, I decided to just say I was at a restaurant. Aiden didn't like when I had to spend time with her and I didn't want to get him all ruffled up.

At a restaurant, getting ready to leave. When I get home, I'm going to skype you. Have the lube ready.

LOL, okay, big boy.

I'll call you later, I typed as Kathy was returning to the table.

Bye, he typed.

I smiled down at it before I slipped my phone into my pocket. "Are you ready to go?" I asked Kathy.

"What's the rush? Don't you want dessert?" she asked, taking a seat.

I shook my head. "Dieting. I have to cut weight and don't like having to cut too much to stay in my class."

"Well, maybe I want some dessert," she pointed out.

"We can get it to go. You know I don't care for all of this exposure.

Since 'dating' you, I've had more cameras in my face than I like," I fussed.

"Oh my god, are you still mad at me over that party shit?" she asked.

"No, but I don't want us to go overboard with this shit," I said.

"How's Aiden?" she asked, and the question threw me off guard because it seemed to come from nowhere.

"He's fine. Why'd you ask?"

"Because we're doing this for him. You're my friend, so I don't mind. I just hope he appreciates the sacrifices we're making and not giving you a hard time for being with me," she said.

Well, Aiden didn't attempt to hide his dislike of Kathy... but I thought we were working past that. I just had to make sure he knew how much he meant to me. "He's fine with all of this."

"Well, that's good to hear. I'm actually surprised he is. I mean, I'm sure he'd rather be in my place, sitting here with you having a delicious dinner out in the open. Instead of having to sneak around in the shadows for the scraps of time you can give him."

"You're overstepping and I'm ready to go. If you want to get dessert, better order it now," I said, scowling. I didn't like that last comment she had said.

"I'm sorry, Macio. I didn't mean anything by it," she backpedaled, but I knew there was something behind her words. "We can go."

We both rose and left the restaurant. Again, the paparazzi were there with their cameras and questions as we waited for the valet to bring my car around. As soon as my Mustang pulled up, we climbed in and I was ready to take her home. When I got to her house, I walked her to her door and she entered without trying to kiss me. I went back to my car and drove home. As soon as I got there, I called Aiden and got nice and naked with my lube ready.

"Hey baby, how was your day?"

"You were with Kathy at the restaurant?" he asked, which made my cock go limp because I could tell by the tone of his voice, he wasn't happy.

"Yes, just one of those publicity dates. Nothing more," I said.

"Why didn't you tell me?"

"Because I didn't want you stressing out about it. I know you don't care for her, and you don't like it when I mention her name. I wasn't trying to hide anything from you," I said.

"You looked like you were enjoying yourselves," Aiden said, and I could hear the jealousy in his tone.

I sighed. "Aiden, we've been through this. She's just my beard, we have to look like we enjoy each other's company. Plus, I've known her for six years, we're friends in real life. We were just talking about silly shit. I'm gay, Aiden. I love cock and man ass… yours in particular. We can't keep having this conversation. I'm doing all of this so we can be together," I stated.

"I know, I know… it's just…"

"What?"

"I guess I'm just envious that she gets to sit down in that restaurant with you out in the open, smiling and laughing at whatever you were talking about in this picture, and I can't," Aiden said sadly, and his words hit me like a fucking Mack truck. It was as if he was channeling Kathy as he pretty much repeated her words to me. It hurt.

"I'm sorry, Aiden. I wish it could be you, too. It's not easy for me to play this part with her when the whole time I'm doing it, I wish I was living my life with you. But we knew what we were getting into and it's doing us no good to keep dwelling on it," I said. I didn't want to talk about how we had to live our truth in the shadows while I lived a lie in the open. It wasn't like we didn't know when we decided to throw caution to the wind and date. "Aiden, are you still there?"

"I'm here, Macio. Look, I will call you tomorrow. I'm still really busy."

I felt he was avoiding me because those damn pictures put him in a mood. Damn, with the internet, people could gossip that much faster. Sometimes I hated that fucking thing. I couldn't even get home and make myself comfortable before some bloodsucking media jerk blasted my private-public life on some dumb blog for all to see. I decided not to press him right now.

"Okay, baby. I love you. Call me tomorrow."

"I love you, too. I will," Aiden said before hanging up.

Well, at least he said he loved me too. That made me feel better. I was in the mood to jack off before, but now I wasn't. I tossed my tube of lube in the drawer and turned on the television. I had some more tough training tomorrow, as I had to defend my championship in a month and my competition was going to be brutal. Jaxon Hardy, he was a former champion and had been talking a lot of shit about how he was going to get it back. I was actually looking forward to the challenge.

"Are you going to be at my match next week?" I asked Aiden as I washed his back in the shower.

He nodded. "I wouldn't miss it for the world," he replied, then tilted his head back for a kiss. I happily obliged and slapped his plump ass for good measure. "I appreciate you giving me another exclusive for my magazine."

"You're special," I said, grinning.

I turned the water off and we both climbed out and toweled off. I pulled a pair of sweat pants from my drawer and put them on, then walked over to the bed, sprawling on it to watch Aiden get dressed. He was leaving in an hour, but I had enjoyed our weekend together, which surprisingly enough, was uninterrupted. Of course, Barry wasn't happy about me not training for those two days, but I promised not to have a life for the next week leading up to the fight. That appeased him. Aiden was all dressed now and I hated that he was leaving, but I took solace in knowing he was going to come back in a week.

"I have to fly to New York for the Knicks game for that exclusive with Derek Houser."

I pouted. "He's not better than me."

Aiden laughed. "No, he's so not."

I climbed off the bed and walked over to him, taking him in my arms and giving him one hell of a knee-weakening kiss. "I can't wait to see you again."

He pinched my pierced nipple and I quaked. "I miss you already."

I smiled and slapped his ass, then walked him to the door when his cab honked. I watched him driving off and felt that damned loneliness settling in again. If he lived with me, I could take him having to leave for a story better, because at least then I'd know he was coming back to me to stay. God, I was hating having to say goodbye, but for my career, I had to make sacrifices.

The week passed by, and in no time, it was fight night. The weigh-in got wild when I made fun of the pudge surrounding my opponent's stomach. He rushed me and we collided into the crowd, which made the media sharks go crazy. They loved that kind of shit and so did our promotor. It really sold tickets when a rivalry looked like it would be life or death. Kathy was with me, playing the part of a supportive girlfriend. Rupert and Barry, along with the commission officials, were there as well, making sure everything was on the up and up.

I was waiting for Aiden to show up for his exclusive interview before the championship bout. He could ask five questions and had fifteen minutes. Like the professional he was, he entered my dressing room and got right down to business, as time was of the essence. I was getting my hands wrapped up while I answered his questions. I wished the fucking commission officials weren't in the room, because if they weren't, I would have kissed the hell out of Aiden. Instead, we both had to play it cool.

It was a nice interview and I had a good time doing it with him. Fact was, we just made a dynamite couple. Barry put my gloves on and we tapped fists. With that, we wrapped up the interview and I did a few practice moves to get my blood pumping. This was the first time Aiden got to see my pre-fight routine. I was happy he got to see this part of me.

"Okay, kid, let's go kick some fucking ass," Barry said.

"Fuck yeah!" I growled and huffed, then walked out of the dressing room with Barry and the commission officials, along with the rest of my corner behind me. It was game time.

CHAPTER FOURTEEN

Aiden

A MONTH HAD PASSED SINCE MY LAST LITTLE TANTRUM OVER Macio having dinner with Kathy. A lot had changed – well, I had changed – since then. Hearing the slight edge of frustration in his voice when he had to defend his time with Kathy for the umpteenth time, followed by the disappointment when I cut our conversation early, triggered something inside of me. I was sick and tired of hurting all the time and feeling like a third wheel in my own relationship with the man I loved; a man who I knew damn well loved me in return.

That night after our argument, I sat in the quiet of my home and thought about my relationship with Macio. I couldn't help but compare it to the failed relationship I'd had with Geoff. I had promised myself that I'd never let myself fall for a man who would deny me in front of his friends and family, yet there I was with Macio. Then I realized that it really wasn't entirely the same thing.

In my relationship with Geoff, no one knew that we were anything other than friends. To be honest, I don't think Geoff had admitted to himself that he was gay. He always said he didn't want to put a label on our relationship. I didn't know if he was ashamed of himself, thought it was a phase that would pass, or was too confused to know what the fuck he wanted. All I knew was that he made me feel cheap and dirty. Those were things that Macio never made me feel.

While it was true that Macio wasn't out publicly, the people closest to him, except his brother, knew about our relationship. Beside Rico, Barry and Rupert were the closest thing to family that Macio had. He rarely spoke to his father and I didn't think he cared too much what the man thought about him. Rico, however, was another story. He idolized his brother and I knew he worried about losing him. Yet, Macio didn't seem eager to take Kathy home to meet the family either. It seemed it was a line he refused to cross, and though I suspected the reason, I needed to hear it from him.

"What does Rico think about your relationship with Kathy?" I asked the next night on the phone. I was certain that the two brothers must've talked about his new relationship. There was no way Rico hadn't seen their pictures blasted all over the internet and social media.

"Aiden," Macio said on a sigh. "I really don't want to talk about this with you. I don't want to fight with you."

"That's not what this is about," I assured him. "I just…" I struggled to find the right words to say without leading him into the answer I wanted to hear. I needed it to come from his heart.

"Rico thinks she's pretty and that she conducts herself well publicly. He likes that she comes across as an intelligent woman with a lot of passion and knowledge of the sport, rather than some groupie." Macio chuckled then and I felt the deep timbre of his voice roll through my body. I was almost distracted by it.

"What's so funny?" I asked him.

"Rico doesn't think she's the one for me."

"What? Why?" My heart sped up and I sat a little straighter in my chair.

"He said that I don't look at her the way he looks at Macy and I never bring her up in a conversation." I didn't think Macio could say anything else that would make my heart happier than it was, but I was wrong. "He also said that if I was as crazy about her as the media reported, I wouldn't make excuses for why I couldn't bring her to meet my family."

A few days prior, I would've been stuck on the fact that Rico wanted to meet Kathy and wouldn't have heard the rest. "Why do you make excuses?" My voice was barely above a whisper and raw with emotions only Macio could make me feel.

"I love *you*, Aiden. If I can't take *you* home to meet Rico, Macy, and the kids, then I'm not taking anyone. I don't like this charade I play with Kathy, it feels wrong to me, and I'm not going to complicate it even more by dragging it home to Rico. Besides, I would never deliberately hurt you like that. I know how hard this is for you and I know how bad that douche hurt you. I'm not him; I'm not that guy." God, his words were like a warm hug through the phone connection and were the spark I needed to get my head out of my ass.

I wouldn't lie and say that I never had doubts after that, but I stomped them beneath the heels of my expensive loafers Macio hated so much. The first thing I did was turn off the Google alert that told me anytime a new story about Macio popped up. Then I deleted the fake accounts I set up so I could follow Kathy's social media accounts. It was next to impossible to believe that what I had with Macio was real with those pictures in my face all the time. Kathy loved social media and it appeared she liked the attention she got from posting pictures of them together. I knew I was the one Macio loved and it was past time that I acted like it. I wasted no more of our precious time whining about Kathy.

I knew that my access to Macio would be limited the week leading up to his big fight with Jaxon Hardy. I understood that he needed to focus all his energy on his training because it would be his greatest challenge. Jaxon was a former champion himself and he wanted that title back more than his next breath. The cocky bastard thought he could easily take down my man to get it.

Instead of moping around my house from missing Macio that week, I went out with Seth or friends from work. Not every night, but more than usual. We went to bars to watch a few games or grabbed a bite to eat. My clubbing days were long behind me, so I easily turned it down when it was brought up.

"You still aren't going to tell me who *he* is?" Seth asked over dinner.

"There's no one to tell you about." It wasn't lost on me that *I* was the one denying Macio's existence. It felt horribly wrong and I hated it, but I had no choice. I loved Seth and knew I could trust him, but I would never betray Macio that way.

"If you say so," Seth said in a sing-song voice.

"I do." I sang right back to him.

I went about my week without a hitch until the night before I was supposed to head to Vegas. Seth had left the bar to use the restroom, so I checked my messages. The smile on my face when I saw I had one from Macio grew even larger when I opened it up. There was a picture of him and Caesar lying in bed with a caption that read: *We miss you.*

I stared at the photo longer than I should have. I started to respond to the message when I realized that Seth had returned to his stool. I quickly locked the screen and set my phone on the bar before I turned to smile at Seth. My heart froze when I looked into Troy Danver's devious brown eyes instead of Seth's guileless blue ones. Troy looked down at my phone and then back up at me. Fuck! How much had he seen?

I couldn't stand bottom-feeding photographers like him. He wasn't an artist; he was a damn paparazzo. People like him didn't care whose life they destroyed as long as they got their cash. I'd be damned if he got to Macio through me. The only expression on my face was one of disgust. "What the fuck do you want, Danvers?"

My hostility didn't seem to faze him one bit. His sneer for a smile made me want to kick him right in the gonads. "I hear you're interviewing Macio again before his big fight."

"And?"

"That's two exclusive interviews with the extremely private fighter," he answered.

"And?"

"I want to know why you, of all people, seem to be his favorite. You'd think a guy like him would steer clear of the controversial gay reporter," Danvers replied. "It appears that the two of you have… bonded."

I refused to be baited by him. I was controversial to some, but not many. I couldn't get a feel if he had seen the photo of Macio on my phone or if he was just fishing. "And you want to know what the macho fighter and the limp-wristed reporter could possibly have in common." I let my voice soften from the arctic tone I'd used earlier. I wanted him to think I was softening too.

"You're damn straight," Troy replied.

"But I'm not," I reminded him playfully.

"Spill it, James." Troy used my last name as if we were best buds. "What's your secret to getting access to the champ?"

I crooked my finger at him and he leaned closer. I crooked it again and he came even closer still. I leaned in the rest of the way until my mouth nearly touched his ear. "It's our deep admiration for Superman and our immense dislike for assholes like you." I sat back in my chair and looked into his stunned eyes. I wasn't a guy who was easily pushed around and it was time he learned it. "Get. Lost."

Troy started to speak, but Seth returned from the bathroom then.

"I believe you heard the man," Seth said when it looked like Troy had no intention of moving.

Troy looked him up and down, as if calculating to see how big of a threat Seth was to him. "Who are you?"

"None of your damn concern," I told Troy.

Troy acted as if he hadn't heard me. "Are you his boyfriend?" he asked Seth.

"Yep."

It was all I could do not to groan out loud. I knew if I did, it would only encourage him more. "Don't tell him anything, Seth. He's a fucking photographer for Dirty Laundry. He's looking for an exposé on my life." It was partially true.

Seth's eyes darkened with anger. "Do as the man suggested and get lost or I'll help you along the way."

Seth was several inches taller than Troy and had a much bigger frame. He could appear quite menacing when he wanted to be, and that night was one of those times. It worked because Danvers got up without another word. I saw the question in Seth's eyes, but he didn't say anything. Instead, we went about our night as if Troy's intrusion had never happened.

It was too late to reply to Macio's message when I got home. I was a little bummed because I knew he would be on lockdown, as I referred to it, for the twenty-four hours leading up to the fight. I chose to focus on the bright side, which was that I would be in his arms in just two more days.

I was both excited and nervous when I was shown into Macio's dressing room. I had seen him at pre-fight conferences, but never so close to the actual event. Only Barry, Rupert, and Kathy were permitted to be around him minutes before a match. As happy as I was to be in the same room as him, I was bummed that I couldn't give him a good luck kiss or even a fucking fist bump. We couldn't take any chances with the commission officials in the room.

I made certain not to look into Macio's eyes when he answered my questions. I feared I wouldn't be able to keep the longing out of my expression, so I chose to keep my eyes on the notes I was taking. Before I knew it, Macio was taped and ready to go. He followed Barry out of the room without a backwards glance at Kathy, Rupert, or me. I smiled inwardly because I might not have received any pre-fight affection, or even acknowledgment, but neither did Kathy.

I turned to face Kathy, prepared to thank her for what she did, but my gratitude dissipated as soon as I saw the calculating smile on her face. She was a woman with an agenda. I had no idea what she was up to, but I was sure I'd be the first, or second, person to know.

"Busy week?" she asked me. The innocuous question didn't match the sarcastic tone of voice she used. I looked questioningly at Rupert, but he shrugged as if to say he didn't know what was going on.

"Sure was," I replied. I had no choice but to play along.

"Me too. I've been fighting off reports that I'm pregnant." Before, her words would've been a knife to my heart, but I was smarter and stronger.

"Wow, another immaculate conception," I replied with wide eyes. Rupert snorted, earning a death glare from Kathy.

She turned her smirking glance back at me. "This is how you repay my kindness?"

"You're right, Kathy. I should be more appreciative." I took a deep breath. "I appreciate how you put yourself on the line by going out to fancy dinners and parties wearing expensive shoes and dresses that Macio feels obligated to buy for you." She blanched at my words, obviously unaware that Macio had told me every single fucking detail of their agreement. He felt strongly that Kathy shouldn't have to pay for any expenses related to her part in the charade.

She smiled acidly, then said, "I meant for not showing him the photos of you on the town with your *boyfriend*." She crossed her arms over her chest and tried to go in for the kill. "I understand why Macio has a beard, but fail to see why you need one too." I was about to ask what she was talking about, but she didn't need prompting. "I'm talking about your dates with Seth this week."

"Seth is just my friend, Kathy. Macio knows that."

"Well, according to the article on Dirty Laundry's website, you're much more than friends." *That fucking twat Troy Danvers!* "There were a few pictures included that made it look like you and Seth couldn't wait to go home and rip each other's clothes off."

I rolled my eyes at that one. "Because every photo posted in the media is the truth and should be trusted." I looked pointedly at her and smiled inwardly when I saw some of her confidence unravel. "Like the pregnancy bullshit," I said, in case I wasn't clear enough.

"You're lucky he didn't see the article before his match. He needs to be focused on his opponent in the ring and not doubting your loyalties. If he lost a match because of you…"

"First of all, I resent that you think Macio is so fucking weak that he can't block out the bullshit and focus on his fight. Unlike you, I trust him to be able to tell the difference between fact and fiction." The balls on that woman riled me up to levels I had never experienced before, but I wouldn't let her ruin my weekend with Macio. She was about to see the side of me that first caught Macio's eye. "It's in your best interest to make sure that he's not bothered by that shit anyway."

"How do you figure?" She looked at me like I was dumber than a box of rocks.

"Who do you think the media will blame if Macio stumbles in the ring? Me, who they don't know about, or you, who they see on his arm multiple times a week?" I laughed derisively as what I said started to sink into her pretty head. "You forget that I'm a sports reporter, honey. I've lost track of the number of times a wife or girlfriend got blamed for an athlete's poor performance. They go from media darlings to pariahs in a blink of an eye. They get booed in public, harassed on social media, and lambasted on the internet. Is that what you want?" The sour look on her face was the only answer I needed.

"Macio is in love with me. It's time you accept it." I looked at my watch and saw that the match was due to start in under ten minutes. "You better get out there and look pretty, darling. We don't want the sharks starting to speculate that there's trouble in paradise."

"Asshole." Kathy flipped her hair over her shoulder and headed for the door. "Are you coming, Rupert?"

I looked over at Macio's publicist and found him watching me with his head tilted slightly to the side. He looked at me as if he were seeing me for the first time and didn't know what to make of me. He was so lost in his thoughts and hadn't heard Kathy speak to him.

"Rupert," she yelled shrilly.

He jumped and followed her without a word, which was okay with me. I needed a minute to gather myself. Regardless of what I said to Kathy, I knew Macio wasn't going to like Troy's article. He was going to like the possibility of Troy having seen the message he sent me even less, but it was something I would need to tell him.

CHAPTER FIFTEEN

Macio

I DREW CLOSER TO JAXON, ARMS RAISED DEFENSIVELY, BUT ALSO offensively for when an opportunity presented itself for a strike. I'd watched numerous video tapes of Jaxon's ring performance. He was a damned good fighter and I had to pay him proper respect or risk making a rookie mistake. I was already bleeding from a shallow cut on my left brow and we were at least two minutes into our third round. The longest match I'd had before this one was only nine minutes and nineteen seconds, which was pretty much two rounds.

Jaxon was huffing and puffing as he inched closer to me. This fight was taking its toll on him too, but he was more conditioned than I'd given him credit for at the weigh-in. I stepped forward, then jumped back, guard up, blocking a right kick from him. He tried to follow that up with a leg sweep, but I dodged that one too, and landed a blow to his temple. It wasn't a good one, as my distance and angle wouldn't let me get enough power behind the punch, but he still felt it. His nose was bleeding profusely, I'd broken it in the second round and I was going to make sure I followed up on it since it was already injured.

The crowd was thriving with an energy that I was feeding off of as we fought. They were hyped up big time and loving this championship battle. Seeing as we were now in the third round, I was sure they felt like they were getting their money's worth. I threw a kick that Jaxon blocked, then followed it up with a punch to his midsection. He tucked in his elbow, protecting his ribs, which left him open for another blow to his face, which I tried to capitalize on, but he ducked, catching me with a blow to my abs.

I puffed out the air and stepped back to size him up again. It would seem that he had been studying my fight videos as well. I was going to need to get his ass into a ground game. He charged me and I blocked the first blow, but his second blow caused me to lose my balance and I fell back against the gate. That was when he hit me with a right hook that knocked me down. There were a few stars floating, but I wasn't completely out.

He was on me then, punching furiously, but I was blocking him effectively and as soon as I saw an opening, I grabbed his fist, then locked my legs around his neck in a triangle chokehold. One of my favorite maneuvers. My thighs were like steel vices as I tightened them around his neck. I could taste the copper flavor of my own blood as it leaked into my mouth from my busted nose. Jaxon was exerting a lot of energy in his attempt to break out of my hold, but he wasn't going anywhere. I switched my grip on his arm to where I could apply pressure to his elbow joint. If he didn't tap out, I was going to break that fucker.

The referee was in our faces, waiting for the moment when Jaxon submitted or his arm broke, whichever came first. We were both screaming and growling, but for different reasons. Finally, he couldn't take the pain anymore and tapped out. The referee hit my biceps twice, ordering me to release my hold. I did, and then shoved Jaxon away from me before rising to my feet. I threw my arms up victoriously as I jumped around the octagon. I was running on pure adrenaline and loving every minute of the excitement the crowd was giving me.

Lights flashed, cheers roared, there were a few boos, too, but fuck them. My corner came into the ring, congratulating me. I only wished Aiden was here and I could hug him in front of the world and that would be acceptable. As it was, this was a man's sport and according to hearsay, not a place for fags. I hated hearing shit like that, and sometimes I wondered how they'd feel knowing this fag kicked their fucking teeth down their throats.

Ah well, I may not be able to celebrate openly, but I was planning on giving Aiden a few rounds in the bedroom, or on kitchen counter, or even in the shower tonight. I stayed in the ring for a few minutes, doing a quick post fight victory interview with ETC promotion president, Shane Dixon. He was asking me questions I knew I'd have to answer again at the post-fight conference in a half hour. However, this was part of my job—granted, the part I hated—but my job, nonetheless.

"This was your longest fight ever, almost going into the fourth round. Was there any moment during the fight that you thought this might be it, I'm going to lose?" Shane asked me.

I shook my head. "Hell no. I never enter the ring with any thoughts of negativity. Fuck that," I said, using the towel Barry had draped over my shoulders to wipe away some of the sweat that was dripping into my eyes. My entire body was slick with it and I couldn't help but wonder just what kind of dirty thoughts were floating through Aiden's mind as he looked at how my body glistened with it. He really got off on the sweat I could work up fucking him… hell, I did too.

He laughed. "With this being your longest bout, how did it weigh on you physically and mentally?"

Barry patted me on my back and I turned to him, smiling, before facing the camera again. "I train like a fucking beast before every fight. I mean, look at these abs," I said, pausing to do a little flexing. I could hear the women in the audience get louder than the men at that point. "It was rough, but I knew I could go the full distance if need be. We could have done the full five rounds and I'd still have energy to fight some more. There was no fucking way I was giving up my championship."

"What do you think of your opponent?" Shane asked.

"He was tough, I mean, I'll give credit where credit is due. He's a tough son of a bitch, but this wolf was hungry and I don't give up my bones," I said, holding my championship belt up for all to see.

"All right, Champ, I'm going to let you go," Shane said, and I was relieved.

I did a little bit more grandstanding for the audience's benefit, the president had informed me that he liked for me to play up to the audience more, so I did. After that, I went back into my dressing room. My corner followed me, which was Barry, Mike, and Victor, along with my ring cut doctor, who immediately looked at my wounds.

"Nothing is broke," the doctor said after checking my nose. I sat there letting him patch me up a bit, then took a quick shower. He looked over my wounds again, determining that I didn't need stitches. He did bandage up the shallow cut over my brow. My eye was starting to swell a little, so I had an ice pack for that. I got dressed quickly and made it to the post- fight conference where I answered a lot of the same questions Shane had asked me and a few more.

Finally, that was over and I could head to my hotel. I was planning to spend the rest of the weekend at the hotel with Aiden, and then go back to Vegas on Monday. I'd already made arrangements for Aiden to be waiting for me inside my hotel room. I thought that would be easier. Right now, I was climbing into the back of the rented limousine with Kathy. Normally, Barry and Rupert would be with me, but they stayed to celebrate with the president of the promotion. I was invited too, but no way was I going to keep my baby waiting.

"That fight was amazing," Kathy said as she slid in closer to me.

I smiled. "Hell yeah... shit, it was the hardest one I've had to date, though. That fucker almost knocked me out with that right hook," I admitted. It wasn't easy for me to do, but I did.

"I was so scared when he had you up against the gate, and then when he punched you and you went down. My heart just stopped beating," Kathy said, putting her hand over her bosom.

I nodded. "Yeah, I knew I had to work my ground game at that point."

"I know you've got to be charged after a fight like that," she said.

"I am. I'm still like, floating high on adrenaline." I smiled thinking about how I was planning on spending all of my pent-up energy.

"I could totally help you," she purred, and out of nowhere, her hand slipped between my thighs.

I grabbed her wrist, stopping her fingers, which were only inches from my cock. "What are you doing?" I frowned. She kissed me and I pushed her back and kept my hand on her shoulder to keep her at an arm's distance. "What the fuck, Kathy?"

She huffed. "Oh come on! Are you telling me that you feel nothing for me?"

I shook my head. "Jesus Christ, I knew this was going to backfire on me."

"What does that mean?" she snapped.

"You and I pretending to be a couple."

"Are we really pretending, though?" she asked and tried to scoot closer, but I kept my arm up, keeping her at bay.

"We are not a couple, Kathy. I am gay. I'm also in love with Aiden. I thought you were over me anyways," I said.

"I was… but then I felt a connection between us the more we hung out together," she said, then sat back against the seat cushion. I lowered my hand and released her wrist because it looked like she was giving up her seduction.

"We're friends… that's all I wanted to be with you, Kathy. I have no interest in being anything more than that," I said, trying to make myself as clear as I could on the matter.

She huffed and crossed her arms over her chest. "I don't see how you can cancel women out, I mean, have you ever tried having sex with one?"

I shook my head because the blows she was dealing me were more powerful than the ones I got in the ring tonight. I was actually feeling lightheaded at the moment. "Kathy, I get that you have feelings for me, but I'm not interested. I think we need to end this arrangement. We can do it quietly and we can even blame it on me if you want to. Say I cheated on you with another woman if it makes you feel better. But I'm done pretending to be your boyfriend."

There was no way I could continue with the charade with her lusting after me the whole time. I was hoping this wouldn't happen, I did like hanging out with her. But what I viewed as a good friendship, she was making it out to be something more.

"I don't see why you're willing to give up everything to be with someone who's playing you for a fool," she said, which sparked my curiosity.

"What the fuck are you talking about?"

"Aiden and his boyfriend, Seth."

I scoffed. "Seth is just his friend."

"According to Dirty Laundry, they are more than just friends. Seth was quoted saying that they were lovers. Now, I know why you needed a beard, but what's Aiden's excuse? My guess is he didn't think he'd be caught cheating on you," she said.

"Where's the article?" I needed to see this shit with my own eyes.

She reached into her little purse, pulling out her cell phone and doing some searching. "Here." She handed me her cell and I read through the sleazy article and saw the pictures of Aiden and Seth together. The two looked to be out enjoying dinner. From what I could see, they did look very intimate.

"See, he's cheating on you. He wants to be with someone who can take him out in the open. Not with someone he has to hide in the shadows with. Someone who has to pretend like he's straight in order to be with him. You need to move on from him, Macio. He's going to ruin you, trust me," Kathy said. "I mean, even if it's not me you want to be with, it shouldn't be him."

I tossed her cell into her lap and turned away from her. My mind was swimming with thoughts of Seth touching my man and I was pissed that Aiden hadn't told me about the article. Was he trying to hide something from me? I didn't see him cheating on me... I mean, he'd been completely honest with me about everything. He wouldn't cheat, I just wanted to know what Seth's deal was. Was he trying to move in on my fucking territory or what?

"I'm just trying to look out for you, Macio," Kathy said.

"I just want to be left alone, Kathy, okay?"

"Fine." She sat on one end of the limo and I sat on the other.

When the driver pulled up to our hotel, we both climbed out. I didn't bother to hide that I wasn't as happy as I was when I first left the arena. The media flashed us with their cameras as I led her inside, ignoring all of their questions. We made it to our two bedroom suite. She slept in one room and I had the other, and both rooms were separated by the length of our suite. Since we were a couple, having one room made sense just in case anyone started prying.

I opened the door to see the living room and dining room empty. Kathy went into her room and I walked towards mine. When I opened the door, there was Aiden sitting on the bed.

"We need to talk," he said.

"I agree." I closed the door and placed my jacket and championship belt on the chair. This wasn't the kind of reunion I had been looking forward to, but I knew we needed to talk about Seth. I bet that was what he wanted to clear up. "You go first."

"I didn't appreciate coming to your hotel room, only to find an escort naked on your bed," Aiden said.

I frowned. "What the fuck are you talking about?"

"When I came here, as soon as I opened the door, there was some brown-haired, blue eyed escort laying butt ass naked on your bed.

Said he was already paid for. Of course, I kicked him out, but I'd like to know why he was here," Aiden snapped.

"I didn't hire any fucking escort," I stated. "The only thing I can think of is Rupert or Barry hired him. That's how I used to do it before I met you."

"Why would they have him for you when I'm here?"

I shrugged. "I don't know. I didn't fucking ask them to get me one. Shit, for all I know, they probably thought we'd broken up after seeing that article about you and Seth in Dirty Laundry looking all lovey-dovey," I shot back.

"Oh, give me a break!" Aiden yelled, throwing his hands up. "I told you, Seth and I are just friends."

"Yeah, then why was he quoted as saying you're more than that?"

Aiden sighed and lowered his head as he massaged his temples. "That scumbag Troy Danvers was spying on me and asking questions about us. When Seth came back from the bathroom, he started asking questions about him, and Seth claimed we were lovers before I could say anything. But after it was done, I thought maybe it was best if he believed that. I was going to tell you about it, but I'd just found out about the fucking article myself tonight. Your girl Friday was more than happy to show it to me."

Shit! I sighed and sat down on the foot of the bed with him. "Kathy showed me the article in the limo and I let stupid shit go to my head."

"You thought I cheated on you?" he asked with an outraged tone.

"No, I had hoped not. I just know that you and Seth are close and he can…" I turned away, feeling a little bit like I wasn't worthy to be with him. I was asking a lot of Aiden and he'd been a trooper having to deal with everything I was tossing his way. As it turned out, his suspicions about Kathy weren't unfounded since she tried to fuck me in the limo. This night was not ending the way I had hoped.

"You were saying?" Aiden asked, placing a hand on my knee.

I looked up at him because he deserved my eye contact. God, he was beautiful and I loved him so much, sometimes I couldn't breathe when I thought about how much I missed him when he wasn't with me. "He can be the man to you that I can't be and I guess when I saw the pictures of you two together, I got jealous."

Aiden took my head into his hands. "You're all the man I need, Macio. I love you." He leaned forward, kissing me.

I wrapped my arms around him, holding him closer as we kissed. I pulled back smiling, because this was more like it. "I love you too, baby. I just wish I could be as free with you as he is."

He slipped his arms around my shoulders and kissed me again. "I know, me too. Sometimes when I think about it, I do get jealous when I see you out and about with her."

I sighed and shook my head. "That won't be happening anymore."

"What happened?" he asked with a frown.

I knew the only way to combat people spreading rumors about us was if we were completely honest with each other, so I told him about the limo incident. "But I stopped her and ended our charade. I even told her she could blame it on me. Say I cheated on her with another woman or something. It's not like that's unheard of among athletes in the sports world." I could see his nostrils flaring as his anger rose and I knew he wanted to march into her room and probably pull some hair, but I wasn't going to let him out of my sight.

"That bitch!" he snarled.

I laughed. "I like when you get angry-protective of me." I nuzzled his neck, licking and sucking his soft flesh.

"You're trying to distract me so I don't go into that bitch's bedroom and yank her head bald," he said, then moaned as I struck a sensitive spot.

"Maybe," I teased. "But to be honest, all I could think of all day was getting to spend time with you and being inside of you."

"Mmmmm, what about the escort?"

I chuckled. "What about him?"

"So you really didn't know anything about him?"

I pulled back to give him eye contact again, so he'd know I wasn't lying. "I had no idea. I haven't been with anyone since I've been with you. Why do you think I have blue balls every time I see you? Don't believe me, feel for yourself." I grinned as I grabbed his hand, slipping it between my legs so he could feel how hard my cock was. "My balls are filled with a load I've been saving for you all day. And I'm going to give it to you nice and hard."

Aiden smiled. "Okay, I'm convinced."

"You know I'd never lie to you," I said, then pushed him back onto the bed.

"I know. I'd never lie to you either," he promised.

I leaned down, kissing him passionately. Just one look from him could set me off and drive me horny out of my mind. I took both of his hands, pinning them to the bed above his head. "I hope you brought extra clothes," I said before ripping open his button-down shirt. He gasped in a mixture of shock and lust as the clear buttons went flying in all directions. Now that I had his taut chest exposed, I leaned down, licking, sucking, and nibbling his flesh like the feast he was.

When I got to his pants, I pulled them down roughly and yanked them off completely. Aiden sat up and grabbed my shirt, pulling it over my head, before I shoved him back on the bed. I kissed and sucked both of his inner thighs as I worked my way toward his crotch. I loved how he squirmed on the bed while I mastered his body to both of our delights. He arched off the bed, gasping as I tongued his hole. I loved the way he tasted, every inch of him was delicious and I was hungry!

"Oh god!" he panted as his fingers gripped my hair. "Oh Macio, feels so good."

I played with his cock as I rimmed him and I loved how hard he was. I sucked and licked his tight hole a bit longer, then moved up, taking both of his juicy balls into my mouth.

"Ooohhhhh shiiit!" Aiden moaned, and I loved watching him

from my vantage point. "Yeeeaaah," he purred when I took him into my mouth.

I sucked him down slowly, making sure to twirl my tongue all around his shaft. I'd been thinking about sucking him off for a whole week and I was going to savor this moment. I loved how he squirmed on the bed and all of the sexy sounds he was making. All of this was for me and I didn't want to ever imagine anyone else making Aiden feel this way... as if they could. Aiden was mine. I smiled when I felt him grow harder in my mouth and he cried out loudly as he released. I swallowed, enjoying the flavor of my man as he gushed down my throat. He quaked hard and I held onto his hips as he rode his orgasm out.

When he was drained, I pulled back, and that was when he got a little aggressive, grabbing me and pulling me onto the bed. "My turn," he said, then slipped off the bed, down on the floor between my legs. I laid my head back and enjoyed his mouth on my cock. Ooohhh, yes, damn... his lips and tongue were working their magic. I was so riled up from all of my lusty thoughts about him, I knew I'd probably blow this first nut out quickly.

"Yeah, baby, suck it," I moaned, giving him encouragement, not that he needed it. He was all over me like my cock was a popsicle on a hot summer's day. Our fingers locked together as he sucked me off and I loved the connection we shared. "I'm gonna cum."

He sucked me harder and faster, and my grip tightened on his fingers as my orgasm rushed through me. I cried out and bucked as I unloaded three days' worth of spunk into his mouth. I could feel him swallowing and that set me off even more, making my climax especially intense. His masterful lips milked me dry and it was going to take me a few moments before I was ready to go again. Aiden climbed back on the bed, grinning at me with wet lips.

I grabbed him by the back of his head and kissed him deeply. I could taste my own cum on his tongue and I loved it. I loved him. I was surely going to have my way with his sexy ass all night. Let

Kathy hear that. Maybe then she'd get that I was just not that into you, as they say. Two hours passed with me fucking Aiden on the bed, against the wall with his legs wrapped around my waist, against the large glass window the way I knew he loved it, and finally, in the bathtub where we were supposed to be soaking after our vigorous workout, washing up.

Afterwards, we were both exhausted and well spent and it didn't take us long to pass the fuck out. I woke up to an urgent knocking on my bedroom door a few hours later. I had to untangle my limbs from Aiden's body in order to climb out of the bed. I slipped on my sweats and opened the door to see Kathy standing there, fully dressed.

"Rupert wants to see you," she said, then I saw her gaze cut to my bed behind me and her frown deepened as her disapproval reared its ugly head.

"Okay. What time is it?" I asked as I wiped the sleep from my eyes.

"Time for me to leave. No way am I going to stay in this hotel and listen to you throw your career away," Kathy shot back, then walked away.

I rolled my eyes. It was probably for the best that she left, since we were breaking up. I stepped out of my bedroom, closing the door behind me. I didn't want to wake Aiden up, lord knows I had put him through a four round fuckbout. I walked over to Rupert, who was sitting on the sofa. I took a seat in the chair opposite him.

"Did you hire an escort last night?" I asked, getting right to an issue I wanted answers on.

He nodded. "I thought you'd want some company."

"Bullshit. You knew Aiden was here."

"For the interview, yes. But I'd read the article about him having a boyfriend. I'd just assumed you two broke up and you just didn't want to tell me. I was only looking out for you, kid," Rupert said.

I rolled my eyes. "Maybe you're looking out for my private life a bit too much, Rupert. I knew about Seth, Aiden and I don't keep secrets. By the way, I hope you got your deposit back on the escort."

"Nonrefundable, I'm afraid."

I shrugged. "Serves you right."

"Next time, I'll make sure before I do something like that in the future, fair enough?" he asked.

I nodded. "Yeah. Okay, so what's up, why are you here? What time is it anyway?"

"Three in the morning, and I'm here this early because I've got some very disturbing news," he said.

I frowned. "What kind of news?"

He licked his lips and lowered his head as though he didn't want to have to tell me what was going on.

"Rupert, what the fuck?" I snapped. "What's going on?"

"Some pictures have surfaced of you and Aiden… together."

Those words shut me down. It was as if I wasn't sure I'd heard him correctly. "What pictures?" I asked. We'd been very careful, Aiden and I. I couldn't even think of a moment when we'd slipped up.

Rupert picked up the envelope he had on the sofa next to him and handed it to me. I took it and removed the two photos that were inside. There in color and HD were two images of me kissing Aiden in my home in Vegas. We were in my hot tub, making out. I remembered this night, it was a month ago when Aiden had come out there to visit me. Holy shit… I felt my life flash before my eyes as I looked at them. My heart began thumping in my chest like a piston and I looked up at Rupert.

"Who sent you these?"

He shrugged. "I don't know. There wasn't any return address or note or anything. Just the photos."

"Do they want money?" I asked, thinking someone was trying to shake me down.

"If they do, they haven't demanded it yet. Listen, kid, this is what I was worried about. Things like this always find a way of coming out. We have to bury it, but I won't be able to bury it if Aiden is still in your life."

"Bury what?"

We both turned to see Aiden standing in the doorway of my bedroom. This wasn't good at all and I really didn't know what to do or think. My mind scrambled for logic, but I just couldn't think logically at the moment. Why… why did shit like this have to happen to us?

CHAPTER SIXTEEN

Aiden

THE LACK OF MACIO'S BODY HEAT WOKE ME UP. IT AMAZED ME how quickly I became addicted to his touch and the way I sought him out in my sleep. Overnight stays were not something I had with many guys in my past. I was used to waking up alone, yet my subconscious knew when he was supposed to be near.

"Macio," I said into the darkness of the hotel room. I understood his need for the hotel, but I would much rather have gone to his home after the fight. I sometimes resented sharing him with his team, but never with his dog Caesar.

I decided to look for Macio when it was obvious he was neither in the bedroom or the adjoining bathroom. I had a feeling that something was wrong, but wasn't sure what it could be. Sure, we had that minor disagreement about the escort and that article about me and Seth, but we got over it. We had grown a lot in such a short time that even though our situation wasn't ideal, I had faith that we were going to make it work.

I heard raised male voices when I approached the bedroom door. I couldn't imagine what the hell Rupert was doing in our hotel room so early in the morning. What was so important that it couldn't wait?

"Do they want money?" I heard Macio ask when I opened the door and looked out into the living room.

Rupert shrugged and said, "If they do, they haven't demanded it yet. Listen, kid, this is what I was worried about. Things like this always find a way of coming out. We have to bury it, but I won't be able to bury it if Aiden is still in your life."

"Bury what?" I asked. I saw Rupert holding an envelope while Macio looked at photos in his hands. The ominous feeling from seconds before grew until I thought I would be physically sick. The devastated look on Macio's face when he looked at me did nothing to make me feel better. "What's going on?" I looked back at Rupert when Macio stood silent. I blanched at the triumphant look that briefly crossed Rupert's face.

Then Rupert's expression morphed into one of deep concern. "Seems the two of you weren't as careful as you thought. Someone is blackmailing Macio with photos of you."

"What?" I asked. Macio said nothing in response, but he handed the photos to me with a trembling hand when I reached for them. The frightened look in his eyes nearly killed me. I reached for him, hoping to comfort him, but he stepped back from my touch and shook his head. It would have hurt me less had he stabbed me in the heart.

I looked down at two photos of Macio and me kissing while in the hot tub at his house. I forced the fear that I was losing Macio out of my mind so I could focus. Investigative journalism had been my first love, so I let my natural instincts kick in. I looked at the pictures with an observant eye and picked up a few things. One, the pictures were taken in Macio's backyard – his very private backyard that very few people had access to. Two, they were very poor quality, which told me an amateur took them and not some seasoned paparazzo like Troy Danvers.

Macio walked over to the large windows that overlooked the city. I saw his reflection in the window and the guarded man that I met at our first interview had returned. Gone were the laughing eyes and blinding smiles; instead, I could see him building a wall between us brick by brick. I knew I had to think fast or lose him forever. So, I told them the two things that struck me as odd. I was encouraged when Macio turned and faced me.

"What do you think it means?" he asked.

"Can I see the blackmail note?" I asked Rupert. I could tell a lot about a person by their grammar and word choices. Rupert turned a slight shade of pink and then admitted that none existed. "And this envelope just showed up at your hotel room at…" I looked at the ornate clock on the wall, "three o'clock in the morning?"

"I…"

"Don't you find that odd, Macio?" I cut Rupert off before he could answer. Something was really wrong about the entire situation.

"What do you mean?" He came back to the middle of the room where Rupert and I stood.

"If I were going to blackmail you and had access to your publicist's hotel room, then I'd take a little bit better advantage of the situation." Macio tipped his head to the side and I hoped I was getting somewhere with him. "First of all, I wouldn't have sent the photos without a demand for money…"

"Maybe that's next," Rupert said, cutting me off. "Could be they're just waiting for the right moment."

"Come on, Rupert. You're smarter than that." I looked at Macio and ignored the other man who sputtered in shock. "These pictures were taken when, babe?"

"A month ago," Macio answered.

"Exactly. This person, who has shitty photography skills by the way, took a money shot like this and held onto it until *after* your championship fight? Wouldn't they ask for the money before? Not only does he or she show up after the fight, but slips this through Rupert's door in the middle of the night? This floor isn't accessible without an elevator key." I reached for Macio and was encouraged when he didn't pull away from me that time. "This isn't some outside guy threatening to expose you, babe. This is someone getting back at you because they didn't get their way."

"I don't think I like where this is going." Rupert's response was nearly a snarl and so different from how he usually spoke that Macio and I both turned to look at him. "Who are you accusing and what are you accusing them of?"

"Relax, Rupert," Macio said. "Let him talk."

I ignored Rupert's outburst even though it only made the entire deal look shadier to me. "Macio, think about it. Kathy's behavior in the limo, the escort in the room, and then her showing you that stupid story Troy Danvers wrote about me. Doesn't it seem like too much of a coincidence?"

"Kathy's behavior in the limo?" Rupert asked in concern. "What's he talking about?" Macio told him about Kathy hitting on him and learning that she hadn't gotten over him like they thought. He told Rupert that they were ending the charade. "It won't matter now that these pictures are going to get leaked," Rupert said bluntly. "Everyone will know that she was your beard. She's going to be hounded in the press something fierce." He shook his head sadly. "Barry will be heartbroken when his daughter's name and reputation gets dragged through the mud."

"Who says they're going to be leaked? Where's the threat to go the press?" I challenged.

"It's obviously a silent threat," Rupert fired back. His chest puffed out as he labored to breathe during his righteous indignation over the situation. "Macio, you've known Kathy for a long time. She's not the kind of person to do something like this." He looked at me and raised his voice even more. "That leaves Barry and me. Which one of us are you accusing of trying to ruin his career - the very career that both Barry and I depend on? You're the only one with nothing to lose."

"Do you even hear yourself right now, Rupert?" I asked.

Rupert advanced on me with pure hatred in his eyes and I braced myself for his attack. "Listen, you little arrogant..."

"Stop it," Macio yelled, cutting Rupert off. He stepped between Rupert and me, blocking Rupert from my sight and physical reach. My heart sank when I met Macio's dark eyes. I saw so many emotions in their depths – sadness, fear, and the one that hurt me the most, regret.

"Macio." I was ready to plead for him to not give up on us. It just couldn't be the end.

"Aiden... we need to take this seriously," Macio said. "What I see is someone, one of those parasite fucking journalists to be exact, found a way to capture photos of us on my private property. Who knows how many photos they have of us?" He sighed, then he turned from me, running his hand down his face. I could tell he was going into full panic mode.

"I'm sure this is just their warning photo, letting us know that they—whoever they are—know about you," Rupert added, fueling Macio's paranoia.

"Jesus fucking Christ," Macio swore as he turned around to face me. "Baby, maybe we need to calm it down a bit."

"There's no way in hell this shitty photo is the work of a professional. Look," I pointed at the poor quality of the pictures, "I'm not even sure people will recognize us." I turned and addressed Rupert. "Macio lives in a gated community that requires a passcode to get in. How did a paparazzo get in to take these photos?" I could feel my frustration rising as I realized how close I was to losing Macio.

"You're asking me? How would I know how some scumbag got access to his home? Maybe he bribed the security. Maybe he climbed the gate. Maybe it's someone inside of the community who saw you two. I mean, how careful were you?" Rupert shot back. "Look, this is what I was worried about, kid. You know what this will do to your career. It's as good as over if these images get out. Maybe whoever sent them is just warning you. Maybe that's why there wasn't a note."

"We can't take the chance, Aiden. I can't lose the belt. This is my livelihood, it's all I know. It's what I train for. If those pictures get out, regardless of who sent them, I'm ruined. My career is ruined."

"Babe, I am taking this seriously, but it's important that cooler heads prevail here and we don't panic. You have to acknowledge that there's something off about the whole situation."

"I don't care! I... I just need time to think, damn it!" He looked up at me and his expression softened. "Aiden, I...." His voice cracked and his words broke off. "I need time, Aiden. This is my career, it's everything to me. I worked my ass off to win that title and even harder to keep it. I can't lose it."

My heart plummeted to my feet as I took a step back from him and then another. I suspected that his request for time really meant that we were over. I knew all along that it could happen, that my love wouldn't be enough to risk his career over. I had hoped that he'd someday learn that he could have it all. Loving me and being a fighter didn't have to be mutually exclusive. I knew nothing else I had to say would make a difference and could only hope that time and space would make him see that what we had was worth fighting for.

"Okay, Macio." Tears burned the back of my eyes, but I refused to show my grief in front of Rupert.

I went into the bedroom and quietly packed my bag, hoping that Macio would come into the bedroom and say goodbye to me privately, but it didn't happen. I walked out of his hotel room with my head held high. If it was going to be the last time he saw me, then I wanted him to see a strong man worthy of his love and devotion.

That strength lasted until I made it to the car where I felt safe enough to let my grief flow. I vowed it was the last time I drove home in the middle of the night with tears streaking down my face from Macio breaking my heart.

CHAPTER SEVENTEEN

Macio

"WHAT THE FUCK DID I JUST DO?" I ASKED MYSELF AS I STARED at the closed hotel door that I let Aiden walk out of.

Rupert came up behind me, clasping my shoulder. "I know this was hard, kid. I know how much he meant to you. And who knows, once this dies down… you two might be able to get back together."

I turned from him, shaking my head. "Maybe we weren't meant to be together. Maybe I was being selfish in thinking we were. He's out in the open and I'm in the shadows." Maybe this was best. At least that was what I was trying to convince myself of. I thought we were playing it safe, but then who in the fuck took those pictures?

"I'm just glad they sent the photos to me instead of some tabloid," Rupert said, and I nodded.

"How did they know that you'd be here?"

"I'm trying to figure that out myself. Although, it's not like I was in hiding. I'm wondering if it's some groupie of yours that doesn't want you with a man," Rupert speculated, shrugging. "Not all stalkers are professional paparazzi."

My mind raced with a million thoughts and every last one of them made me want to puke. I felt sick to my stomach and my head was throbbing. I hated seeing the pain in Aiden's eyes when he looked at me. Oh god, what had I done? My heart felt like it'd been ripped from my chest and stomped on, kicked across the room, then pushed back into my body by the Hulk. I knew Aiden and I were playing a dangerous game, and I think that was part of my excitement. I also felt like I deserved the happiness he brought me and I felt good knowing I brought him happiness.

Jesus, did I just throw all that away?

"Macio, I can see you're stressing, but you need to stick to your guns on this one," Rupert said. "You need to let him go before you two get in too deep."

I plopped down on the sofa. "It's already too late for that. I love him, Rupert."

There was a hardness to Rupert's expression when I said that. Of course, I wasn't surprised. He'd been against Aiden and me from the beginning, but he always kept it professional and kept our secret.

He sat down on the sofa beside me. "I know this hurts, kid. But this is best. Like you said, you're living on two sides of a coin. He's openly gay, you're not. He can go on dates with guys and no one really gives a shit. You get caught kissing an openly gay public figure, Shane will go crazy. MMA isn't a sport that will accept you being gay, you know this."

"Fuck, I know! Damn it, does that mean I have to always be alone?" I shot back. I was angry as hell. Angry at whoever took those fucking pictures. Angry at the MMA sports world for forcing me to live in the closet. Angry at a society that wanted to shame two men in love. But most of all, I was angry at myself for being so damned weak!

"You have to choose, then. Once you make your decision, you stick to it. Aiden or your career, because that's what this comes down to, Macio," Rupert said.

I looked at him and he was staring at me with a stern expression. I thought about how happy Aiden made me, how much I loved being in his presence, the scent of him next to me and how intoxicating it all was. I thought about how his smile could brighten my day and the sound of his laughter warmed my heart. I thought about how great it felt to be inside of him, bringing him pleasure and seeing that look of ecstasy on his face when that moment came.

Then I thought about what I'd be giving up if I chose him. Millions of dollars in endorsements. My promotion might not want to promote my fights. Other fighters would have a shit ton of issues, no doubt. Fans would turn on me and eventually, I might be asked to take a dive just so they could give the belt to someone manlier by their standards. These fears weren't unfounded. I didn't know of one MMA fighter who was openly gay. Also, it wasn't just me I had to think about. Rupert, Barry, my whole crew made money through me, too. I couldn't let them down. Maybe it wasn't meant to be, after all. Maybe I was just being selfish in wanting to keep Aiden to myself. I forced him to go back into a closet just to be with me, and for what? A few weekends of shared passion and endless phone calls? That was no life, not for either of us. Rupert was right.

I looked at Rupert. "It's over," I said.

Rupert nodded. "Then we can move on from this point." He slapped me on my knee. "Let me take care of these photos, kid. I want you to focus on your career, that's what's most important here."

"What are you going to do?"

"I'm going to do my own investigation, see if anyone saw who dropped these off. In the meantime, try to get your head straight." He got up and walked out of my hotel room, leaving me alone with those thoughts I wished I didn't have.

God, I needed a drink.

It had been a week since I let Aiden walk out of my life without so much as a fight. That was seven days of me feeling like I had made the biggest mistake of my fucking life. That was one-hundred and sixty-eight hours of me laying in my bed at night, holding on to the pillow Aiden had slept on at the hotel. I couldn't shake the feeling of deep regret and I couldn't help but miss him so damned much.

I sat down on the bench and let Mark, my ju-jitsu coach, tape up my hands. He didn't know I was gay, but he did know I had something on my mind and it wasn't about the MMA world.

"You okay, Macio?" Mark asked me. "You don't look like you're all here."

"I've just got shit on my mind," I said.

"Yeah, I bet, that break-up with Kathy was ugly. It was all over the media. Bitches were tripping like you broke up with them personally and shit," Mark stated.

I snorted with a smirk. "Yeah, I had plenty of hate mail from a few of them."

It was true, women hated that Kathy and I had broken up. To them, it was a bruiser and Cinderella story. I wondered how many of them put themselves in her thousand dollar shoes I'd paid for. She hadn't talked to me since storming out of my hotel room that day, but her name was synonymous with mine lately. Of course, the amount of feedback I was getting for breaking up with Kathy I knew paled in comparison for what I'd be getting if those photos were exposed.

"Yeah, well, you did what you needed to do. To be honest... and this is just between us... I felt she was too fucking clingy, man. I mean, she was all over you. I like Kathy, got nothing against her, but I just didn't see you two as a lasting couple. There just wasn't any connection," Mark stated.

"Yeah, my brother said the same thing," I replied with a chuckle as I thought about what Rico had said. Of course, my brother called to give me his support over my break up. He said some comforting things that made me feel worse, because what he didn't know was that I did have a break up, but it wasn't with Kathy.

"All right, you're all taped up. Okay, it's time for you to put that shit in the back of your head now, Macio. I'm going to whoop your ass out there. I'll teach you for lowering your guard in the ring."

I flexed my fingers, making sure I could move them just fine. I put on my gloves and stood up, ready to follow Mark to the mat. "I underestimated Jaxon a little."

"Which is something we've told you time and time not to do. Never underestimate your opponent. Motherfuckers underestimate you all the time and look what happens?" He smiled as he proved his point.

I nodded. "It won't happen again." I followed him to the mat and took up my position. Barry sat backwards in the chair, resting his arms on the back of it as he watched us spar. Of course, he understood why I had to break it off with Kathy and supported my decision. He also got wind of my real break up with Aiden and supported that too, especially after he saw the photos.

It was Barry who urged me to cut off all ties with Aiden. That meant all social media links I had with him, just in case someone hacked my site. They didn't want any incriminating social media trails that could prove those photos real. Aiden was right about one thing, those images were blurry as fuck. Barry pointed out how that worked in our favor. You really couldn't see the faces clearly, but he didn't want to press the issue.

I hated having to cut off all ties to Aiden. I wanted to see his photos in magazines and read his articles. On several occasions, I'd masturbated to a photo I'd taken of him with my cell phone while he'd slept naked in my bed. I should have deleted the damn thing, but I couldn't. I tried several times, but couldn't never press the "delete" button. Aiden had been so beautiful laying on the rumpled covers.

We'd shared hours of hot lovemaking and were exhausted. He looked so peaceful as he slept, too. That photo felt like the last thing I had that was ours. I couldn't bring myself to get rid of it. Instead, I sent it to my Google drive. At least it wouldn't be on my phone anymore.

Mark took me down easily when I didn't see the move he used to sweep my leg out from under me. "What the fuck is this, Macio? This is bullshit, man. Get your head in the fucking game. I'm not here to play with you," he snapped as he let me up.

"I know, I'm sorry," I said as I climbed to my feet.

Mark grabbed me by the back of my head, forcing me to look at him. "I know you're hurting, Macio. Channel that shit into your fists, bro. Make that pain work for you." He let me go and punched me in the chest in his motivational way.

I nodded and jumped up and down, trying to work that fire back inside of me. I'd given up the love of my life… quite possibly a love that I may never have again, all for my career. It was my decision and I needed to put myself into it one hundred percent. I needed to let Aiden go if I was going to move forward. The good news was, no more photos came in the past seven days, so I was keeping my fingers crossed. I shoved my pain into the closet I was hiding in and put my focus on Mark and taking him down.

"That was a great training session, bro," Mark said, slapping me on my shoulder as we walked out of the shower room.

"Thanks, man. Loved seeing you on your ass," I taunted.

"I had your ass on the ground more, teaching you that new shit," Mark bragged.

"Yeah, yeah," I said, then toweled off. We both got dressed quickly, and I walked out of the locker room, running into Barry.

"We need to talk," Barry said.

"I'm tired, Barry, can this wait?"

"No."

"Shit. Fine." I followed him into his office and he shut the door behind me.

"I've just gotten off the phone with the president of ETC and he's loving you, kid. The fans are loving you, that last fight drove everyone wild. It made a lot of money for the promotion, too. People want to see you fight, they want to see you win. Hell, even the ones who want to see you lose are still paying to see you fight. You're a pay-per-view draw, kid. That means you can get even more sponsorships. I was talking to Rupert and he's working on a multi-million dollar deal for you with Hyperion automotive."

"Holy shit, are you serious?" I asked. Hyperion cars were expensive as fuck.

"Yeah, serious as a heart attack. It's a delicate deal, he's really trying to build you up, so that's why we don't need any scandal going on with you right now. You breaking up with Kathy isn't that big of a deal since no one knows the reason why. That's all going to blow over soon, especially when you get in the ring with your next opponent. What we need to do is get you an opponent and a feud that's really going to hype up the fans. You've got to do some shit talking, buddy, really pump it up, and we need to make sure you can back it up. That's why I need your head in the game."

"My head is in the game, Barry."

"Good, because I'm here to make sure you succeed, Macio. I love you like you're my own son."

"I know." He did support me no matter what. Barry was telling me about an opportunity of a lifetime. I had to take it.

"Dirk Calder's been wanting a shot at you for a while, ever since he won his contender match, and now the opportunity is finally here. He's been talking a lot of shit, too." Barry laughed.

"Fuck that bitch, I'll wipe my ass with his face," I stated.

Barry laughed harder. "Yeah, I know... but watch out, because he has a mean right hook and his ground game is better than your last three opponents.'"

"So, I'll beef up my ground game."

"And your aikido."

"That's tomorrow's training. Okay, can I go now? I'm hungry as fuck."

"Watch those calories, Macio."

"I will." I wanted a steak—rare and spinach salad so damn bad. I gave Barry a hug, then left the gym. My body was a little sore, seeing as Mark hadn't pulled his punches, and Hiko wouldn't be pulling his punches tomorrow during my aikido sparring. I drove to a favorite steakhouse of mine and ordered my food to go. When I got home, I ate and got on Twitter to look at Aiden's account. I needed to stop torturing myself, but I needed to see him.

Damn it, would I ever get over him?

CHAPTER EIGHTEEN

Aiden

T FELT LIKE I WENT THROUGH HALF OF THE STAGES OF GRIEF IN THE first few hours upon arriving home in L.A. after walking out of Macio's hotel room. I was in shock that Macio and I could be over and wanted to deny it had happened. I was angry – at Macio, Rupert, the universe – and was willing to bargain anything I had to get him back. Depression and loneliness hit me upside the head like a two-by-four and left me feeling dizzy and disoriented. It didn't help matters when I tried to drown my sorrow in a bottle of booze. I woke up the Monday after the breakup wondering how soon I could expect the upward turn, the reconstruction, the acceptance that we were over, and the hope that I'd find happiness again someday.

I cried myself sick as I typed up the interview I had conducted with Macio. It was embarrassing how many times I replayed the recording just so I could hear his voice. I kept checking my phone to see if he had texted me. I read every text message he ever sent me at least twice before I opened my Messenger app. I had planned to read through all of them, too, but I noticed the conversation thread was gone. My heart sank when I searched for Tyler Johnson and realized he'd deleted the one secret way he had of communicating with me.

It was then that I realized Macio had made his decision. It was his way of severing all ties and moving on without me. I tried to do the same by deleting his contact information, but I wasn't strong enough yet. I equated the pain from deleting his photos and messages from my phone to losing a limb. Fuck, I thought I might recover from the physical pain quicker than the emotional.

I threw myself into my work and took every traveling assignment I could to keep my mind off of Macio. At first, it didn't work. I thought about him just as much as I did when I was at home and there wasn't enough activity in the day to keep my thoughts from turning to him – wondering how he was doing and if he ever thought about me. In addition to the traveling, I turned over the fighting assignments to the new reporter Jerry had hired and refused to read any article or on-line report that I thought his name would even appear in. No Google searches, nothing. Macio had made a clean break and I needed to do the same.

Eventually, it paid off. I stopped looking at the pictures of him on my phone and I even went complete days without thinking about him. I congratulated myself when I realized after three long months, I had finally reached the upward turn phase of my grief. I was ready to embrace the reconstruction phase and hoped it might include some up close and personal time with a guy who wanted to be with me – and not just when no one was looking.

I realized I wouldn't meet that special someone by spending all my time hiding inside my house when I was home. I stopped ignoring dinner and dancing invites and hit the town with my friends. It felt awkward the first time a stranger pressed his body against mine on the dance floor. My heart screamed that it was all wrong and only

Macio had the right to touch me so intimately. The hard truth was that he didn't want me enough to love me openly, so I forced myself to ignore my reservations and threw myself into the dance. I didn't leave the club with my dance floor partner, but it was a step in the right direction.

I wasn't fooled into thinking the first guy who showed interest in me would be the one I fell head-over-heels for, but I had to admit it felt good to have a man look at me with naked interest in his eyes, especially if it was in a crowded café in the middle of the afternoon. The date wasn't what I had hoped it would be because the guy was clearly only looking to hookup.

I needed much more out of life than a guy who was just looking to pick up men from an app. I wanted to find a guy that I had a lot of things in common with, but someone who could also push my boundaries a little and perhaps interest me in non-sporty things like art and movies. I wanted a guy who could stimulate me both sexually and intellectually. I thought just maybe I had found my opportunity when Seth introduced me to a colleague from his office.

"Where the hell have you been hiding him?" I demanded when tall, dark, and dreamy went to use the restroom. Garrett Connelly exceeded every item of my wish list for a serious boyfriend. He was educated, funny, quick-witted, and drop-dead gorgeous, but above all those things, he was out and he looked at me like I could be someone special to him.

"You weren't ready to meet Garrett because you were too busy getting over a guy you swore didn't exist." He pinned me with a look that said he dared me to argue with him. The dramatically arched brow reminded me of a pro-wrestler we both used to lust after when we were younger.

I was laughing hysterically at his shenanigans when I felt a light tug on my sleeve. I turned my head and looked into Kathy Vincennes' crystal blue eyes. I jerked with surprise, which prompted a soft smile from her. "Kathy?"

"In the flesh." She smiled softly at me, which threw me for a curve. This was a woman who had once been at odds with my happiness, but you'd never have known it by looking at her that night. "How are you doing?"

"I'm… um, good. How are you?" I asked her.

"Is there somewhere we can talk in private?" she asked. There could only be one topic that we had in common and it was a place I didn't want to go. "Please. It's really important." The soft plea in her voice worried me that something could be wrong with Macio. No matter how things ended between us, I would never wish misery and unhappiness for Macio.

"Sure." I rose from my chair and tilted my head for her to follow me. I led her to a patio off the side of the restaurant that wasn't busy that time of the year due to the cooler night air.

"How are you really, Aiden?" she asked once we were alone.

"I'm fine, really." I felt tension bunching up the muscles in the back of my neck and raised my hand to try and work them out.

"I think you're as miserable as Macio is." She held up her hand to stop me when I started to respond. "He's a mess, Aiden. He's been a wreck since he broke things off with you and I'm worried for him." She blew out a soft puff of air and looked away for a few seconds as she pondered her words. "People who don't know him wouldn't recognize just how on the edge he is, but I see it and so does my dad. I think Rupert is the only one who thinks he's doing okay, but that's because he wants it to be so." The disdain in her voice told me she wasn't Rupert's biggest fan. It was nice to know I had something in common with her, even though it was too late for it to count.

"I'm not sure what you want from me, Kathy. It's been three months since I last saw Macio. He's made no move to talk to me or get in touch with me in any way. He's made his decision and moved on with his life and I'm trying to do the same thing." Then a thought occurred to me and I asked, "How did you even know where to find me?"

"It was fate." She smiled like she was truly pleased to see me. "I've been debating calling you for some time now, but I kept talking myself out of it. You'd been hurt enough and I didn't want to cause you any more pain." I was sure I gawked at her when she reached over and rubbed my arm comfortingly. I was getting a glimpse of the kind-hearted Kathy that Macio knew. "I'm in town for my friend's wedding and she picked this place for the two of us to have dinner before things get crazy when the rest of the bridal party shows up tomorrow. And here you are."

"And here I am," I replied.

"Aiden, he needs you. Can you please call him?"

It killed me to hear that Macio was hurting so badly, but I wasn't willing to risk my heart to him again. Maybe one day far off in the future it wouldn't hurt me to see his face or hear his voice, but I wasn't there yet. If I truly wanted to move on and find happiness, then I needed to stay away from him. "I can't, Kathy. I'm sorry."

I didn't stick around to hear anything else she had to say. I returned to my dinner companions and tried my best to push the things that Kathy said about Macio out of my mind. I had thought I was further along in my healing process over our breakup, but I realized how wrong I was after a few words from Kathy. Still, contacting Macio after all the time that had lapsed would only lead to two things: misery and heartache. I decided the only chance I had for a happy future was to move on and never look back.

I was pleasantly surprised when it seemed that Seth hadn't noticed I wasn't as engaged in our conversation as I had been before Kathy interrupted us. The same couldn't be said for Garrett. "You're still getting over someone, aren't you?" he asked when Seth left us alone to say hello to someone he knew at the bar.

I was going to deny it, but then I looked into his honest green eyes and couldn't do it. "Busted."

"We've all been there." Garrett reached across the table and placed his hands over mine. "I think something truly amazing could develop between us, Aiden, and I'm willing to wait for you as long as I need to."

"Garrett, I can't make you—"

"Any promises. I know." He smiled patiently at me. "How about you agree to have dinner with me next weekend and we see where things go."

I studied him for several long moments, looking for any sign that he wasn't as sincere as he seemed. The last thing I wanted was for him to later say that I misled him when I couldn't give him what he wanted from me. I knew I wasn't in the right frame of mind to attempt a relationship right then, but that didn't mean I would turn away an offer of friendship that could lead to something pure and meaningful down the road. So, I agreed to dinner.

I was a nervous wreck until I reminded myself that it was dinner between new friends, not a date. I relaxed and let my guard down a bit. In fact, he was easier to talk to than Seth because he didn't know my dating history. He didn't push for names and details when I told him about trying to move on from someone who was closeted and didn't show any signs of wanting to love in the open.

It wasn't exactly a unique situation, so I wasn't surprised to learn over steaks and lobster tails that he had been through a similar experience in his not too distant past. Instead of crying into our beers, we laughed at some of the predicaments we had found ourselves in. It felt good to laugh with someone who knew what I had been through.

It became quite obvious that our waitress was ready for us to move on when we lingered too long over dessert and coffee. Neither of us wanted to leave and we both were unsure of the next step. Our dallying around was cutting into her earning potential and it appeared to make her nervous. We left her a generous tip for her trouble when we couldn't delay our goodbye any longer.

"Can I call or text you while you're in Spain covering soccer?" Garrett asked when he walked me to my car after we left the restaurant.

"I'd like that."

Our friendship picked up from there over the next month. We tweeted and flirted publicly via Twitter and Instagram, which was a welcome change from having to hide all the damn time. Garrett was on my mind a lot when I had down time and his texts or calls never failed to bring a smile to my face. We went to lunches, dinner parties, museums, and many other places together. I finally got a glimpse of what a healthy relationship looked and felt like. Yet, it was Macio that came to me in my dreams.

I tried so hard to move on from him completely, but it seemed that he still owned a chunk of my heart. Regardless, I could never have what I truly wanted, so I tried to force things with Garrett to prove that I could be physical with someone other than Macio, but it backfired. It started off okay with a sweet kiss on my couch, but I knew it wasn't right the minute his tongue touched mine. I pulled back from our kiss and just stared at him in defeat.

"It's okay that you're not ready," Garrett said sympathetically. "There's no expiration date on pain and no guaranteed timeframe for a heart to heal." He brushed his thumb over my cheekbone comfortingly before he dropped his hands to his lap.

"Why are you so good to me?" I ran my hands through my hair in frustration.

"Because I've been there, Aiden. I want to be someone special to you someday and I'm willing to wait for you if you think there's a chance for us." His captivating green eyes held so much promise and I wanted so badly to tell him that I was sure we had a chance, but... "Tell you what," he said, interrupting my thoughts, "let's talk when you get back from your road trip. Take some time and think it over, okay?"

"I will," I promised.

I had every intention of doing just that during my ten-day road trip that ended in New York. I vowed I would excise Macio's ghosts from my heart and move on with a man who could give me the life I always wanted. Instead, I ended up crying my broken heart out to

Garrett on the phone a few days later.

"It's so stupid to still be in love with him after everything that he put me through. I mean, I haven't known him that long, so why is he so hard to get over?" I asked Garrett.

"I don't think it matters how long you knew him," he said softly. "My grandparents only knew each for three days before they got married in 1941. They were married for sixty-five years and died seven months apart, ten years ago." I heard the longing for that kind of love in his voice.

"You're not really helping me, Garrett," I said wryly. "You're supposed to tell me that someone I knew for such a short time couldn't possibly be the reason I would never be happy again. You're supposed to tell me that there's someone else out there for me."

"What if there's not someone else, Aiden?" Garrett asked.

My heart fell to my feet. "Do you mean that you don't think I'll ever find someone else to love who will love me in return?"

"No, that's not what I meant." Garrett let out a soft sigh before he said, "What if this guy is the one? Maybe you can't get over him because you're not meant to. Perhaps he misses you just as much and needs more time. Maybe he regrets the decision he made but is too afraid to call you." I never told Garrett Macio's name or his profession, only that I had fallen for a closeted guy. It wasn't his fault that he didn't know the entire situation or that his words gave me false hope.

Garrett and I realized that a romantic relationship wasn't going to develop between us. Instead, I gained a wonderful friend who I could talk to about things that I couldn't with anyone else. In a way, it made me feel worse that I couldn't fall in love with Garrett.

At night, I'd often replay Garrett's words and wonder if he could possibly be right. Did Macio miss me? And would anything change after more time passed? If not, I was well and truly fucked because I had finally accepted that I would never get over Animacio De Niro.

CHAPTER NINETEEN

Macio

SWEAT DRIPPED OFF MY BODY AS I POUNDED THE FUCK OUT OF the punching bag, trying to burn the rage out of my system. I'd successfully defended my championship and was making hand over fist in financial endorsements, but I was as unhappy as any man could be. My life felt unfulfilled because I'd given up on the one thing that brought me joy. The one man who was willing to give up his own freedom for me. I came to the conclusion after the last four months of pain and suffering that I might be a badass inside of the octagon, but I was a fucking pussy-ass coward out of it.

My muscles ached as I released my fury on the sand-filled leather bag in a flurry of jabs and kicks. I was pissed at everything and everyone. I'd been this way since the day I let Aiden walk out of my life without engaging in the only real fight that mattered. I was mad at society for not accepting two men wanting to share their lives together. I was mad at the sport I had dedicated my life to that said a man wasn't a real man if he could be in love with one. But in the end, I was mad at myself for punking out. I gave the bag one more hard blow before I gave up, finally exhausting myself. Unfortunately, I was still angry and unhappy.

"I don't know what that bag did to you to deserve such an ass whooping, but I'm sure it had it coming," I heard a soft, feminine voice say.

I didn't even need to turn around to know that it was Kathy. Since our little mishap four months ago, we'd made up and put all of that behind us. She'd been pressing me for the past month to talk to Aiden and I'd been doing my best to ignore her… and avoid her. Thinking of Aiden was far too painful, even though he was all I could think about.

She walked over to me. "You need to talk to him, Macio. Before it's too late."

I knew what she was talking about. I'd already seen the pictures of Aiden and some other guy named Garrett smiling and flirting all over Aiden's Twitter and Instagram accounts. I'd managed to destroy two cell phones after looking at how happy they were. Perhaps I was already too late, as it looked like Aiden had moved on.

"It's already too late," I growled and threw one more punch at the bag. It was weak, just like my excuses.

"So, I guess you're giving up on the one person in this world who made you complete," she pressed. "I guess all is going well for you then. Must be why you're all alone in my father's dimly lit gym beating the shit out of a punching bag."

I looked at her. "What do you want me to do? He's already got another boyfriend and I can't necessarily give him what he deserves. We just weren't meant to be," I said.

"Do you really believe that?"

I didn't respond. I'd been telling myself that lie for four fucking months and I still didn't believe it myself. How could I expect her to? "You should be at home. It's late."

"I see," she said. "I only care for your happiness, Macio. You're a great guy and you deserve to be with him. Don't give up on what you two had. Especially not out of fear."

I stared at her, at a loss for words because it seemed as though Kathy could see right through the walls I had put up. This really was amazing, coming from her. "I'm surprised that you're pushing me to talk to him so much. It wasn't too long ago when you wanted Aiden out of the picture. When did you become his white knight?"

"Now you're just being an asshole," she remarked.

"I'm still curious."

Kathy laughed. "I was arrogant to think I could change you, Macio. You made it quite clear that you are strictly dickly." She giggled at her own joke, then sighed as she grew more serious. "I didn't respect you or Aiden or either relationships involved. I can admit when I'm wrong... can you?"

I snorted. "That's just it. I have and I share that pain with no one else but myself, because everyone else has stock in what I can bring them. Through me, everyone else makes their living."

Kathy held her hands up, cutting me off. "Oh, so you're the martyr here."

"I'm the breadwinner."

"Do you really even know what will happen if you two get back together?"

"If he's even willing to do that. I broke his heart, K. Not only that, he doesn't deserve to have to live in my shadow."

Kathy stepped up to me, grabbing my face in her delicate hands and forcing me to look at her. "Then don't make him. Get your man back, Macio, and both of you walk out into the light. Let society be damned. Take the blows, stand up to the challenge, and make the change."

Fear struck my heart at the thought of what she was telling me to do. I could imagine my brother and father's disapproval, the ridicule from the public. Not to mention the backlash from the promotion.

Could an openly gay MMA fighter even be marketable? I pulled away from her and turned, storming off to the locker room.

"You don't know what the fuck you're talking about, Kathy. Go home," I growled. I took my time in the locker room, showering and getting dressed. The whole time I was in there, I was praying that Kathy had left. When I finally walked out, I was all alone in the gym again. I locked up and went home to my empty house, save for Caesar, who came running up to me, jumping on my chest.

"Hey big boy!" I greeted as he licked my face and I rubbed his ears. We did our ritual and after I gave him a doggy treat, he ran off to his special place under the stairs to eat it. I tossed my gym bag into the corner of the room that also held my two bags of luggage. I had a championship fight to go to in New York in a week, which meant I needed to get there for all the pomp and circumstance beforehand. That consisted of conferences, a weigh-in, and promos. All the shit I hated. I went to my fridge for a cold beer. After a few swigs, I looked over my mail and stopped at a magazine featuring one of Aiden's articles.

"Why are you torturing yourself?" I mumbled as I turned to the page where he was featured, only to see his photo inset on the page. God, he was beautiful and everything I'd ever wanted. My chest felt tight and that constriction traveled up my throat as I fought back the tears. I'd shed plenty since we parted ways. The doorbell ringing gave me a much needed distraction. "Coming," I called out, heading towards the door. I checked the peephole, only to see Rupert on the other side. "Shit... what the fuck does he want?"

I opened the door, giving him a slight smile. "What can I do for you this time of night?"

"I just came to give you some company, kid. I'm here under a friend's capacity," Rupert said. He was holding two bottles of the good shit, and that was just what I needed to drown my sorrows, at least for a night.

I waved him in. "Make yourself at home."

"Thanks." He entered and I closed the door.

He was dressed pretty casual in a pullover and jeans, which was rare for Rupert. God knows he loved his suits. He walked into my living room and I followed. "I'll get us some glasses," I offered after Rupert took a seat and turned on my seventy-five-inch screen TV.

"Cool," Rupert said, grinning.

I walked into my kitchen, grabbing two wine glasses and a corkscrew, then returned to the living room, taking a seat beside Rupert. "Here." I handed him the corkscrew, and he popped open the wine and started pouring. "So, how's the wife?"

He shrugged. "Having a good time spending my money, as all women do."

I smirked. "Shit, I know a few twinks who can put most women to shame when it comes to shopping," I said.

Rupert laughed. "Oh, I bet." He held his glass up. "What should we toast to?"

I had to think about that, because I didn't have shit to celebrate at the moment. "How about we toast to finding our way," I suggested.

Rupert smiled. "I'll drink to that."

We clicked our glasses and started drinking.

Two hours later, and two bottles empty, we were both good and drunk and talking about all kinds of shit. I hadn't laughed that hard in so long, it felt good to just let it all go and live again, even if it was temporary.

I chuckled at something Rupert said and shook my head. "Hey, buddy, no one told you to dress up like a hotdog that year."

"Your dog thought I was one of his stuffed toys!"

We both burst into drunken laughter as the memory came back to us of Caesar, in his early puppy days, gnawing on Rupert's hotdog costume at my Halloween party a few years ago. Rotty's had death grip bites and my pup made that hotdog, and the man inside, his for the night. When I'd finally gotten Caesar to let go, there was a big hole in Rupert's costume that left his ass exposed. We all had a good time laughing at the whole incident that night.

"That was great," I said, smiling as I thought back fondly.

"It really was," Rupert agreed. "It's nice to see you smiling and laughing again, Macio."

I looked at him. "Yeah, it feels nice."

He put his hand on my knee. "I just want you to be happy. I care about you a great deal."

"I know."

His hand moved up my leg, getting closer to my crotch. "I mean, I really do care about you. I'd go out of my way for you."

"Rupert, what's going on?" I asked, even in my drunken state, I was confused by what was happening. He leaned over, kissing me. I pulled back. "What are you doing?"

"Let me give you what you need. When was the last time you got off?"

"Fuck... you—you're straight," was all I could say.

"I have a wife, but I'm not straight," Rupert said, then he grabbed my crotch and I jumped. "It's time you moved on, Macio." He kissed me again, this time more forcefully.

My mind was swirling with the boatload of information I was struggling to process. Meanwhile, my cock was growing harder as Rupert massaged my groin. He pulled away from me, kissing my neck and sucking on my ear.

"Just let me give you pleasure, Macio," he whispered into my ear. I felt his fingers unzipping my pants and he reached inside, pulling my erection free.

Jesus Christ! What the fuck was happening? I felt like my mind was cloudy and I was having a hard time focusing. Just when Rupert lowered himself towards my cock, Aiden's face flashed before my eyes and it cleared away all of my haze. I grabbed Rupert's shoulders, forcing him to sit up.

"Stop," I said.

"I want you, Macio. Don't you see? We can be discreet about this. No one has to find out," Rupert said.

"Holy shit," I grumbled as I climbed off the sofa, fumbling with my wilting erection as I shoved it back into my underwear. I zipped up my pants and turned back towards him. "Are you fucking serious right now?"

"I… I thought you would be open to this," Rupert said.

"To fucking you?" I roared.

"I only wanted to make you happy. You seemed so lonely."

"I feel sick," I mumbled as I staggered away from him. "Get out. Go home to your fucking wife."

Rupert stood up with a bit of a wobble. "I—I'm sorry, Macio. I… I didn't mean—"

"Just go," I said, then directed him toward the front door.

"I'm too drunk to drive," he pointed out.

Shit, he was right. "Then call yourself a fucking cab and go." No way was I going to let him stay here after the stunt he just tried to pull. "As a matter of fact, I'll call." I pulled my cell phone out of my pocket and fired up the app.

"I'm sorry, Macio," Rupert was saying as I typed in my information and his.

"Yeah, I bet you are. I can't believe you tried to fuck me," I said, still in shock by that fact. "How long have you been lusting after me?"

"We don't have to talk about this. I made a mistake in my drunken state. I didn't think it through. Please forgive me, Macio."

I plopped down in one of my plush chairs. "Look, let's pretend like this shit didn't just happen. A cab is on its way. Go home, get some sleep. Tomorrow is a new day," I said. He made a mistake and I was too drunk to try to think about how bad things could have gotten had I not stopped him. But really, I stopped him because he wasn't who I wanted. He wasn't who my heart desired. Aiden was as much a part of me as my flesh and bone… he was that deeply rooted. If anything, this debacle made that very clear to me. We sat in silence for ten minutes before there was a honking of a horn outside my home. Rupert apologized one last time before leaving and I took my drunk ass to bed.

When I woke up the next afternoon, I knew what I wanted. I had to hurry up and get dressed because my flight to New York was departing in two hours. Luckily for me, I'd packed my bags already, so that was one thing I didn't have to worry about. I called my cab and when it arrived, I made my way toward the airport. Caesar was sad to see me go, but the dog caregiver would make sure he wasn't lonely while I was gone. I met up with Barry at the airport and when I approached him, he checked his watch.

"Cutting it pretty close, ain't cha, buddy?" he asked, giving me a curious eyebrow.

"With good reason. Look, we need to talk."

"Here?"

"Now."

He sighed. "Are you feeling okay, Macio? Please tell me you're not nervous about the fight?"

"Hell no, I'm going to wipe the floor with Tony Romero's ass. This is much more important," I said.

Barry nodded and we walked over to a seating section that wasn't too crowded and took a seat. "Okay, what's going on, kid?"

"I want Aiden back."

"Jesus Christ. I thought you were getting over him."

"I can't and I don't want to, Barry. I haven't been happy since we broke up and that was the biggest mistake of my life. I let him go because I was afraid. I'll never forgive myself if I lose him forever."

"Macio—"

"I don't need your permission, but I do want your support. I'm going to pursue Aiden. I'm going to get him back."

Barry was quite for a few seconds as he studied me. "You're

serious."

I nodded. "I've never been more serious about anything in my life."

"I can tell. I see that look in your eyes and I know what it means. Macio... you know I'm with you every step of the way. But you have to know, if you two somehow get back together and it gets out, it's going to be some tough storms coming your way. So, I need you to really... I mean *really* think about this."

"I did."

"Think about it some more and if by tomorrow your mind is unchanged... then we take whatever comes our way head on, fair?" Barry asked.

"Fair. But just to let you know... my heart is what's unchanged and that's why my mind is made up. But I'll give you the twenty-four hours you're asking for. After that, I'm going back for my man," I said. I was determined to get Aiden back by any means necessary. I was sick and fucking tired of living my life in fear of what others thought of me. My family included. The shit that happened with Rupert gave me an epiphany. He lived a lie. His wife had no idea he was bisexual and I was sure she didn't know that he wanted to sleep with me, his number one client.

I was going to tell Barry about what Rupert had done the night before, but decided against it. I said last night that we could and should forget it ever happened. In spite of that lapse in judgement, Rupert was an amazing publicist and he was fair by me. He messed up, but he deserved a second chance. I messed up and I only prayed that Aiden would give me a second chance. If I wanted Aiden to forgive me, I had to be able to forgive Rupert.

When Rupert met us at the airport with a nervous expression on his face, I was happy I'd kept what happened between us a secret. Barry greeted him as he normally did and I saw the nervousness fade from Rupert's face. When Barry made one last trip to the bathroom, Rupert turned to me.

"Did you tell him?"

I shook my head. "Like I said last night, it never happened. Let's leave it at that."

"Okay… thank you."

"Just don't try that shit again," I warned.

He looked at me and nodded.

We sat in silence until Barry returned, then the three of us took our luggage and boarded our plane heading for New York. Not only was I excited to kick some ass and defend my title, but I was looking forward to flying to L.A. afterward and claiming my man.

CHAPTER TWENTY

Aiden

MY TEN-DAY ROAD TRIP FELT MORE LIKE TEN MONTHS BECAUSE I was still reeling from the acknowledgement that I wasn't over Macio and might never be. New York was my final stop and I was beyond ready to conclude my interview with the starting lineup of the New York Knicks and get back home. I had been looking forward to the interview before things blew up in my face because I wanted to showcase the men's charity work and good deeds for their community. I still wanted to do that, but I also wanted to get the fuck out of Dodge before I ran into someone I didn't want to see.

I wasn't ignorant of the fact that a major fight was going on in the city that never sleeps and I saw several members of the press who covered the fights in the same hotel I was staying at. The last thing I wanted was a run-in with Macio or anyone on his team. I kept my head down and made a beeline for the exit when it was time for me to head over to the basketball game. The plan was for me to watch the game, interview the starters, and head back to my hotel early so I could get some sleep before I needed to head to the airport for my ass-crack-of-dawn flight.

The game was a nail-biting, buzzer-beater win over their biggest conference rival so the guys were too excited to talk about their charity work directly after the game as planned. They talked me in to going out to dinner with them and promised I could conduct the interview over steaks and seafood. I was famished and it sounded like a good time, so I gladly went along. The interview went great and I had a better time than I would've ever predicted, but it was really late when I got back to my hotel room.

I was too wired to sleep once I crawled between the sheets, so I decided to get a head start on writing my article for the following week's edition of Ringside. I laid everything out and then went into the hallway to get a bottle of lemon-lime soda from the vending machine near the elevator.

"Damn it," I said when I saw it was out of order. Going downstairs to the one I had seen on the main floor seemed like such a pain in the ass, but I was thirsty and tap water didn't sound the least bit appealing.

I trudged down the few flights of steps, rather than take the elevator, and entered the ground floor near the hotel gym. I could hear the whirring of the treadmill and the fast footfalls of someone who sounded like they were running from their personal demons. Hell, I knew that feeling all too well and commiserated with the person. I couldn't help but glance inside the gym when I approached it and then stopped dead in my tracks, certain my eyes were playing tricks on me.

It wasn't just anyone running from their demons, it was Macio – my tormentor and the other half of my broken soul. He must've sensed he was being watched because he looked in my direction. The cartoon-like widening of his eyes when he saw me would've been funny if I also didn't notice the signs of distress written all over his beautiful face. I realized how true Kathy's words were and it broke my heart.

I wanted to go to him, to offer some comfort, do something, but I wasn't sure what he would accept from me. His actions four months ago said we were over and I had no reason to believe he felt any differently until he stopped the treadmill and crooked his finger for me to come to him. My body went to him on its own accord, as if drawn to him like a magnet.

He stood before me with his body glistening from sweat and his gym shorts riding low on his hips so the top of his V was on display for my lonely eyes. "Aiden." There was so much feeling in that one word – relief, hope, and the same longing that had rocked my world for the past four months. "Fuck, I've missed you."

I closed my eyes and reopened them, sure that I had been dreaming once again. Then I felt his fingers caressing my face and knew he wasn't a figment of my imagination or a vision that would vanish the moment reality pulled me from my slumber. "Tell me you're real," I heard myself say.

"As it gets, baby." Macio pulled me into his arms and held me tight. At first, I was so excited to be in his arms again that I forgot where we were and that someone could see us. I tried to step back from him, but he just held me tighter. "I was coming for you when I got back home, Aiden. I had decided enough was enough and I was going to claim what belongs to me."

"Macio." I honestly tried to focus on his words and not the masculine smell of his sweat or his half-naked body pressed against mine. I could feel Macio's body reacting to my nearness just as strongly as mine was to his. "Show me," I told him.

"Not until you're truly mine. I won't share you…"

"There's no one else, Macio." He looked so doubtful and I wasn't sure why. "There's been no one since you. I promise."

Macio wrapped his hand around my wrist and pulled me behind

him into the stairwell. He was on me as soon as the door closed. He pushed me up against the wall and pressed the full weight of his body against mine before he captured my lips in a fierce kiss. Macio's tongue sought entrance and I opened to him immediately, eager to re-learn his taste and the texture of his tongue against mine.

I was panting heavily and my dick was leaking large amounts of pre-cum by the time he pulled away. The wicked smile he gave me promised me a night I would never forget as he took my hand and led me up the stairs to the next landing. He repeated his kiss until I was weak-kneed and shaking from head to toe.

Macio opened the door and looked into the hallway to make sure we were alone before he led me to the elevator doors. I could feel his need for me vibrating off him as we waited for the elevator to arrive. Once inside, he removed his penthouse access card from his shorts and pushed it into the card reader slot.

I wanted him to kiss me again, I was sure my eyes begged him to do it, but he wouldn't risk getting caught on camera and I honestly understood how he felt. "Things will be different this time, Aiden. I promise you."

Maybe I was stupid for getting lost in the depths of his dark eyes and wanting to believe in him once more, but I couldn't stop myself even if I had wanted to. My soul cried out for him and it felt like my heart was whole for the first time since I'd walked out of his hotel room in Las Vegas.

Any miniscule amount of hesitation I might've had faded the second we were alone in his penthouse suite. I expected him to throw me over his shoulder and carry me off to his bed, but instead, he pressed his forehead to mine. Desire and longing clawed my guts and I felt his answering need for me ripple through his strong body.

"I love you." His declaration was a broken whisper against my lips. "Tell me you believe me, Aiden."

I could've blamed it on my need to be with him, to be filled by him, but the truth was that I heard the difference in his voice. Hearing that he loved me wasn't new, but the way he said it was; as if the confession had been ripped directly from his soul. "I believe you, Macio."

It was the catalyst he needed to lead me to his bedroom where he removed his workout gear and my clothes, then laid me on the bed. "I'm going to wash the sweat off me. You better be here when I get back or I'll search the entire hotel until I find you."

I snagged his arm before he could walk away. "Don't bother showering. I want you just as you are." I proved it by lifting my head and licking a path of salty, wet skin from his collarbone to his jaw before I sucked his earlobe into my mouth. I tugged until he collapsed on top of me. "Show me with your body what words could never express."

There wasn't an inch of my skin he didn't kiss or part of me he didn't touch, including the ones deep inside my soul that a human hand could never reach. Macio took his time readying my body with oiled fingers to receive him, even though he shook with the desire to claim me. He was proving to me that things were different and that his needs went well beyond the physical.

Macio's lips never left mine when he positioned himself between my spread thighs and pushed inside me. I couldn't help but cry out when he penetrated me and I struggled to adjust to his girth. It had been so long since he had been inside me and he was harder than I'd ever felt him before.

Macio cupped my face in his hands and looked into my eyes. "Mine." He began to move inside me in long, slow glides, making sure I felt every inch of him rasping over my sensitive, stretched entrance before he brushed against my prostate.

"Yours," I replied. I lifted my legs higher and wrapped them around his waist, holding him as tightly as I could.

Macio slid both of his hands into my hair and lowered his lips to mine so he could make love to my mouth as surely as he did my body. I felt him in every part of me, from my curled toes to the tips of my hair.

From that moment on, most of the talking was done with our

bodies. I touched him everywhere I could reach with my hands while he worked in and out of me. I felt my hot tears streaking down my face and tasted his in our kiss. My orgasm built inside me and I wanted to fight it off, to make it last, but I had been too long without him. I felt Macio's desperation in the way his body shook against mine.

"I want you to fill me, Macio."

"Aiden," he groaned.

Pleasure coiled around my spine and spread through my veins until I knew I would come if he didn't stop and pull out of me. The wicked gleam in his eyes told me he could tell how close I was to coming all over myself and he wasn't about to let up.

Macio moved his hands to cup my ass and lift it higher so he could change the angle of his penetration. Instead of grazing my prostate, he pegged it repeatedly until I roared his name and came so hard my vision dimmed.

"Give me everything, Aiden," Macio said as stream after stream of my cum hit my chest and stomach. He dropped down and licked a drop that even hit my chin. "How did I live without your taste? Never again," he vowed.

Once my balls were empty, Macio growled deep in his throat as his orgasm ripped through him and he came inside me. He pumped his hips over and over until there was nothing left of him to give me before he collapsed into my waiting arms.

"Jesus, Aiden. Tell me you're real," he said, repeating my words from earlier.

Instead of using his same words back at him, I said, "As a heart attack, baby," which made his body shake with laughter.

"I need a shower," Macio groaned, but made no move to roll off me.

"I think we could both use a shower and maybe we should do some talking now that we took the edge off," I suggested.

Macio inhaled deeply as if he either didn't want to talk or feared what would be said. If we were really going to make a relationship work between us, we needed to communicate openly or we were destined to repeat our breakup. I, for one, doubted my ability to recover if that happened again.

Clean up time turned into playtime, which resulted in earth shattering blow jobs that left us both leaning against the shower wall, gasping for air. "Too much for the champ?" I asked teasingly. I knew he had to be running on fumes by that point after a fight and two powerful orgasms.

"I got your champ right here," he said, cupping his cock and balls.

We got back in his bed once we had toweled off, and laid down, facing one another on our pillows. I fought sleep because I was sure that he wouldn't be there when I woke, that everything that had transpired was a cruel visage of things I wanted to happen, not the life I would truly have. Macio's eyes softened with understanding as he brushed the back of his fingers over my cheek.

"I'll be here," he promised, "and we can talk in the morning."

"I have a flight to catch in like… two hours," I told him after a huge yawn.

"You'll just have to catch a later one, because I'm not ready to turn loose of you yet. I… can't. I need more time."

"Okay." I snuggled tighter against him and let the heat of his body and the solid rhythm of his heartbeat lull me to sleep.

Sunlight streamed through the windows when I next opened my eyes. I was a bit disoriented at first and confused when I woke up in a hotel room that clearly wasn't mine because my accommodations weren't nearly as luxurious. Then I recalled every second of my reunion with Macio when it played through my mind like it was a movie. I was disappointed that he wasn't sleeping beside me and a bit annoyed because he promised to be there. Then again, he didn't necessarily promise to be in the bed, just that he wouldn't disappear.

I heard a familiar voice coming from the living area of the penthouse suite and I whipped back the covers in furious indignation.

Dread didn't begin to describe the feeling in the pit of my stomach as I yanked open the bedroom door and locked my gaze on Rupert, who raked his eyes up and down my nude body. I had been too fucking pissed at his presence to bother with putting on clothes or a robe.

"You again," we both said accusingly, at the same time.

CHAPTER TWENTY-ONE

Macio

HADN'T BEEN THIS HAPPY SINCE THAT NIGHT IN VEGAS WHEN I
last held Aiden in my arms. I couldn't believe I let him walk out
of my life four months ago. I'd done some pretty stupid shit in my
lifetime but that was the dumbest. All that seemed to be behind me
now, because I had him in my arms once again. This time, I wasn't
going to give him up. I nuzzled my face in the crook of his neck,
inhaling his natural scent along with the refreshing smell of soap.
Aiden stirred with a soft moan and I smiled as I pulled back a little,
not wanting to wake him up.

I couldn't believe my eyes when I looked up and saw him standing on the other side of the glass wall of the gym. In that moment, I
knew for sure there was a God, because he was giving me the opportunity for a second chance. And when Aiden came to me, I saw the
look of longing in his eyes. He missed me just as much as I had been

missing him. The moment I touched him, my heart swelled so much inside my chest, I thought it might explode. Then, when we kissed... it was like we were never apart. I've never loved anyone as much as I loved Aiden.

I was just about to tighten my grip around Aiden and go back to sleep when I heard a knock on my hotel door. With an agitated groan, I released Aiden, then climbed out of bed. I quickly donned a bathrobe and made my way to the door, opening it once I saw it was Rupert.

He took one look at me, eyes traveling down my body as if he was drinking me in. I thought about the last time he'd had that look in his eyes and what almost happened between us and decided to close my robe just a little bit more to hide what skin I could. When he saw me adjust my robe, he seemed to come out of a trance.

He gave me a quick smile. "You're still in bed? That's not like you."

"I had a late night. What's up?" I replied, wanting him to get to the fucking point of why he was here.

"Your fight last night was amazing, Macio. So much so, I was able to get you a meeting with another possible endorsement." Rupert gestured towards my hotel room. "Mind if I come in and go over the details?"

"Now is not really a good time," I said.

"It will only take me a few minutes. They want to meet with you in two hours, I just want to go over a few things."

Shit... I didn't need this right now, but since it was business, I let him in. "Fine." I stepped to the side and he walked into my penthouse and took a seat on the sofa. I took a seat far opposite him. I knew I could defend myself if he somehow lost his mind and tried to make any moves on me, but I felt it was best to keep our distance.

"All right, I know you've heard of OnyxTime," he began.

Oh yeah, I'd heard of them. They had some of the hottest sport watches on the market. Stylish and functional. "Yeah."

"Well, with your winning streak and marketability, they are

looking for you to be their spokesman. They want to see their watches on your wrist and are willing to offer you a substantial amount of green for the privilege," Rupert said.

"Well, shit… that is amazing. I love their watches, so this is actually an endorsement I can get down with," I said, feeling a little excited about this one. I had turned down one two months ago, after my last fight, because the company was known to be anti-LGBT. No amount of money would make me sell my soul anymore. When Aiden left me because I was afraid of losing my career, I felt like a total loser despite my winning streak. I had lost more than my integrity that day. I'd lost half of my heart and soul. I'd lost my partner and the love of my life. Never. Fucking. Again.

I had done a lot of growing up in the last four months, that was for sure.

"So, I'll set up the meeting. We should have it in your hotel room, keep it all private," Rupert said, which brought me back to the present.

I nodded. "Yeah, um, that works. You said in two hours, right?"

"Yes… one o'clock. Make sure you're dressed, though," he joked.

I could tell he was making the effort not to look at my body… much. I'd caught a few glances at my legs here and there while he was talking. I really couldn't help but wonder if his wife knew about his sexual orientation. Part of me wanted to ask her, but it was best that I stayed out of it. I turned when I heard my bedroom door open and saw Aiden stepping out. Shit, I was hoping to avoid these two meeting. Not because I was trying to hide Aiden… those days were behind me. Nope, it was because whenever Aiden and Rupert were in the same room together, the temperature went up. It was evident they really disliked one another.

"You again!" they said at the same time as they glared at each other.

I jumped up from the chair, ready to put an end to the storm before it began. "He was just leaving, baby," I said, hoping to calm Aiden down.

Rupert stood up, adjusting his suit as he glared at Aiden. "I was." He turned to me. "We'll speak later." With that, he left my hotel room and I was still feeling the rage emanating from Aiden.

I turned to him. "He was only here to tell me about a possible endorsement deal with OnyxTime. They want to meet with me in two hours to go over it." I said, being completely honest.

Aiden crossed his arms over his naked chest and I smiled as I looked down at his body. "I don't trust him."

"I don't know if I like you showing off my goods," I teased. "Come here."

Aiden's scowl began to fade as he approached me. I took his face into my hands and kissed him. I kissed his neck, shoulders, and chest as I moved further down. I licked his perky nipples, sucking on each one gently as he moaned in pure satisfaction. I loved how his breathing deepened as I moved lower until he gasped when I took his cock into my mouth. I sucked along his shaft with deliberately slow movements, which I knew drove him crazy, and was rewarded with a squirt of precum and a moan from him. *Yeeeahh, baby... I want more of that from you.* I slipped my hand around him, gripping both of his firm, plump ass cheeks. His body was for my eyes only. I didn't want anyone else to taste him, he was mine!

Aiden's fingers tightened in my hair as he reveled in the blow job I was giving him. I looked up, watching his flushed face go through all of the expressions of ecstasy, and seeing his pleasure made me horny out of my mind. My own cock was jutting through the folds of my robe, ready for action. I pulled back, kissing the tip of Aiden's cock, then stood up, removing my robe. I grabbed his ass cheeks again as he wrapped his arms around my neck, securing his grip. He knew exactly what I was going to do. We were so in tuned with each other. I smiled as I hoisted him up and he wrapped his legs around my waist.

"I love you, baby," I said as I aimed my cock at his hole. I had so much precum leaking from my cock, I wouldn't need lube.

Aiden threw his head back, moaning as I entered him. "I love you too, Macio," Aiden panted out, which hit all of my triggers. Whenever my name left his lips, it was music to my ears. Yeah, he knew who he belonged to. Now and forever.

I kissed him again with all the passion I was feeling as I fucked him in the middle of the living room. We both grunted and moaned in sheer pleasure as we made love. I loved looking at his muscles flex under his smooth, sweat-sheened skin. Aiden's hard cock rubbed between us, leaving smears of precum over our stomachs. I knew by how vocal he was that he'd be cumming soon.

"My cock feel good to you, baby?" I asked, kissing his chin and neck.

"Fuck! Oh god, yes!" he cried out as I made sure to hit his prostate over and over. "I'm so close."

Yeah, I knew just how close my boyfriend was, too. I wrapped one arm around his back, giving him more support as he began bouncing on my cock, which was driving me crazy.

"Oh, hell yeah, ride me, baby," I growled.

"Oh shit, I love when you growl," he moaned as he bounced.

I laughed and buried my face in his neck and growled on his flesh, making him cackle and squirm because the vibration made him ticklish. From there, I licked, sucked, and kissed him until he cried out.

"I'm cumming!"

"Yeah, shoot your load all over me," I encouraged. It didn't take long for Aiden to comply. His body went ridged in my arms as he quaked in pleasure. I looked down in time to see his beautiful cock coating my toned abs with his cream. "Yeah, that's it... just like that." I looked up at his face, wanting to see him in the throes of ecstasy, and he looked so perfect to me. I grabbed him by the back of his head, kissing him again.

Once his orgasm faded, I walked us over to the large window, pressing his back against it, and really drilled his ass as he held on. It didn't take long for my own climax to erupt from me and I roared and grunted as I filled him with my seed. He was begging for it the whole time, which totally set me off. I was panting heavily now and kissing him... I couldn't get enough of kissing him. Aiden unraveled his legs from around my waist and I let him get back on his feet.

"That... was amazing," I said, grinning like a fool.

Aiden smiled and nodded as he kept his gaze locked on mine. "It was."

I kissed his forehead, then pulled back. "We need to shower and eat something. I also have to get ready for this meeting." I walked over to my robe, picking it up off the floor.

"Yeah... after that morning workout, I need some refueling. I'm happy about this endorsement deal for you. I hope it's everything you want," Aiden said.

I looked at him. "Thanks. Me too. I turned down a pretty profitable one a few months back because the company was anti-gay. As far as I know about OnyxTime, they're on the up and up."

Aiden nodded, then his expression grew serious. "While we have some time, we need to talk."

Ah shit, I'd been dreading "The Talk", but knew we needed to have it. "Yeah, you want to go first?"

He nodded and walked into the bedroom. I followed and took a seat beside him on the bed.

"Seeing you again, being with you, has made me extremely happy... but I'm also equally worried. There's a reason why I never wanted to get involved with a closeted guy. When I first met you, Macio... I ignored all the warning signs because of how I felt about you. The more time we spent together, the more I felt like I could make living a closeted life work. But then it all blew up in my face and I broke apart in a thousand pieces."

God, hearing him say those words to me hurt like a million stabs to my heart, but I didn't interrupt him. I owed him respect and I had to take the blows because I'd earned them. No deflecting or countering in this bout.

He went on. "I love you, Macio... so much. I tried hard to get over the heartbreak, but couldn't. There hasn't been anyone else in my life who could replace you and I never wanted any one to. However, if we do this again... if I open my heart up to you again... it can't be like it was before. I have to know you won't ditch me when things get rough."

He was now looking at me and I could tell he was giving me time to respond. I wasn't much for words; I was a bruiser, not a poet. All I could give him was my honesty and I was sure that was all he wanted from me.

"I fucked up. I panicked like a little bitch and I made the biggest mistake of my life when I let you walk out of my hotel room. I'm never going to do that again. I thought my career was more important than my happiness, but I was wrong. I also got scared of what would come my way. I could get into an octagon with a brutal opponent and not feel one ounce of fear. But the thought of being outed and having people I knew and didn't know looking down at me... well... that thought terrified me."

"Do you think it was easy for me to publicly come out?" Aiden asked as he put his hand on my knee.

I shook my head. "I envied your courage. But I also felt that we lived in two different worlds."

Aiden sighed and nodded. "That's true, and it was one of the reasons why I was so willing to live in yours."

I reached up, caressing his chin. I loved everything about him, even his stubble that scratched my skin. "I'm not afraid anymore, Aiden. I'm not sure if I'm ready to share you or what we have with the public just yet. But I'm not going to run away ever again. That, I can promise you. Whatever comes our way, we wade through it together from now on."

Aiden smiled and leaned forward, kissing me. When he pulled back, he punched me as hard as he could in my jaw, snapping my head back. Pain shot through my face and more than one tweety bird flew around my head for a second before I cleared my senses. I looked at Aiden as I massaged my jaw.

"That's for breaking my heart. I love you. Okay, you know what I like for breakfast." He got up from the bed and sauntered into the bathroom to shower.

I was left there with my jaw stinging from a blow that I should have seen coming, but hadn't. I laughed as I rubbed my aching jaw. Looked like my baby has a nice right hook. I flexed my jaw as I dialed for room service. Once I placed the order for our breakfast, I joined Aiden in the shower. We actually just washed up this time, no han-ky-panky. Aiden and I enjoyed our breakfast, then he rescheduled his flight. I hated to see him leave. At one, I had my meeting with OnyxTime that went very well. The deal was for a million dollars for five ads over the course of a year. Which worked out to two-hundred grand per ad.

After the meeting, I could tell Rupert wanted to get into it about Aiden, but I shut him down and kicked his ass out of my hotel room. I didn't want to hear anymore anti-Aiden shit right then. When I told Barry if I could get a second chance, I wasn't going to blow it, I meant it. I decided to go down to the gym and burn off a few calories before I hit the city for the sights.

"So, you really are in love with Aiden?" Barry asked me as he held the punching bag while I kicked it.

I nodded and threw in a knee.

"Oh, that's a good one. You really need to work on switching your offensive tactics. Strike low, then go high with the knee, that's a good stunner," Barry said, breaking from the conversation about my love life to give me fight pointers. "Okay, back to what I was saying... I didn't really want to bring this up, but since your next championship fight ain't for another two months—"

"Spit it the fuck out. What are you talking about?" I snapped, throwing a few powerful blows at the bag.

"Rupert has been sitting on this for the last two weeks, not wanting to worry you. However, I think you should know about it."

I stopped throwing punches and gave all of my attention to Barry. "Stop pissing around the bush."

"It's beating around the bush," he corrected.

"I know, but I like 'pissing' better. Now, get to it."

He sighed as he let go of the bag, then rubbed his eyebrow. "He's been trying to figure out who this person is that's sending him photos of you and Aiden. There's been new ones since you two got back together."

I huffed. "Why didn't you tell me?"

"I'm telling you now."

"How long have you known?"

"About a week. We both didn't want to bother you with this if we could figure it out and stop it. But then the son of a bitch sent another photo, this time to me with a blackmail demand," Barry said.

I actually growled at that. "What's the fucking demand?"

"The letter said…" Barry sighed as though he didn't want to tell me. "It said, 'Fags don't fight in MMA arenas. If you don't want your dirty little secret getting out, I want one million dollars. You're rich, I know you've got it, so give it, cocksucker.'"

Oh, that pissed me the fuck off. I punched the bag so hard it hit Barry, knocking him to the side from the impact. He almost lost his footing, but caught his balance.

"Damn, kid."

"Fuck this shit! Fuck whoever sent that bullshit, too. They ain't getting a motherfucking dime out of me. I want to see the photos and that note. Call Rupert, get his ass here, now!" I raged. I snatched off my boxing gloves, tossing them to the floor.

"See, this is why we didn't want to bother you with this shit," Barry stated.

"Well, now I'm bothered and I'm about to do something about it. Call Rupert and tell him to bring all of the photos he has received." I stormed off to the locker room to shower up and get dressed. The hot water pelting my skin normally gave me relaxing vibes, but not right now. I was fuming and ready to murder a motherfucker. How dare someone tell me that bullshit! "Fags don't fight in the MMA"! Well, this one does, bitch, and if I ever meet this guy, I'll show him what a fag MMA fighter can do. All I could see was red and I was so enraged, I punched the shower wall, cracking the tile.

Shit, Barry was going to be pissed about that. I would replace it. I was mad as hell, but couldn't take it out of his livelihood. I finished showering and got dressed. When I met back up with Barry, he was in his office.

"Have a seat," he said, gesturing to the chair.

I did. "Is Rupert coming?"

He nodded. "He's on his way. What happened to your hand?"

He nodded at my right hand, and I looked down to see that it was slightly bruised from me striking hard tiles with bare flesh. "I owe you a shower tile."

"Damn it, kid… don't break your fucking hand because you're mad. Not with a gym full of shit you can beat on," Barry complained… which made a lot of fucking sense.

"I won't."

"Okay, now… try to keep your calm. I like my office the way it is. This is the photo that was sent to me along with the letter."

Barry handed me a brown envelope that looked like the one I'd seen before. I took it and pulled out the photo and letter. I read the letter first and felt the rage boiling over in me. How dare someone try to blackmail me. I refused to live in fear again. Next, I looked at the photo. It was a bit clearer than the first photo I'd seen of Aiden and me in the hot tub, but I knew it was us. Our faces were more distinct, and we were in my bedroom while I was fucking him in the window like he loved. The kinky bastard. Anyway, it was us for sure and I was ready to rip the balls off the person who had the audacity to violate my privacy then demand to be paid for it.

I tossed the shit back on Barry's desk. "Fuck them, and fuck those photos."

"What are you going to do?" Barry asked. Right at that moment, Rupert walked through the office door. "I was just getting our boy here up to speed," Barry told him.

"Good," Rupert said, taking a seat next to mine. "Here." He handed me two more brown envelopes.

I looked at the photos inside. All recent with Aiden and me together at my house and one of me kissing him goodbye in the doorway. "I want to know who the fuck is climbing onto my private property and taking these photos. I'm going to initiate an investigation into this."

"But what about keeping your secret?" Rupert asked.

I shrugged. "It's a secret I'm not worried about keeping anymore. I've decided to come out."

"Now hold on, Macio. Think about what that means. You could lose endorsement deals," Rupert pointed out.

"This isn't something I just came to the decision about five seconds ago, Rupert. I'm done hiding who I am because I'm afraid of what *might* happen."

Rupert shook his head. "Not might, *will*."

"Look, if you want to bail to avoid what's coming, now is the time to do so," I said. "But I'm coming out. I will not be blackmailed. I will not be ashamed of being gay, and I'm not going to give up Aiden again just because some asshole doesn't like us together. Fuck all that bullshit."

The whole time Rupert and I talked, Barry was sitting there, silent. I looked at him. "Don't you have anything to add?" I challenged.

Barry shrugged. "I knew you were going to do this when I showed you the photos. I've been preparing for you to come out the moment you told me you were going to try to get your boyfriend back. I told you then, kid… I'm with you for the full ride, rough or smooth… we'll kick ass together."

I smiled at Barry. It felt great to have his support because I respected and loved him so much. He was like the father I never had. To know that he was going to stand by me gave me even more courage to come out. I looked at Rupert, waiting for his response.

"So, are you in or not?" I asked him.

"You're throwing your life away for a piece of ass. Granted, an attractive piece of ass, but a piece of ass all the same," he shot back.

"Are you saying that because you're jealous it's not your piece of ass?" I snapped.

"Ummm what? Did I miss something?" Barry asked, looking between both of us.

"I wasn't going to mention it, but Rupert and I got drunk one night and he made moves."

"So much for not mentioning it," Rupert said, frowning.

"I always wondered why you seemed to hate Aiden so much. You don't even know him. But I've figured it out. You were jealous that I was fucking him and not you."

Rupert jumped out of his seat. "That's fucking ridiculous!"

"Is it?"

"You've fucked plenty of guys," Rupert stated.

"Escorts that meant nothing to me. But Aiden was different, wasn't he? Aiden meant something to me and that's why you've been giving him shit since you two met," I said. "I'm going to say this one time. Get over it. Aiden is in my life and he's not going anywhere. If you really consider yourself my friend and care for my wellbeing—as you've said—then you'll accept this. Are you in or out?"

"I'm in, but you're making a huge fucking mistake," Rupert said, then stormed out of the office, leaving me alone with an awestruck Barry. I was pissed at Rupert for his attitude toward Aiden; that was why I threw down the gauntlet. From now on, things were about to change and I needed to know who was going to be on my side.

"Are you okay, Barry?" I asked.

Barry blinked several times, then nodded. "I'm trying to get over the fact that Rupert hit on you. I suspected he had a serious attachment to you, but I thought it was because he saw you as one hell of a meal ticket. Didn't know he wanted to fuck you. I wonder if his wife knows."

I shrugged. "I'm sure she doesn't. Look, if they send you another photo or letter demanding money, you can tell them I said to 'suck my dick, they ain't getting shit'. Dumb asshole didn't even put any contact info in the letter." I stood up, adjusting my sweats.

Barry looked up at me and nodded. "I'm proud of you, kid. I'm worried for you, but I'm also proud too."

"Thanks, Barry." I smiled because I had never felt so free in my life. I was about to finally be me and I couldn't wait to share this moment with Aiden. Of course, he was out of town at the moment, but he'd be back tomorrow and back at work, writing up a story. I left Barry's gym, went home and tried to sleep, but couldn't... I was so excited. Finally, I had to take a pill in order to get some rest and I woke up around ten in the morning. I got up quickly, packed a bag, and called Barry to let him know I was taking a short break. He didn't argue because he knew it would have been futile. I was going to see my man.

I made my travel arrangements, got to the airport, signed some fan autographs and boarded my plane, first class. A few hours later, I was in L.A. I rented a car, putting my bag in the back. I didn't bother to get a hotel room. I was going to stay at Aiden's. I drove to Ringside Magazine's building, parked, then walked inside. My body was buzzing with more energy than when I headed into the ring. I was inside the belly of a media beast about to take my man out for a surprise dinner.

I walked up to the front desk and the girl behind the counter grinned at me. "Wow, I can't believe it's actually you."

I smiled. "In the flesh. Listen, I'm here to see one of your staff members, but I don't want him to know it's me. Can you see if Aiden James is available?"

"Oh, okay… sure." She dialed a number and waited. "Yes, hello Mr. James. You have a guest that would like to come up and see you. Is it okay if we send him up?" She paused as she awaited his reply. "Sure. Not a problem. Bye." She hung up and looked at me. "He's waiting. Oh, before you go, can I get your autograph?"

"My pleasure," I said. I signed the piece of paper, took the visitor's badge she gave me, then made my way to his floor, following her directions. The doors opened and I stepped off and looked around. The space was full of cubicles like a little maze. People were busy walking this way and that, some stopped when they noticed me walking through the aisles.

I had to ask one guy where Aiden's desk was and he looked at me in shock, then pointed in the direction.

"Thank you," I said, then made my way over to where my baby was working diligently. I could see his fingers flying over the keyboard as he typed away on his latest story. I stood over his shoulder and he didn't even know I was there. This was going to be awesome. Boy, I was charged as hell to finally be coming out and on my Own. Fucking. Terms. "Hungry, baby?"

CHAPTER TWENTY-TWO

Aiden

I WAS AN EXHAUSTED MESS WHEN I ARRIVED AT WORK. REUNITING with Macio was the happiest day in my life, but it had taken me on an emotional rollercoaster full of twists and turns that left me feeling dizzy and disoriented worse than any buzz from alcohol.

I experienced the joys of being in his arms again, the fear that he would be ripped out of my life again, and the worry that our late-night talks were having a negative impact on his training. I hoped he was sleeping better than I was and that his dreams weren't filled with uncertainty and doubt. During the day, I was sure of our love and that we'd have the life we both wanted, but that all disappeared the second I slipped into dreamland.

I hit the coffee hard and kept it coming all day long. I worked through lunch so I could leave early and start my mini vacation. Macio didn't know it, but I took an extra day off so I could extend my stay with him and Caesar in Vegas. I existed on peanuts from the vending machine and an endless flow of coffee. As the afternoon wore on, the growling of my stomach was loud enough to garner looks and comments from my coworkers, but I just kept my mind on the prize – a long weekend with Macio.

The receptionist called up to let me know I had a visitor and I fought down my annoyance at the unexpected intrusion into my day. Didn't this person know I had a hot stud to get to? I was so flustered that I didn't even ask who it was, I just told her to send them on up. I hung up my phone and went back to typing my interview so I didn't lose any more precious time.

"Hungry, baby?"

I sighed out loud because that voice did so many things to me. It warmed my heart, it turned me on, and it made me love stronger than I ever dreamed possible. I heard a warm chuckle and turned my head. Oh god, I had starved myself until I had become delirious. I wanted Macio so badly, my psyche imagined him standing in my cubicle looking at me like I was his next meal.

"Surprise." A huge smile spread across Macio's face when he saw the confused look on my face.

I jumped to my feet and threw my arms around his neck without even thinking about it. "Macio."

"Hi, baby." He wrapped his arms around me and held me tightly in the middle of my office like he did when we were alone. "I missed you and decided I'd gone enough days without seeing you."

Surely, I was dreaming. I just knew my alarm was going to go off at any minute and he'd be gone. I did the only thing I could think of to prove that Macio was real and in front of me. I pinched the skin at his waist and twisted, but not too hard in case I wasn't delusional or dreaming.

Macio growled low, then said, "I'm going to make you pay for that later."

"Promise?"

"I'm real – we're real – and soon you won't need to pinch me to know the truth," he replied.

"But we're standing in the middle of my workplace with your arms around me."

"Aiden, they're all so busy, they don't even know I'm here. Even if they did, it wouldn't matter to me. I'm done hiding."

I looked around the room and saw that what he said was true. Everyone had their eyes focused on their computers in front of them. My heart pounded in my chest as his words about not hiding penetrated my poor, starved brain. "What does that mean?"

"I'll show you," Macio said. "Can you leave now or should I..."

"No! I'm ahead of schedule on this article, so I can go." I packed up my messenger bag and we walked together to the elevators. My stomach growled embarrassingly loud, causing Macio to scowl at me. "I was coming to see you tomorrow. That's why I was working so hard to get ahead of my Monday deadline."

"You don't skip meals, babe. It's bad for every part of your body, especially your beautiful brain." He hooked his arm around my neck and pulled me to him for a quick kiss while we traveled down to the ground floor.

I snorted. "Yeah, let's pretend that's what you think is beautiful."

Macio's expression grew very serious, and then he said, "It wasn't your looks or your phenomenal ass that hooked me, Aiden. It was your wittiness, your sass, and the sparkling orneriness I saw in your blue eyes. As handsome as I think you are, and as much as I love your ass, it's your personality that snagged my heart. That's how I knew you were the one." *The one.* That was some serious shit. "I have a huge surprise for you – one that will show you just how serious I am."

I followed Macio to his rental car and stored my bag in his trunk before I got in the passenger seat. I wanted to ask him a million questions about where we were going and what we were doing, but I could tell by the firm set of his jaw that he wouldn't answer them. He wanted to surprise me and that was final.

I was shocked when we pulled up to the valet parking line for Bogard's. It was the most expensive and exclusive restaurant in Los Angeles. People waited for months to get a reservation, but I guess if you're Animacio De Niro, you didn't have to.

"Wow," I said as I got out of the car. "I can't believe you brought me here."

The valet parking attendant handed Macio a ticket, then drove off in the luxury rental. Macio turned to face me and reached for my hand. "One of the things that always hurt you the most was that we couldn't be like any other couple and eat dinner together in a restaurant. I know how much it hurt you to see photos of me with Kathy doing the things that we never could. That all ends."

"Macio." I had to close my eyes to ward off the tears that threatened to spill. I kept them closed until I had myself under control. "Babe, I would've settled for a fast food joint."

"Not for my guy." Macio stunned me even more when he held open the door for me so I could precede him inside. He placed his hand on my lower back and guided me to the hostess station where we were greeted by an adoring fan. Macio graciously signed an autograph for her and then said, "I have a reservation for four."

"Four?" I asked. All of my happiness deflated out of me like a balloon when I realized that it was probably Rupert and Barry joining us for dinner.

"The other party has already arrived, sir. Follow me."

Macio's wide smile eased my dread a bit as I followed behind the hostess. I was absolutely shocked, and I mean you could've knocked me over with a feather, when we headed to a table where Macio's brother and sister-in-law sat. Rico's eyes briefly met mine, then shifted and lingered on his brother.

Rico rose to his feet when we got closer to the table. I could tell by the expression on his face that he wasn't expecting my presence at dinner. I looked at Macio over my shoulder to gauge his emotions and all I saw were smiling eyes and a grin that radiated joy. His happiness caused my steps to falter.

Macio leaned forward and softly said, "I told Rico and Macy that I was bringing someone special to meet them; a person I loved more than any other. That won't ever change no matter what happens here tonight or the days that follow. It's me and you together versus the world, if need be."

His words bolstered my courage and put a smile on my face for one of the most important introductions in my life. It was true what they said about only getting one chance at a first impression. I wanted Rico and Macy to see what Macio did when he looked at me – a man worthy of his love.

"Rico," Macio said once we stood directly in front of him, "this is Aiden. I thought it was time you met the man I want to spend the rest of my life with."

Rico shifted his eyes to me and said nothing, didn't move – not so much as a blink – until his wife let out an unladylike snort followed by a giggle. Rico turned to his wife and said, "I'm not giving you twenty dollars because you were only partially right. You said he was gay, I said he was gay *and* in love with Aiden."

"Fine," Macy said with an exaggerated eye roll. "Keep your damn money."

Rico turned his attention back to us and I was happy to see that Macio was just as shocked as I was. "It's nice to finally meet you, Aiden. I've heard a lot of wonderful things about you."

"You have?" Macio and I asked at once, making Rico laugh.

"Dumb ass." Rico looped his arm around Macio's neck and pulled him in for a hug before he extended his hand to me. "This lovely woman," he nodded in the direction of his wife, "is Macy."

I thrusted my hand toward Macy, but she waved me off, then launched herself at me for a hug. She hugged Macio next, then said, "It's about time you came to your senses. You were miserable without him."

"I wasn't aware I mentioned Aiden that much to you guys," Macio said once we took our seats.

"That's how you know it's real, sweetheart," Macy said. "Talking about him was effortless and came naturally to you. Hell, you weren't even aware you were giving so much away to us. I kept waiting for you to finally tell us you're gay, but you never did. Then there was that Kathy debacle." Macy shook her head.

"That wasn't my brightest hour," Macio replied. "I'm lucky that Kathy and I can still be friends. I'll have to give her a heads up when I go public with my relationship with Aiden. I don't want her to get caught up in the media storm, but I think it's unavoidable."

"You're going to go public?" Rico asked in a concerned voice.

Macio bristled in his chair. "What? It's okay to have a gay brother as long as it stays private?"

"Don't put words in my mouth, little brother. You're not too big for me to settle this like we used to when we were kids," Rico warned.

"Enough, you two," Macy admonished. "Aiden isn't used to our dynamics yet." She turned to Macio and said, "Rico is only concerned about the impact it will have on your life, Macio. He loves you no matter what. You know that."

"Apparently he doesn't know that, Macy." Rico was looking down and his fingers were picking at the linen napkin in his lap. "He didn't trust me enough to tell me he was gay. He didn't tell me about Aiden or the truth about Kathy." Rico raised his head and looked into Macio's eyes. "I'm trying really hard not to take it personally, but I can't seem to help it."

"Rico, I promise that we'll have the big heart-to-heart we should've had years ago this weekend. Tonight, I just want to show you the highest amount of respect I can by bringing Aiden to meet you. I want to show Aiden how much he means to me by bringing him home to meet the only family that I have."

"Don't forget our little monsters," Macy scolded playfully.

Rico looked at his wife and snorted. "Who the hell could forget those two?" He turned his focus back on Macio and asked, "Why didn't you tell me? Just answer that for me and we'll put it behind us for the night. We can hug it out at our house this weekend when you bring Aiden to meet your niece and nephew."

"Straight up fear, Rico. I was afraid I would lose the only family I had and it scared me into a hiding who I was. I am sorry that I hurt you by not telling you the truth, but I thought it was the only way."

"Fair enough. Let's enjoy this adult night out because it won't be nearly as peaceful…"

"Or elegant," Macy interjected.

"With the kids around," Rico finished.

"Bring them on," I said. "I adore kids."

The waiter brought us a basket of bread and glasses of water while we perused the dinner and drink menu. "Everything looks so good," Macy said. "I'm not sure what to get."

"One of everything, baby, because Mr. Money Bags is picking up the bill," Rico teased, smiling at his brother over the top of the menu he held in his hands.

My surprise date was one of the best nights of my life. Having dinner with Macio and his family in a public restaurant meant the world to me. Rico and Macy both seemed interested in what I did and I told them some behind the scenes funny stories, but without revealing the identities of the people involved, of course. Hearing Rico and Macio laugh and joke while telling stories of one another made me smile so much my face hurt by the time the valet attendant retrieved Macio's rental car.

Rico and Macy hugged us both and made us promise to be at their home at seven for dinner the following evening. I couldn't wait to meet the kids that had their uncle wrapped around their little fingers. I somehow doubted they were little monsters, but then again, their parents saw a different side of them than we would.

"This has been a wonderful night, Macio," I said once we were inside his car. "Thank you so much. Meeting your family means the world to me and if you have time on Sunday, I'd love for you to meet my family too."

"I wouldn't miss it, baby." Macio leaned forward and gave me a kiss before we set off.

"My house is that way." I pointed to the street we passed.

"I haven't forgotten where you live, Aiden. Our night isn't over yet. I have one more surprise for you." The excitement I heard in his voice made me smile. "I can't wait!"

"I've only seen you this excited about sex," I told Macio. "Please tell me we're not going to a sex club. That's not the way I'd prefer to make our debut as a couple."

"Fuck no," Macio said. "I'm not letting anyone get a look at what belongs to me. You're mine, Aiden. I'll never share you. Ever."

"You'll never have to."

Weekend traffic was heavy, so it was another forty minutes before we reached our destination. "I don't believe it," I gushed when Macio turned into the entrance for the drive-in theater. "I haven't been to one of these in years."

"When I searched nighttime things to do, this popped up and I thought it would be cool. Then I checked to see what movies they were playing and I knew it was fate."

"What movies?"

"Superman movie marathon. We're going to eat popcorn, drink sodas – okay, I'll probably drink water – and make out," Macio said.

"It sounds like a perfect night."

And it was. We did exactly what Macio had said, but we added in some groping and teasing in the mix. I'd never had a hard-on for as long as I had that night, nor had I ever wanted to suck Macio off as much as I did then, but I waited until we got home in the wee hours of the morning.

We didn't make it very far inside my house before we starting ripping each other's clothes off. Macio bent me over the couch and fucked me with every ounce of frustration he'd had from holding back for several hours. It was fast, dirty, and everything I'd been begging for every time I stroked his dick through his jeans.

Macio growled in my ear and I whimpered every time he pounded my prostate with the broad head of his dick. It didn't take him long to make me come all over my leather couch or for him to fill my ass with his spunk.

We took a quick shower and climbed into my bed with the intention of sleeping until late morning or early afternoon. I had no idea what time it was when pounding at my front door woke me up.

"I swear to God, if that's Rupert, I'm going to kill him," I growled.

Macio laughed and said, "There's no way Rupert is at your front door. It's probably your buddy Seth or even *Garrett*." The jealous way Macio said Garrett's name made me smile.

"Doubtful," I replied. "I guess there's only one way to find out."

I got out of bed and slid on my robe and heard Macio do the same. I wasn't sure what the hell I expected when I pulled open my front door, but finding Troy Danvers sure as hell wasn't it.

"Hey, kids," he said nonchalantly, as if he expected to find Macio in my home.

"Worse than Rupert," I said to Macio over my shoulder.

"Oh, that's just mean," Troy said, clutching his chest like I had stabbed him in the heart. "You're going to change your opinion about me once I tell you why I came."

"Okay," I replied. "Why are you here?"

"Can I please come in?"

"Say no, he could be a vampire," Macio said in mock horror.

"Again with the insults," Troy said in a wounded voice. "Fine, I'll just go on back on home and let Macio find out the hard way that his publicist is planning to stab him in the back." He turned and started down my porch steps.

"What?" I asked.

"Get back here," Macio growled. "What the fuck are you talking about?"

"Rupert contacted me yesterday and told me he had a story to sell me. I thought it was about another fighter and agreed to meet him for dinner. Imagine my surprise when he handed me this photo." Troy reached into jacket pocket and pulled out the photo of Macio fucking me against the windows in his house.

"Get in here." Macio grabbed Troy by the collar of his shirt and pulled him inside my house. "Start from the beginning and don't leave a fucking thing out."

CHAPTER TWENTY-THREE

Macio

COULDN'T BELIEVE WHAT THE FUCK I JUST HEARD OR WHAT THE hell I was seeing. Both Aiden and I sat down and listened to everything Troy Danvers was telling us about his meeting with Rupert. My heart was aching like I'd been stabbed ... or maybe it was my back that was hurting since that was where Rupert planted the fucking blade. I trusted him, I loved him as my friend and it hurt me to know he wanted to do something so devious to me. What the fuck had I ever done to him to make him want to betray me like this?

"I never liked or trusted his ass," Aiden said, slamming the photo of him and me fucking on the cocktail table. "That first photo was highly suspect. Even then, I wondered if he took it himself and tried to pretend like someone else did. That would explain why he got so defensive at the time."

Aiden made perfect sense. I sat back on the sofa and looked at

Troy. "So, are you here out of the kindness of your heart, or do you want something for this information? I mean, you've been stalking me for months, trying to get a scoop like this. Am I to believe you've grown a soul and a conscious?"

Troy sighed. "Maybe I don't like what Rupert's trying to do to you. Maybe... just maybe I have some integrity."

"Bullshit."

Troy frowned. "I do have integrity."

"Since when? I find that hard to believe, not after the scandals you've been behind," I shot back.

"Maybe I have a conscious."

I gave him the side-eye. "This would be one hell of a story, though. MMA champion who's a closeted gay, dating an out reporter for Ringside Magazine. Why are you passing up on it?" I needed to know what his damn angle was. I was still trying to wrap my mind around Rupert's betrayal, I didn't need any more surprises.

"I respect you, Macio." He turned to Aiden. "I respect you, too. Maybe in the past, I did sell my soul for a story and made a lot of enemies."

"Ain't no 'maybe' to it," Aiden clarified.

Troy huffed and sighed. "Look, I'm trying to do the right thing here, give me a break."

I studied him, looking for any tale-tell signs that he was being anything but honest at the moment. So far, everything he said seemed genuine. I leaned forward, picking up the photo again, examining it. "Son of a bitch!" I snapped. "All of those other photos he showed me, claiming some mysterious asshole was sending them to me, was actually him." I turned to Aiden. "You know, after we broke up, I didn't get any more photos, then as soon as we got back together, here came the photos again."

"Why didn't you tell me?" Aiden asked.

I shrugged. "I had just found out about it a few days before we got back together. At the time, it came with a blackmail note, but no contact info. I didn't give a shit anyway, because I had already made up my mind to be with you regardless." I turned to Troy. "Thank you for letting us know, Troy. How did you know to come here?"

"Rupert told me you were coming out here to see him. Wanted me to get some images, clearer images of you two together. I told him I would because I didn't want him going to anyone else with this story who would take him up on his offer." Troy looked at Aiden. "He really doesn't like you."

"Like I give a fuck," Aiden stated. "I hate him for what he's doing to Macio."

"I'm going to handle this shit," I said, thinking that I was about to come out on my own terms, no one else's. I looked at Troy. "Since you're freelance, would you be interested in taking our first official couple photos?"

Troy cocked both eyebrows. "Are you serious? You want me to take your pictures?"

I looked at Aiden. "What do you think?"

Aiden seemed to mull it over. "I'm okay with it."

"Well, I'm honored, but who am I taking the photos for?" Troy asked. "I mean, I'd like to get paid for these photos. My generosity only goes so far."

I rolled my eyes. "Ringside Magazine. It's the biggest sports publication out there. Aiden, you can write the story about our relationship and have it on the website's daily blog in a few hours." I wanted to grab this bull by the horns.

"Are you sure, baby?" Aiden asked. "I mean, this is a really big move."

"I was sure about this move before I flew out here. All Rupert's done is put a little fire under my ass," I stated.

"Okay… well… if you're ready, I'm ready," Aiden said, giving me his support.

Knowing that my brother was all right with me being gay made coming out even easier. I was actually really looking forward to it.

"Okay, let's get dressed and you get your cameras ready."

Troy nodded. "How soon will Ringside be able to pay me for these images?"

"True to nature," I taunted.

"Hey, you make a living beating people's asses. I make a living taking photos of celebs. But that doesn't mean I don't have a heart. I split a lot of the money I make off my photos and donate it to the local LGBT center for youths," Troy explained.

I cocked an eyebrow. "Are you gay?"

"Maybe I am. Ever wonder why, out of all of my scandalous photos, I never outed anyone? Like I said, I have integrity. Now, I don't give a shit about some asshole cheating on his wife or her husband. I'll expose them all day long," Troy said.

Now that I thought about it, he had never outed people. The magazine he worked for a lot seemed to have no problem with that. But they were a sleaze rag and I wasn't going to give them this exposé. "You're right. Okay... fair enough. Are you ready?" I looked at Aiden. He was still fuming over the photo Rupert had taken of us, but he nodded. We waited for Troy to return with his camera and told him to make himself at home... on the sofa. Aiden got him something to drink and we both left him alone to go get dressed.

"He better not get too nosy down there," I said as I slipped on my t-shirt.

"He's not going to find anything but family photos and nick-knacks, but let's not leave him down there too long, okay?" Aiden replied as he slipped on a pair of khakis.

I loved the way his ass looked in those pants. I was hoping to wake up to some afternoon nookie, not this bullshit, but I was about to put an end to this right now. There was one thing I wanted to talk to Aiden about before we went back downstairs.

"He did this because he's jealous of you," I said.

"I know." Aiden finished buttoning the last button on his lilac shirt. Not many men could pull off that color and look damn good, but he could. "I knew the moment I met him that he had an unhealthy attachment to you. I was highly suspicious of that first photo he brought to you. And when you broke up with me, I could see the happiness in his face as I walked out of the hotel."

It was all making sense to me now. "I was so clueless about him. Listen, Aiden… baby, I've got to tell you something. Please try not to get mad."

Aiden froze. "Please tell me you didn't fuck him."

"No! Hell no."

Aiden exhaled deeply. "Oh, thank goodness."

"It's just one night before we got back together, I was feeling really down and conflicted about what I wanted to do. He came over my house with wine and… well, we got pretty fucked up. He tried to take that moment to make his move on me. I stopped him before it got too far and kicked him out. But when he did that, I knew for a fact that I wanted you in my life more than anything and I wasn't going to let anyone or anything stop me," I admitted, making my way closer to Aiden.

"What's too far?"

"Nothing happened."

"Not what I asked."

Oh shit… there was that sass I loved. "Some groping and he tried to suck me off, but I wouldn't let him. The whole thing was probably less than a minute before I put a stop to it. I sobered up pretty quickly, I'll tell you that."

"That slimy motherfucker, I knew he wanted my damn man!" Aiden growled.

Well, he was never going to get me. I took Aiden's face into my hands and kissed him. "I love you so much."

"I know. I love you too," he said, smiling back up at me.

"Let's do this."

We returned to the living room where Troy was sitting on the sofa.

"About time… my curiosity was getting the better of me. I almost looked inside your bathroom cabinet," Troy teased, getting his camera ready.

"It's good that you didn't, nothing to see there anyway," Aiden said.

"Okay, how do you want to do this?" Troy asked, getting into his professional mode.

"I figured one or two photos of us looking all couple-like should be good enough for the blog," I said.

Aiden nodded. "That'll work. We'll pick the best out of the selection to feature. First, let me contact my boss."

I nodded and Aiden walked into the kitchen for some privacy while Troy and I talked.

"I had suspected you were gay," Troy said.

I arched an eyebrow. "Oh really? Why?"

He shrugged. "I'm not necessarily out and proud myself, but I'm also not hiding in the closet either. It's just no one is interested in taking pictures of me. Still, most athletes are always surrounded by women. Strippers, escorts, chicks at bars and parties. As famous as you are, you seemed to avoid all of that, but until Kathy, you weren't with any woman. That's rare for an athlete, especially one as young and popular as you are. I know women must throw themselves at you."

"You could say that."

He nodded. "Yeah, I know. Plus, the whole Kathy and Macio thing seemed contrived. People who wanted to believe the relationship was real, really ignored the signs. Not me, I have an eye for that sort of thing. The stiffness when she kissed you. The space between you two when you were together. It was like you weren't comfortable in your own skin when you had to be with her," Troy said.

I smirked. "Kathy and I are friends."

"Friends, not lovers. It was the lovers part you obviously had issues with." Troy shrugged again. "Let's just say, I wasn't shocked when I saw the photo of you and Aiden. It was hot, though."

I growled and he laughed. Aiden returned with a huge smile on his face. "My boss is stoked about this story. He's ready to run it for the evening edition on the blog. He wants us to do a quick story for the blog and a more in-depth one for the magazine. Oh, and he's willing to pay you top dollar for the images." Aiden looked at me. "He's also willing to pay you for the exclusive interview."

"Well, far be it from me to turn that down."

Aiden nodded, then looked at Troy. "He wants you to contact him." He gave Troy his boss's information.

"Cool," Troy said, making the call.

Aiden looked at me. "You too." He gave me his cell with his boss' number ready for me to call.

This was all kinds of tedious to me. Normally, Rupert handled all this, but I couldn't call him anymore. I contacted his boss and went over the details with him and settled on an amount that was pretty decent for this exposé. We had to work out the details, but when we did, both of us were satisfied. Finally, with the business end having been worked out for both Troy and I, he was ready to get started.

No doubt, Troy was happy with the deal he made for the number of photos Ringside wanted. Now it was time to pose. We took pictures sitting on the sofa, smiling and kissing for the camera... and each other. We took photos in the kitchen while Aiden made lunch and I hugged him from behind. We took photos of me kissing his neck while he smiled for the camera. It was very lovey-dovey, in your face kind of shit. But very tasteful, too.

Afterward, we sat down and picked out the best photos, then Aiden did what he did best and got those fingers to blazing over the keyboard. Troy left after lunch and for the first time ever, I didn't think he was so despicable. He seemed like a decent enough guy, which was odd considering he was a paparazzo.

I sat down, answering all of the questions Aiden asked me so that he could complete his short article. It was concise and to the point. I looked over his article, making only a few minor changes. It was perfect and conveyed exactly what I wanted it to. Fuck whoever didn't like me being gay. I was out, bitches, and I had never felt such freedom or happiness.

I called Barry. "I want to get rid of Rupert," I said as soon as he answered the phone.

"Hold on, what the fuck... what's going on?"

"You're right. I've got a lot to tell you. First off, I'm coming out in a blog post on Ringside Magazine at five this evening."

"Holy shit, kid. Is this what you call giving me a heads up?"

"Yeah."

"Remind me to put you through extra hard training when you get your narrow ass back to Vegas. Okay, so you're coming out tonight. I might close the gym up early to avoid the media sharks. Now, what is this bullshit about Rupert?"

"This motherfucker has been playing us." I told Barry about what Rupert had done and he was pissed.

"That lowdown, dirty son of a bitch!" Barry roared. I let him rage for a few minutes because I knew how pissed he was. I was just as pissed when I found out. "Let me deal with Rupert," he said finally.

"I don't care about the contract I had with him. If he wants to try to take me to court on that shit... I've got some dirt on him that might give him cause to not make a big deal out of us parting ways," I said.

"Luckily, the endorsement deals he worked out with you won't be affected. That was one thing I was always adamant about. It's probably why he was trying to get even closer to you. I can't believe this shit," Barry stated.

"I know. Listen, I have to call Kathy and let her know. I just wanted to keep you updated."

"On some last minute shit, yeah. Be careful, kid."

"I will." I called Kathy next, but got her voicemail. I left her a message letting her know that I was coming out. I also sent it via text. I turned to Aiden and he was closing his laptop.

"Okay, the story has been sent and we just have to sit back and wait for it to post," he said.

I was looking at him and loving everything about him. I felt so close and connected. Last night, being out on the town with him, not afraid of who might see us, was the best night of my life. That and the night he took me back.

"Well, we have dinner at my brother's tonight. What do we do with ourselves until then?" I asked with a wiggle of my eyebrows.

Aiden laughed and leaped into my arms, wrapping his legs around my waist. It took me by surprise, but I grabbed him and made sure to have my way with him on the sofa again, then we took it back to the bedroom for round two. After a short nap, we both woke up ready to see our article on Ringside's website. Aiden got his laptop and we refreshed the page over and over until it popped up.

"Holy shit... this is really real," I said, beaming. I felt all kinds of butterflies fluttering around in my body because this was the biggest and most important thing I'd ever done publically. It didn't take long for the hits to start coming or the comments. Some were very positive, actually most were... but then there were plenty of haters making their opinions known. Still, an hour after the debut of the article, it had over a million hits and over three thousand comments. I was finally out.

My cell phone started ringing as well. I climbed out of bed and looked at it. "Hey Barry."

"Shit's hitting the fan, kid. Ask me why I decided to be your manager and head coach again?"

"Because you're a great guy with one hell of a soft spot."

"You give me more gray hair than my daughter—naw, I'm not going to tell that lie. But you're up there."

I laughed. I knew why, too. It was because he loved me like I was his own son. "So, what's going on, Barry?"

"I just got a phone call from the president of ETC. He's not happy that his Light-heavyweight Champ came out publically without giving him a heads up. I had to tell him you were impulsive and just barely let me know. I did let him know I had tried to warn him on your behalf, but he probably didn't listen to the message. Anyway, he's been filtering calls from the media about it since the article posted."

"Is he okay with it?" I asked. I mean, I cared because it was my livelihood, but I didn't care, because I was happy to be out.

"Ehh, hard to tell at this point, kid. He's just frustrated right now. He's probably concerned about how he's going to market your up-coming fight against Martinez."

"I'm sure a lot of gay men watch MMA," I said.

"Oh, no doubt. Watch and participate, but it's just not wide-ly known… or accepted. There's a lot of testosterone in this sport. However, you knew that already. Just keep doing what you're doing. Keep training and we'll wade through it all. I just wanted to let you know to expect the media to be in your life a lot more, at least for a little while."

"Thanks for the heads up."

"Yeah, see… that's how it's done."

I laughed. "Bye, Barry."

"See ya, kid."

I looked at Aiden. "I'm hungry. Ready to go to my brother's?"

He nodded. "Can't wait to meet your niece and nephew."

"You'll love them." Again, my cell started ringing. It was my brother. "Hey."

"So you came out."

"News sure travels fast."

"Yeah, especially because of the media hounds camping outside my house for a story. I could have used a heads up, little bro."

Apparently, I sucked at giving those. "I'm sorry. Yeah, I should have told you. It just happened. I'm not going to let that stop me from seeing you, though."

"All right. Just know you're going to have to fight your way through them."

"I figured."

I ended the call with my brother, and Aiden and I got dressed. When I got to his house, I noticed a few media trucks camped in front on the street. I sighed.

"Maybe this isn't such a good idea," Aiden worried.

"What do you mean?" I was hoping he wasn't having second thoughts. It was too late for that.

"I hate that they're bringing your brother into this."

"That's why I hate the media. But maybe if we give them what they want, they'll leave them alone."

Aiden nodded and when we climbed out of my rental, they were on us with flashing lights and questions. I took Aiden's hand as I crossed the street to my brother's home, then turned to address them.

"All right, I'll answer just a few questions, then I would ask that you leave my brother's home. He doesn't know anything more than you," I said.

"Did you brother know you were coming out?" one of them asked.

"No. He's shocked."

"How long have you two been together?" another asked.

"Didn't you read the article posted?"

"Were you dating when you were with Kathy?" came another silly ass question.

"Yes. Kathy and I are still very good friends."

"How do you think the public will feel having been deceived by you with your Kathy ruse," a rude ass woman asked.

I looked at her. "I stopped worrying about what the public thinks about who I'm dating when I decided to come out. I got tired of hiding who I really was because I was concerned about what everyone else would think. This is me. I'm the badass motherfucking MMA Light Heavyweight Champion who's gay and in a gay relationship with the love of my life. Take it or leave it. Now, goodnight."

I turned with Aiden's hand still in mine and we made our way into my brother's home. He'd been standing by the door, waiting for us to finish our "interview".

"Jesus, that's a circus out there," he said. We hugged and he hugged Aiden.

"I know. Fucking vultures," I snapped.

"Hey, language, bro, little ones are around."

I smiled. "Speaking of… where are the munchkins?"

My brother led us into the dining room where the rest of the family were. Hugs and kisses were passed out and a great meal was eaten over a loving family conversation. Eventually, all of the media people were gone and we were really able to enjoy our time. I watched as Aiden played with my niece and nephew, he really did love kids. I did too. I hoped to have some one day. I thought we'd make wonderful parents. As for my brother and I, we needed our heart to heart, so we made our way to the backyard with two beers.

"So, how are you feeling?" Rico asked me.

I took a swig of my beer and smiled. "I feel good."

"You want to tell me why you didn't trust me?"

Okay, he was getting right to the point. That was how we were in this family. I looked at him. "Because of how dad was. The things he would say made me too afraid to come out when I was younger. You seemed impressionable back then and I thought that you were still that way. I thought you wouldn't accept the fact that I was gay."

"Ahhhh, I see." Rico nodded. "Yeah, I was a dumbass teenager back then. I looked up to dad a lot, but after marrying Macy and going off to college, I realized he was wrong about a lot of shit. I also realized he was a shitty father. I made sure I'd never be that way with my own kids. I never want my children to be afraid to confide me in the way we were with dad. I never want my kids to ever question whether or not I love them. They'll just wake up and go to sleep knowing in their hearts that I do."

I nodded and smiled. My brother was an amazing father and one I inspired to be like. "You're a great dad, Rico."

"Thanks. Macy's brother is gay… he came out at Christmas, to no one's surprise," Rico said, laughing.

I laughed too. I'd only met Macy's brother once, but he had more sugar in his tank than an ice cream truck. He was out long before he officially announced it.

Rico wiped the tears from his eyes from laughing so hard. "Ohhhhh, god…. It was hilarious. Anyway, Macy also helped me keep my mind open. So when I saw you parading around with Kathy, I knew something was off. For as long as I'd known you, you were never into girls. Macy was like, 'he's gay, baby'. Then you did the two interviews with Aiden and spoke so highly of him… I started putting two and two together. Aiden was out, you were in… in love, that is. I'm happy for you both, by the way."

I was grinning now. "That means a lot to me."

He nodded and we clicked our beers together. "And fuck dad if he can't accept that, you hear me?"

I was shocked to hear Rico say those words, but it made me love my brother ever more. "I hear you."

"Good. Now, let's go back inside, these damn mosquitos are tearing me up," Rico said, slapping his arm, killing one. "Gotcha, bitch!"

I laughed and followed him back inside. This truly was the best time of my life.

CHAPTER TWENTY-FOUR

Aiden

THE WEEK AFTER MACIO CAME OUT WAS LIKE LIVING A DREAM. Most of the time it felt like a beautiful one that I didn't want to wake from, such as getting to know each other's families. Then there were a few dark spots that felt a little nightmarish, like the hateful voicemail message Macio received from his father or being stalked by the media. As frustrating as those moments were, the good times outnumbered them by a landslide. Macio didn't seem to be too upset about his dad's message and no gauntlet of story hungry reporters were going to darken my days and keep me away from my love.

The chaos outside Ringside Magazine headquarters was more than my editor, Jerry, wanted to deal with daily, so he asked me to work from home until the circus died down. He figured they'd get tired of waiting for a guy who never showed up and would move on. Now, Jerry didn't tell me I had to work from *my* home, so I worked from Macio's.

Macio went off to train daily and Caesar and I worked poolside. It was the kind of life I always dreamed of – I was referring to sharing a life with the other half of my soul, not the luxurious surroundings part. So maybe I did take a midday swim with Caesar every now and then, but I gave as good as I got. I prepared healthy meals for my man every night and pampered his tired body with my hands and lips. The truth was, I would've lived in a tent to be with Macio if I could pick up a Wi-Fi signal so I could work. Hey, he wasn't the only one who loved his career.

I was blown away by the amount of support we received on both the online story and the interview that went into print all around the world. It was hard for me to imagine, but there was most likely a copy of that magazine in nearly every doctor and dentist office throughout the continental U.S. It was doubtful people knew that I interviewed Macio buck ass naked and there was a lot of heavy petting and kinky foreplay going on, but that was okay because people didn't need to know everything. Macio had answered many interview questions for me that day, but two of his answers stood out the sharpest and would be words I'd hold onto for the rest of my days.

When was the first time you realized that it was okay to be gay? Honestly? It was when I met you for our first interview. You were this confident, sassy man who wasn't afraid for the world to know that he was attracted to other men. I thought to myself that I might never be as brave as you, but I at least recognized that it wasn't wrong for me to feel the way that I did.

What made you decide to come out? I could never be the man you needed me to be living in the shadows. I hurt you and subjected Kathy to a lot of negative press with my publicity stunt. There isn't a title belt I could earn that would mean more to me than you do.

I was sure there were fighters who read the article and rolled their eyes or gagged on the sweetness of his words, but they were true and spoken from the heart. Let them underestimate his prowess in the ring since he came out as gay. It would be a lesson they never forgot, that much I was sure of. Surprisingly, there were no fighters who came out and publicly took a stand against him. I wasn't sure if it was because word came down from the top that disrespecting him wouldn't be tolerated or if the men just wanted to avoid a media shit storm like the one we were dealing with more than a week after the online article went live.

Fans of the sport, and people on the internet in general, however, didn't show the same restraint as the ETC fighters did. The comments from the fans ranged from being disgusted by his "lifestyle choice" - which pissed me off because being gay wasn't a choice – to supportive and even jealous. The jealous ones cracked me up the most. It turned out, Macio had a large fan base among gay men that he didn't know about. Some of them thought we were "awwww, such a cute couple," and others were like, "what's he got that I don't?" In the beginning, I often wondered what the hell Macio saw in me that made him want to turn his world upside down, and that was before he came out. My favorite commenter by far was the one who said I was "hot, but what the fuck was up with my loafers?" It was Macio's favorite too.

"I love having you here, Aiden," Macio said one night when we were making out in his hot tub. "Is there any possible way you could move here and still work for Ringside?" His question stunned me so much that I only stared at him for several long moments. "Forget it, baby. I know it's too soon and it's not fair to…"

"I'll talk to Jerry tomorrow," I told him excitedly. "Other reporters do it, so I don't know why I can't. Hell, I can do conference calls for meetings and it's not that big of a deal if I have to travel to L.A. once in a while. It's no different than any other kind of traveling I have to do." I set my glass of wine down and straddled Macio's lap, completely unsurprised to find how hard his dick was. My baby was a fighter *and* a lover. "Are you sure you're ready for this, Macio?"

"Aiden, I'm only happy when you're by my side. I would move to L.A. if I could, but Vegas is the mecca of ETC fighting. I'd have to ask

Barry and his family to relocate or find a new trainer. I would do that if it was the only way to be by your side, but…"

"I'd never ask that. Either Jerry approves of the change or I'll find another job," I told him.

"It's that simple for you?" he asked.

"Yes," I nodded. "It's precisely that simple for me."

I talked to Jerry the following day, and as I suspected, he had no problem with me working from home – my new home in Vegas. I began making plans to move immediately. Step one was to break it to my family and friends and step two was to put my house on the market. My announcement shocked no one and listing my house turned out to be easier than I imagined. My neighborhood was an up and coming one for families with kids and the realtor thought I'd sell it quickly and for a hellacious profit.

Macio and I were in L.A. the following weekend, sorting through my things to see what I wanted to move to his house and what I wanted to sell or give to charity. As much as I had grown to love Macio's house, I thought he could use the warmth that my furniture would bring.

It was a good fucking thing we were in L.A. and not Vegas when Macio found out what Rupert had done behind his back. We thought going public with our relationship would be the end of Rupert and his need to humiliate Macio, but we were terribly wrong.

"Holy fuck," Seth said as soon as I answered his call late Saturday night. "Macio must be fucking furious."

I looked over at my guy who was standing at the refrigerator naked as the day he was born, looking for something healthy to nosh on. "Nope. He's definitely not furious. I'm curious as to why you'd think so."

"Haven't you seen the latest article on The Daily Spew?" he asked.

"Why the hell would I read that shit and why are you? They make Dirty Laundry Magazine look like child's play," I told Seth.

"Okay, you found out about my dirty little secret. I like to read gossip and shit, but man, I hate to be the one to break this news to you guys," Seth said hesitantly.

"Wait a sec," I told him. "Babe," I called over my shoulder to Macio, "Seth stumbled across something on The Daily Spew that he thinks we should know about." Macio came over with a scowl on his face and I hit the button to put Seth on speaker.

"What's up, Seth?" Macio asked. He smiled when he saw the way his no nonsense voice affected me.

"Hey, Macio," Seth said timidly. "Damn, I hate that you're hearing this from me, but I guess it's better coming from a friend." He took a deep breath, then blew our world apart when he said, "Your former manager, Rupert, told The Daily Spew that you weren't as squeaky clean as you'd like people to believe. He told them that, prior to meeting Aiden, he and your coach provided you with gay escorts after every fight. He even got a few of the escorts to share their story, but the magazine graciously used fake names to protect their privacy. It's pretty steamy and damaging stuff," Seth said softly.

Macio looked like he was going to be sick and my head went into spin mode so we could turn this around to our advantage somehow. In order to do that, I had to know what was being said, even if I really didn't want to hear the play-by-play account of some of the escorts. I thanked Seth and hung up the phone.

"Don't, baby," Macio pleaded with me. "I don't want you to read those things, Aiden. I'm not at all proud of who I was until I met you."

"Then that's what you tell people. First, you need to read if the things they said were true. If not, you could sue Rupert for defamation of character or something else."

"Baby, he broke his Non-Disclosure Agreement, so his ass is mine, figuratively mind you," he said when I scowled at him. "I'll let Barry know right away. Damn, I need a new publicist in the worst way. I have to make that a priority," Macio said.

"There are several PR agencies in L.A.," I told him. "Maybe you need to find someone outside your normal circle going forward. You don't really need them in your face 24/7, so having one based in Vegas isn't really a necessity, you just need them to act in your best interest."

"True." Macio took a deep breath and pulled the website up on his tablet and we read it together.

"He liked it I when I called him Champ," Christopher said. "It really revved him up and kept him fucking for hours."

"He was a fucking machine," Nicholas added. "I was sorry to hear he was off the market."

The interviewer went out of his way to try and get Rupert to admit that Macio didn't just have sex with the escorts in Vegas where it was legal, but also in other states where it wasn't. It could've been his self-preservation in full swing, but the dirty bastard refused to admit anything of the sort. He was quoted as saying, "No, no. Escort services were only purchased through legally licensed companies and never outside of Vegas. No laws were ever broken." When asked why he was outing his former client, Rupert said, "He's out there pretending to be this upstanding guy who wants to help teens accept who they are and to give them hope for a bright future where they'll be accepted. That's not who Anamacio De Niro really is, though. He's a user, a man who purchases the services of escorts and only walks tall and proud when he thinks he's going to lose the tight ass he wants to plow."

"Whoa," I said out loud. First, I was angry on behalf of Macio because he really did want to give encouragement to teens who thought there was no hope for a happy life. He wanted to be a beacon for kids like himself and Rupert's comments really made me angry. Then there was the comment about me, as if he still had no clue about how in love we were with one another. I said nothing about either of those things though, because I honestly didn't think anything I had to say would make Macio feel any better. "Sooo, you want me to start calling you Champ?" I asked instead.

"Aiden," Macio said, his voice was equal parts horror and humor.

"Babe, there's nothing really that damaging in that stupid article. The whole world now knows that you're a fucking machine and I'll once again have to read comments about how you're wasting your time with a guy like me, but I'm tough enough to take it." I meant every word I said to him, too. "Macio, if you aren't proud of the fact that you used escorts, then that's what you tell people. If you feel like you owe people an apology for letting them down, then you can say that too. If you don't want to say anything at all, then that's the road you choose. Know this," I reached for his hand and tugged him closer, "I'll be by your side every step of the way. Do you hear me? This changes nothing between us. Except that I know to call you Champ now." I just couldn't resist adding that in.

"Aiden, I don't even know what to say to you right now." He stood up and paced in front of my coffee table. "How can you even love me? I'm a guy who kept you hidden, broke your heart, and now I've embarrassed you in front of your family and friends."

"How have you embarrassed me?" I wasn't following.

"My past deeds impact how people see me, which extends to you by default," Macio said. "Your mom, sisters, your coworkers, and your friends are reading this and wondering why you're wasting your time on a loser like me."

"Macio, you're the furthest thing from a loser I know," I said. "I think you're a winner and not just in the fucking octagon, either. Throw out everything we know about you as a fighter and let's talk about Macio the man – the one I'm head over heels in love with." I rose from the couch and walked to him. "You are a man who speaks the truth from your heart. You are a man who had been raised to hate who he was, but rose above it. So many kids give up on themselves and life before they even have a chance to experience it. Not you, because you're a fighter to the very marrow of your bones." I linked my fingers through his. "If anyone asks why I'm with you, I'm going to tell them that those are just a few of the reasons why I'm blessed to be the one you love."

"Damn, baby," Macio whispered, lowering his forehead to mine. "I crazy love you."

"I crazy love you right back." I lifted my chin and presented my lips for a kiss. "Now, let's fire up your camp and start working on a response or a fuck you, whichever you want, and then make plans to sue the hell out of Rupert so he can't do this to someone else."

"Sounds like a plan," Macio told me.

"Then you can fuck me into the wee hours of the morning, Champ."

Macio was quick, but for once I was quicker. I darted away from him but didn't run too fast or too far because I liked it when he caught me. Calling Barry and the gang ended up waiting until the next morning.

CHAPTER TWENTY-FIVE

Macio

WOKE UP BRIGHT AND EARLY AND READY TO TAKE CARE OF BUSINESS. That bullshit Rupert pulled wasn't going to go unanswered. Not at all. I didn't like my personal business being out there for everyone to read. I knew some of it would have to be when I came out, that just went with the territory of being a celebrity. However, I came out on my terms and only released what information I wanted the world to know. It was very controlled. But Rupert blasting his fat ass mouth off about the escorts and what he thinks of me pissed me the fuck off.

I looked at Aiden, he was still sleeping soundly. I knew he would be because I gave him that champ dick last night… he was down for the count. I climbed out of the bed and handled my bathroom business first, then called Barry.

"Yeah, I was wondering when you were going to call me," Barry said.

"When did you find out about the article?" I asked.

He groaned. "Shit... Last night. You know I don't read that bullshit, half the stories in that rag are made up. I was worried that stupid motherfucker was going to do something like this when I fired his ass. He acted like he wanted to do something to me that day, but he thought better about it."

I snorted. "Yeah, it wouldn't be wise to attack the man who's the head trainer and manager of ETC's undisputed champ."

"Yeah, you could see those gears turning. I was hoping he wouldn't go off and do something stupid like this, though. So, what do you want to do, kid?" Barry asked.

"I want to sue his dumb ass for breaking the disclosure. He's been stabbing me in the back ever since I started dating Aiden. He's done all of this because he's jealous. The motherfucker better hope I don't out *his* ass. If he keeps pushing me, I might just do that. Truth of the matter is, I really like his wife and she deserves a better husband. But outing Rupert for hitting on me puts more of my business out there, and I don't want that either."

"Maybe just tell his wife privately," Barry suggested.

"Ugh! I swear, I don't even want to be bothered with the drama."

"Yeah, I get that. Well, at least the escorts didn't have anything bad to say about you."

"That's because I'm a fucking machine that gives great dick," I joked. Well, half joked, because that shit was true. I was done bragging about my sexual exploits with men who were just there to take the edge off. With Aiden, sex mattered, and the only person whose opinion held meaning regarding my bedroom prowess was his.

"Well, do you need me to do anything?" Barry asked.

"I'm looking for a new publicist right now. Preferably someone who's in the LGBT community or supports it. I don't need anyone giving me homophobic advice because they don't want to rock the boat." I said. "I do need you to contact a lawyer for me so we can get our lawsuit going against Rupert."

"All right, I can get that started. Are you going to address the article?"

"Yeah, I'm sure I'll have a camera and microphone thrust into my face as soon as I step out of the house. Ugh, just when the shit was starting to die down, too. They had their story, they had their pics of Aiden and I out on the town... the hoopla was starting to play itself out and here comes Rupert, out from the rock he'd been hiding under with his hate."

"This too will die down, and soon we can all get back down to fighting business," Barry stated encouragingly. "Especially after we sue his ass. Okay, I'm going to make some calls and get back to you."

"Yeah, me too. Talk to you later." I ended my call with Barry and checked out the publicist companies Aiden had suggested the night before. I found two that I really liked, they had plenty of good testimonials and a great reputation. I made appointments with each for a meeting. I wanted to see what they could offer me. Rupert may be on a jealousy-fueled hate train right now, but when he was acting as my publicist... I had to admit, he was damn good. With his business degree as well as his journalistic one, he did double duties for me. Got me amazing endorsement deals and he was responsible for bringing Aiden and I together – though I was willing to bet he wished he hadn't by now. Regardless, I needed that kind of business savvy and prioritizing from my new publicist.

I heard two footsteps right before Aiden slipped his arms around my shoulders. He kissed the side of my neck, then rested his chin on my shoulder. "What's up, baby?"

This was everything I wanted. To be able to wake up and go to sleep with the man I loved in my arms. To be free to be in love with the person who captured my heart. Everyone deserved to know what this felt like regardless of orientation or anything else. If you were lucky enough to find the "right one," you should be able to embrace them and share your life with them without repercussions from others.

I closed my laptop and turned my head a little so I could kiss his temple. "Just setting up meetings with two possible replacements for Rupert."

Aiden slipped away, only to walk around the sofa and sit on my lap. I wrapped my arms around his waist, holding him close. "Are you going to address that article?"

I chuckled. "Yeah. What pisses me off is that I feel like I have to. Number one, I never claimed to be a saint. I beat people's asses for a living. Not the most noble of aspirations, but I love the rush and I love to win. I was single, so fucking escorts shouldn't even be a big deal, but I know people want to make it into one. That's the only reason why I'm bothering to say anything about it. I don't want my work with teens to be tarnished, and I also have to protect my endorsements— those that backed me up."

"Okay. I'm with you no matter what you decide," Aiden said, then he kissed me longingly as if the time we'd been separated expanded to years instead of only one hour. I loved it. He pulled away and gave me a few pecks on my nose, lips, and forehead. "I'm going to make us something to eat."

He started to rise off my lap, but I tightened my grip, keeping him in place. "What if I want to eat you?"

Aiden grinned. "Well, my big, bad, wolf... I do have some very sweet buns."

I smiled. "You sure do. I was checking them out. Some nice pop 'n fresh ones."

Aiden burst into a fit of laughter. His laugher was so sweet and genuine, it became contagious and I started laughing with him. We both had to wipe tears from our eyes by the time we calmed down from whatever it was that made Aiden lose it.

"That... was the... corniest shit... you've ever said," Aiden managed to say through his fading giggles.

I thought about what I'd said and laughed again, because it was true. "Yeah, it was." I slapped him on one of his sweet buns. "You can make breakfast. I'll eat your buns and the sweet center after."

"Such charming things you say, Champ," Aiden said, then kissed me again. When he pulled away this time, I let him up. My stomach was growling for some grub right about then. I watched him and his sexy ass walk away from me, then I turned and settled on the sofa.

I was so happy with my life now. I thought I was going to really suffer financially when I came out by having some of my endorsement deals fall apart, but only one pulled away. Homophobic sons of bitches. Fuck them and their really delicious chicken. I had to admit, I loved their chicken, but now I saw who they really were and I was glad to bid them farewell. Everyone else supported me and were happy that they now had a LGBT member as well as a MMA Champ as their spokesman. Gay people buy cars, watches, and sports equipment, too, and their money was just as green as everyone else's.

All in all, things were going well for us. I ignored as much of the hate mail that was still coming as I could. Some of those bastards were sneaky with their subject titles. Shit like "I hope you two are happy," then when I clicked on it, they finish it off by saying, "burning in hell with the rest of the fags". Funny how people loved to say things like that as if it made them better than the person they were harassing. Self-righteous people who spewed hate like that weren't going to see any pearly gates either. I also had to get through a few encounters in the locker room with some of my fellow fighters.

I didn't tell Aiden about them, I didn't want to stress him out because it wasn't anything I couldn't handle and wasn't prepared for. Besides, I shut their mouths pretty quickly when I reminded them how I whooped their asses. It felt good to put them in their places. Now that I thought about it, maybe I would tell Aiden about those encounters after all. He could get a good laugh like I had. I got up and went into the kitchen and told him about them, and just as I suspected, he laughed. He almost burned the bacon, he was laughing so hard.

"Oh god, you showed them, baby. Fuck them," he said as he took the bacon out of the pan.

Mmmmm bacon. Loved the slabs of pork sizzling on a plate

covered with a towel. I waited until Aiden turned his back, then quickly snatched one of the slabs from the plate. It was so hot, it burned my fingers. "Ahh shit!"

Aiden turned around just in time to see me drop the bacon on the countertop. "That's what you get, thief."

"I couldn't help it. The food smelled so good. You know how I am about bacon," I whined in my defense. I picked up the piece I'd dropped and blew on it.

"Ah, ah, ah, wait for breakfast," Aiden scolded right before he snatched the bacon from my fingers, putting it back with the other pieces.

"Awwww man, but what can I snack on now?" I asked imploringly as I made my way over to him.

"There's yogurt in the fridge," Aiden suggested.

"Yeah, but there's also cream in your balls," I countered as I dropped to my knees in front of him. I pulled his boxers down a little, just to let his cock free.

"Oh my god, I'm cooking!" Aiden screeched.

"Yeah, and I'm sucking," I said, then shoved his cock into my mouth.

"Ooooh," Aiden purred.

I could hear him struggle to continue to fix our breakfast as I sucked his dick. I loved how hard and smooth he felt in my mouth as I ran my tongue all around his sensitive areas. The sounds he was making drove me wild and I couldn't wait to fuck him afterwards.

"Ahhhh shit... You're gonna make me burn the eggs," Aiden warned.

I laughed, then pulled back off his cock, only to suck his balls into my mouth.

"Ooh shit... that's it, baby. Yeah... just like that," Aiden moaned in ecstasy.

Eventually, he gave up trying to cook and just leaned back against the counter until he cried out in climax. I sucked every drop he gave me, savoring my man's flavor. I loved how his body quaked in pleasure until I licked the last drop from his slit. I smiled as I rose to my feet. "I like my protein in the morning, baby," I said, then grabbed him by the back of his head, kissing him passionately. He melted in my arms because he knew that he was mine and I was his. I ground my hard, aching cock against his, letting him feel how much I wanted him, then I pulled back, growling. "Okay, now you can finish breakfast." Again, I slapped him on his fuckable ass and walked away, leaving him satisfied and hungry for more at the same time.

CHAPTER TWENTY-SIX

Aiden

SETTLED INTO MY NEW ROUTINE IN MACIO'S – OUR – HOME. IT amazed me how comfortable and right it felt to be in the same space as him, sharing meals, a bed, and a life. I could touch him and kiss him whenever I wanted to instead of just wishing that I could. It was everything I had ever dreamed of and more. I kept expecting to wake up at any minute to find out that it had all been an elaborate dream, but instead, I found the love of my life on the pillow beside mine.

Macio's mornings began long before mine, which I didn't mind too much because it meant that he returned to me earlier. He never left for training without kissing me and telling me that he loved me. When he got home each afternoon, he was ready for two things – food and fucking. It was a toss-up daily which one came first; I never complained about either one.

One afternoon, Macio left to visit a LGBT shelter for runaway teens and young adults after his food and fuck time. I stayed behind so I could get some more research done for my next interview with NFL rookie phenom, who was either referred to as a thug or a great guy. I wanted to meet him in person, rather than do a phone interview, so I could see for myself what kind of person he really was.

I had read many articles about his supposed connections to gangs during high school and the community work he engaged in during college. What was true and what was fiction? I thought it was possible that both were true. A lot of athletes overcame adversity from their early years, then gave back to their communities and encouraged teens to avoid some of the things they got caught up in. They were people I greatly admired.

I rose from the sofa where I'd taken up residence to let Caesar out to stretch his legs and do his business. I debated about taking a swim, but decided to get my research done so I could spend as much time with Macio as possible before I had to leave for my trip. I left Caesar to do his thing and went in search of something to drink. I heard the front door open and close and figured it was Macio returning home to grab something he forgot. I mean, it probably took a long time for the blood to return to his brain after the fucking he gave me before he left. I heard his footsteps approaching behind me and decided to have a bit of fun.

"Can't stay away from this," I yanked down my shorts to reveal my bare ass, "can you?"

My wisecrack and ass crack were met with silence and not the sexy comeback I'd expected. A feeling of unease came over me, followed by my hair standing up all over my body. I quickly yanked up my shorts and turned around. The last person I expected to see again in Macio's house was standing in his - our - kitchen with a gun pointed at me.

"You think you're fucking cute, don't you?" Rupert snarled. "You have ruined Macio's life." He was so angry, his hands shook.

That whole saying about your life flashing before your eyes was totally true and my movie reel was way too damn short for my liking. My brain went into survival mode because I had just recently found the guy I wanted to spend my life with and I wasn't about to give that future up easily.

"Rupert, let's talk about this." I raised my hands up in front of me in a surrender gesture. "You don't want to do anything drastic here."

"Don't tell me what I want to do, you little fucker."

Rupert took two steps toward me so that there was probably ten feet or less between us. I saw in his eyes that he wasn't playing around and had come with one purpose in mind - to kill me. With my back against the kitchen counter, my only escape was around Rupert or through him. If he hadn't held a gun on me, I would've tried either option. The gun changed things, though. I tried to discreetly look for something within my grasp to throw at the arm holding the gun like I'd seen in the movies, but there was nothing.

I could only pray that something would distract him long enough for me to charge him and hope for the best. In the meantime, the best course of action was to buy time by keeping my mouth shut and letting him talk. If Rupert was like most TV and movie villains, then he would have plenty of things to say.

"Macio was destined for great things, but you destroyed it, Aiden. It's only a matter of time before he's a sad little asterisk in MMA history," Rupert said.

"How do you figure?" I asked. *So much for keeping my mouth shut.*

Rupert shook his head slowly, as if I was lacking a brain. "Before, when people looked at Macio, they saw a champion they could believe in. Now, all they do is wonder what he likes to do with his dick."

"You sure as fuck didn't help him out there, did you, Rupert?" I figured if I was going to die that day in Macio's kitchen, then I'd at least go out the way I wanted to. "The only one obsessed about what Macio's doing with his dick is you, and it's only because he's not giving it to you. That's what you can't stand. You figured someday you'd be the one crying out Champ while he pounded away." I took a step forward, uncertain when I'd grown such big balls, and said, "It's never going to happen, Rupert. Do you hear me? You can kill me now, but the only thing you'll get out of it is a prison sentence."

"See, that mouth of yours is the reason you're going to bleed out in Macio's kitchen. Imagine how broken he'll be when he discovers your brains all over his floor."

The fact that I worried more about Macio finding my dead body than dying was proof of how much I loved him. I didn't dare close my eyes and imagine how broken he'd be because I wouldn't give Rupert the satisfaction of knowing that his poisoned arrow struck its target.

"My mouth is what captured Macio's attention and set me apart from the others, including you." I stood up taller. "I might die today, but I won't die unloved. I will go to my grave knowing Macio placed his love for me above his career and money."

Rupert laughed hysterically. "I give it a month at the most before he moves on from you. There are so many asses to fuck in the world. You'll be nothing more than a distant memory - a regretted one at that for ruining his career."

As much as it hurt me to think of Macio with someone else, I'd never want him to live without love in his life and revert to emotionless sex. He deserved so much more than that. "Maybe so, but it won't be your ass he chooses."

"Don't be so sure, you arrogant bastard. I was so close once before. I felt his lips against mine and felt him start to harden beneath my hand. Only some misplaced loyalty to you stopped him. If you're dead..."

Caesar must have heard the raised voices, because he began barking viciously and scratching at the back door. It startled Rupert so much, he pulled the trigger and fired a shot. Luckily for me, his arm had jerked slightly in the same direction that his head turned and the bullet hit the cabinet behind me and not me. My eardrums felt like they were going to bust from the noise of the gun blast, the splintered wood from the cabinet, and the shattered glasses from the dishes inside them.

It also spurred me into action. I charged at Rupert, who looked shocked that he'd fired the gun, which was odd because why else had he come? I lowered my shoulder and rammed him in the chest hard enough to knock him on his ass. I heard the sound of the gun hitting the floor but didn't stop running or even looking over my shoulder to see where it landed. I had only one chance to escape him. I sprinted for the front door, hoping I could reach it before Rupert recovered his gun because he would have a clean shot at me.

"Stop, Aiden!" Rupert screamed, as if I was stupid enough to fall for that. "I'm going to fucking kill you. Macio won't even recognize you when I'm through with you."

Macio's house had always seemed large to me, but never more so than in that moment when it felt like I ran and ran, but never got closer to the door. Finally, as if someone turned off the slow-motion feature, I was within a few feet of the door and had hope that I would make it. *I'm going to make it, Macio.* As if I had conjured him up, the door opened and Macio stepped through it. The smile fell off his face when he saw the fear etched on mine.

"Gooooo!" I waved my arm and repeated for him to go.

Macio looked around me to see what the fuck was going on and his eyes widened in fear. I knew then that Rupert had found the gun and was aiming at me. I wanted to be brave so Macio would remember me that way and not as a terrified man who was ready to cry because he wasn't ready to leave him. At least I'd leave this world with Macio being the last person I saw, not that bastard Rupert. *I love you.* I couldn't be sure if I just thought the words to myself or said them out loud.

Macio lunged at me, grabbed both of my biceps in his strong hands, then turned his body to try and knock me out of the way. I heard the loud bang of the gun go off, followed by Macio grunting in pain in my ear. We crashed into the wall hard enough to knock the paintings off it, then fell on top of the decorative table by the door. It wasn't strong enough to support our combined weight, so the table, all the decorations on it, and both of us went crashing to the floor.

I felt shards of ceramic and glass piercing my shirt and stabbing into my skin seconds before my head hit the marble tiled floor hard enough to knock me unconscious. I wasn't sure how long I was out, but it couldn't have been too long because I heard sirens in the distance. I looked into Macio's concerned eyes and was so grateful to be alive.

"Not a dream," I said, trying to convince myself. "You're real."

"As a heart attack, baby." It reminded me of the conversation we had when we first got back together.

I wanted to laugh, but my head hurt too badly. I became aware of excruciating pain in my side and upper thigh, then forgot about it when I noticed Macio's injury. He had removed his shirt and wrapped it around his upper arm to staunch the blood flow, but it wasn't working.

"You came back," I said.

"I forgot my phone in the bedroom. It's a good thing I came back when I did or I would've lost you." The tenderness in Macio's voice was almost enough to make me forget the situation we were in.

I sat up suddenly, then clutched my stomach when it pitched and rolled, threatening to spill its contents all over the bloody floor. I got extremely lightheaded and began to sway as blackness threatened to pull me back under. I needed to stay awake. What if we were still in danger?

"Rupert?" I asked, more like slurred. The sirens got louder as our help got closer.

"Ran like the fucking coward he is," Macio growled. "He's not going to get very far."

"You're bleeding really badly, Macio," I pointed out.

"It's just flesh and muscle. I'm going to be okay," he tried to assure me. I was having a hard time focusing on him because there were suddenly three of him and none of them would stay still long enough. "You have some nasty cuts and you banged your head really hard, but you're going to be okay too. I love you, baby."

"You're so fucking sexy," I told him. "All three of you." Another wave of nausea hit me and I couldn't hold my contents inside me the second time. Later, I would be mortified that I vomited in front of Macio or worried that he saw me as weak, but right then I was too miserable to care.

The cops and EMTs arrived on the scene and separated the two of us to get us ready for transport. Macio insisted that he was fine to walk, even after the blood loss, and insisted on riding on the same ambulance as me. He held my hand and spoke to me and, although I couldn't hear the words he was saying over the loud sirens, I knew whatever he said was beautiful and full of emotion.

I could feel the edges of oblivion creeping up on me and knew I was about to lose consciousness again. It seemed like the harder I fought to stay awake, the heavier my body got and the dimmer my vision became.

"Don't fight it, baby. I'll still be here," Macio told me.

The next time I opened my eyes, it was Barry sitting beside me and not Macio. I assumed the worst when I took in Barry's tired, stressed expression and body language. I tried to sit up, but Barry reached over and laid a calm hand over my chest and gently pressed me back down against the bed.

"Relax, kid," he said gently. "Macio is fine. He's out of surgery and resting in his room next door. The bullet missed bone, but it tore through muscles and ligaments. He's looking at months of physical therapy to get the strength back in his arm."

I reached for the covers, prepared to throw them off so I could go find my man. "He needs me."

"He does need you, and that's why you have to stay here and rest. Aiden, do you trust me?" I did, although I didn't know him well. I always had the impression that he had Macio's best interests at heart, which I could never say about Rupert. I nodded, then regretted the action immediately because of the pain the movement caused. Rupert reached over and patted my hand where it rested on the bedrail. "I'll make sure you two get moved into the same room. Okay?"

It would have to do because I was too sick to be going anywhere. "Thank you, Barry."

"No problem. Now that I know you're okay, I'm going to go check on Macio, then see about moving you guys in as roomies for the night." He pinned me with a serious look, then said, "As long as you both promise to stay in your separate beds and actually do what the nurses tell you."

I had to think hard about it for a few seconds because being in the same room with Macio and not sharing the same bed felt like torture, but he would need his rest. "Okay," I promised, maybe with a slight bit of petulance in my tone.

The next time I woke up, my guy was in a hospital bed parked next to mine. He smiled weakly at me and I thought to myself that he had never looked more beautiful than he did right then. He was banged up and in pain, but he was alive. I wanted so badly to go to him, to run my fingers through his hair and kiss his face, but I had made a promise to Barry and I would keep it.

"How long we in for?" I asked him.

"We're both going home tomorrow," Macio said. "Barry made sure that all signs of Rupert will be gone."

"Have they found him?" The thought of his crazy ass waiting for us to return made me sicker than I already felt. As gimpy as Macio and I were right then, it would've been like shooting fish in a barrel.

"Fuck yeah, they did. He won't be able to hurt anyone ever again," Macio told me.

I released a relieved breath and smiled at my guy. I held up my hand and gestured to our surroundings, then said, "This isn't my idea of a sleepover, baby."

"Mine either, but it's just for a night and then we'll be back to sharing a bed again."

I could handle one more night. In the grand scheme of things, it was no big deal at all. At least he was still beside me and neither one of us were gravely wounded.

"Unless you want to come over here and snuggle against my good side," Macio said invitingly.

"I promised I'd be good," I told Macio.

"Not going to happen," Barry said, walking into the room. He had a blanket and a pillow tucked under his arms and wore a scowl on his face. It was obvious he didn't trust us and had intended to set up a night watch. "I decided not to take any chances where you two are concerned." He pointed his finger at both of us. "Besides, both of your families are coming tomorrow and you'll need your rest to deal with them."

Macio and I both groaned. So much for some peaceful cuddling while we recuperated.

CHAPTER TWENTY SEVEN

Macio

THE MEDIA CIRCUS THAT ROLLED INTO OUR WORLD AFTER THE incident with Rupert trying to kill the love of my life was one for the record books. Aiden and I had reporters shoving microphones in our faces the moment we left the hospital. They were waiting for us at our home, all hoping to catch whatever juicy details they could, simply to sensationalize our lives. Neither Aiden nor I gave them much, because it was our private lives, our business. One of the headlines read: "MMA Gay Love Triangle" as if that was even close to the fact. There was no love on my part for Rupert in that way. I really hated how the media had a knack for twisting facts to make fiction. On the brighter side of the scandal, at least Lisa, Rupert's wife was made aware of her husband's antics. Last I'd heard, she was filing for divorce. Good for her.

As for the media circus, the only rag we gave the truth to was

Ringside. I already had the best reporter who wrote his stories with integrity living right with me, just the way I wanted it. That was also one of their highest selling issues, because everyone wanted the inside scoop on what happened that day Rupert broke into my home in hopes of killing my sexy lover. As if I'd ever choose him after the fact. Crazy ass bastard. As for me, it wasn't all rainbows. Because of my injury, I had been on the mend and trying to get back into fighting shape. I had to forfeit my championship belt because I wasn't physically fit to defend it at the time.

That didn't seem to bother the assholes who fought for it as if they actually earned it. Jacob Kirsey was now the reigning champ, but he wouldn't be for long. I was in the best shape of my life now, and my stamina game was on point. I wore Aiden's ass out on a daily basis. God, I loved him! I couldn't even begin to describe how happy I was now. He was totally supportive of me while I was healing from my injury. He took care of me every step of the way. Aiden gave me encouragement when I had to relinquish my title, which was one of the hardest things I ever had to do.

It was one thing to lose it in a fight to a more skilled opponent. It was another to have to give it up without any fight at all. But my baby didn't let me wallow in pity, not self or otherwise. I finally knew what it felt like to have a soulmate, because that was who Aiden was to me. The other half of my heart, the part of me that breathed life into my lungs and pumped blood into my veins. I never wanted to ever be parted from him again.

"I think you've worked out enough for the night," Aiden said as he entered my home gym.

I slowed down my treadmill to a walking pace and turned down the music as he approached my machine. "Hey baby, what's for dinner?"

"Roast, veggies, and scalloped potatoes, the meal for a champ," he said with a smile.

Just thinking about that meal made my stomach growl. Aiden

was a champ in his own right in the kitchen. I had to be careful of my weight. While I was on the mend, I'd picked up a few unnecessary pounds eating his delicious cooking. Of course, I'd worked it off in time to cut weight to qualify for the upcoming championship bout to reclaim my title.

Aiden smiled. "Sure. I'll fix the table."

"Sounds mouthwatering, can't wait to eat. Just give me five minutes, babe," I said.

"Okay." He turned, giving me a sweet view of that ass of his I was damn sure going to plow tonight. I loved watching him walk away.

As for my career, it had been a long road getting back to championship status. I had to have two bouts and win even before I could challenge the current *champ*-a term I used loosely. He never won it from me, so he was no champ in my eyes. Of course, my fans supported me as I climbed that ladder and the promotion played up my comeback because it sold tickets and pay-per-views like never before. I still had to deal with some levels of homophobia, but it wasn't slowing me down.

Fact was, people wanted to see my fight. My ring prowess was more important to a good majority of fans than my bed prowess. Of course, I was sure a lot of my fans were interested in both. I'd received a lot of fan mail from my gay fans, many with nude photos as if to turn me on and away from Aiden. That was never going to happen, but I did appreciate the loyalty and support. I knew because I had such a strong fan following, it helped secure my place in my MMA promotion. To this day, I was still the only out and proud MMA fighter. Hopefully, one day, more fighters would find the courage to come out also.

As for my upcoming fight against Kirsey, my promotion was hyping it up as the fight of the century in MMA history. They were really eating up all of the publicity I'd been receiving from coming out and being a hero for saving the life of my lover. It was all so dramatized, and actually broke the old ticket sales record my first comeback bout made.

I turned off the treadmill, toweled the sweat off my body, and made my way to the dining room to chow down with my man. As I walked through my home, I took notice of the things that were changed since Aiden had moved in. He never did like my décor, so now our home had his special touch everywhere, especially in the bedroom, patio, den, and living room. All of the places he loved to lounge and work. So, there was a lot of softer colors and more artwork here and there. I liked the changes and it made the place feel more like it was our home, which was good, because it was.

Aiden was pouring two glasses of wine when I entered and I walked over to him, grabbing his waist and pulling him to me as I kissed the nape of his neck. "Hey there, sexy."

Aiden chuckled and turned his head to face me; that was when I kissed him full on, tongue and all. I swear, I couldn't get enough of him in any capacity. I didn't know how long we stood there kissing. At one point, Aiden turned in my arms and we were in full make-out mode.

Finally, my stomach put an end to our passionate display and re-minded me of why we were in the dining room. Reluctantly, I pulled away with a peck. "I'm starving."

"Good, because I cooked my ass off," Aiden said when I released him.

I checked out his ass while he walked to his chair. "Naw, that pretty thing is still intact."

He laughed and pointed to a chair. "Sit."

I did as I was told and he served me my plate. Everything looked as good as it smelled, and I ate to the last drop, savoring every bite. "Damn, baby, you know you can cook."

"I have my mom to thank for that. She always felt it was import-ant for her children to know how to take care of themselves," Aiden said as he finished his meal.

"I love your mom." She was the greatest woman, really. She

welcomed me into her family with open arms. In fact, the only person who hadn't accepted my new life was my father, which was no surprise, but I wasn't about to let him rain on my parade. Either he'd come around or he could go to hell. My brother, his wife, and kids loved me and Aiden, and were happy that we had found each other. That was all that really mattered to me.

After dinner, I made good on my word to put Aiden's ass to work. I had him huffing, puffing, moaning, and groaning in ecstasy from the wall to the bed, and as soon as we busted our nuts, he was down for the count. I looked at him in my arms, so sweet and sexy. So perfect for me. I kissed his forehead, then pressed mine to his and drifted off to sleep.

"Hey, kid, are you ready to go out there and kick some ass?" Barry asked me as I was getting my hands wrapped up. Aiden was in my dressing room too, along with the official.

I nodded. "Fuck yeah, I'm ready to get back what is mine," I said. My body was fully charged with pent-up energy I couldn't wait to release inside the octagon. I hadn't had sex in a week in preparation for this fight, and as soon as it was over, I was going to ravage Aiden's ass, especially since he'd been taunting me with that hot body of his for the past three days.

He'd come out of the shower, dripping wet and posing right in front of me while he toweled off, making sure I was watching his every move. One time, I got weak and walked over to him and he put on the brakes, talking about, "You have to be at your peak for your fight in two days, so no hanky-panky." Then he laughed and slapped his ass as he walked away. Oh yeah, I was going to bang his walls down the first chance I got.

For now, my focus was on my opponent, Jacob Kirsey, and reclaiming my title. He had been talking a lot of shit leading up to our fight about how he wasn't going to lose his title to a pansy-ass cock-sucker like me. I was looking forward to shoving my fist in his face and my foot up his ass. My aikido coach finished taping up my hands and putting on my gloves. We slapped fists together as his way of giving me his encouragement.

"Go out there and kick his ass, Macio," Hiko said.

"Damn straight. His ass will be left crying in that ring, or knocked out, either or is fine with me," I said.

"All right, it's time," Barry announced.

"Give him hell, baby," Aiden said and he grabbed the back of my head, bending me to his for one of his soul-melting kisses. "Win for me, Champ."

"I love you," I said.

He smiled. "I love you too. Now, go out there and do what you do… second best."

I frowned. "Second, what's first?"

His grin turned wicked and full of lust. "What you're going to do to me after the fight."

Oooh, hell yeah. "And you know it." I slapped his ass and he released me. I turned, following Barry out of the dressing room. We made our way to the octagon and I was greeted with mostly cheers. There were some boos, but that was always the case. I didn't care why those people didn't like me. Fuck them. I climbed inside the octagon to more roars from the crowd and flashing lights of the cameras. My theme music blared a little longer as I flexed my muscles for the audience so they could see what good shape I was in.

When Jacob's music came on, there were just as many cheers for him as there were boos. I guessed people didn't appreciate him being the champ without actually winning the belt from the real champion. This match was going to set it all straight, the fighter who actually deserved to wear the belt and title. He entered the octagon, all pumped up and talking more shit. After his theatrical display, we stepped up to each other to hear the referee go over the rules.

"I'm going to beat the fag out of your ass, boy," Jacob taunted.

I laughed. "Bitch, you're about to get your ass beat by a fag," I shot back, then blew him a kiss.

My taunt had the desired effect as he tried to lunge at me, but the referee stopped him. I laughed in his face even more and flexed my muscles to more cheers from the crowd. They were ready to see shit go down, and I wasn't about to disappoint.

The referee stepped back, the bell rung, and the fight began. Jacob threw a right hook that I blocked and he kicked, but I tucked my elbow, protecting my ribs. I let him be on the offense, waiting for him to leave himself open. I'd been watching his fights, and he had a weakness... I just had to wait for him to present the opportunity for me to take him out. I threw a kick, which he blocked; when he went for a left jab, I stepped to the side and countered with a powerful right hook. He took it square on the jaw, which snapped his head back. I followed with a swift kick to his face, which surely broke his nose. Blood poured from his nostrils as he fell to the mat. That was when I pounced on him, throwing a bevy of blows until the referee pulled me off.

I stepped back as the crowd went crazy. The referee checked Jacob out. My opponent looked dizzy as hell as his eyes rolled around in his head. Seeing as he was unable to continue the fight, the ref declared him knocked out to the ring of the bell. I yelled in triumph as I raised my hands in the air. My crew poured inside the gated octagon, crowding around me in their excitement. I was so happy to have not only reclaimed my title in the first round, but I also proved to the world that you couldn't hold me back. To add the cherry on top, I got a kick out of shutting Jacob's homophobic ass down. Let that be a lesson to anyone else who dared to call me a fucking pansy.

I hugged my coaches and crew as they congratulated me on my victory.

"Shit, you knocked his ass out in less than three minutes, kid!" Barry beamed. I smiled and hugged him again.

"Thanks to you never giving up on me, Barry."

"Never, kid." Barry hugged me again, then raised my hand in the air, to the audience's delight.

Even though I was surrounded by people who cared about me and stood by me, I knew someone was missing. I moved through my crew and looked out by the side to see Aiden standing there, clapping and cheering.

"You, come here," I said as I beckoned him with my whole arm.

Aiden smiled and climbed inside of the octagon, then made his way over to me. "Congratulations, baby. I knew you could do it."

I grabbed him by his face. "With you in my life, there's nothing we can't accomplish." I kissed him in front of everyone. The crowd erupted even more; there were some boos, but there were also some cheers, and that was good. Of course, it could have been all boos and I wouldn't have given a shit, but it was nice to know there was some support out there. I pulled away and hugged Aiden close to me as we continued to celebrate.

Soon, we had the official ceremony of declaring me the winner and I stood there, proud as the referee wrapped my championship belt back around my waist, where it belonged. Of course, I had to shower and dress in time for the post-fight interview. I concluded that as fast as I could and when I got back to my hotel, Aiden was waiting on me.

There he was, naked on the bed. "Welcome back, Champ."

Oh hell yeah, life was better than a motherfucker. I smiled as I walked over to him, shedding my clothes along the way. "Are you ready for this dick I'm about to give you?"

"Bring it," he said, then licked his lips.

"Just know, you asked for it. I don't want to hear any complaints in the morning about why you can't walk right."

"Stop talking shit and put your words into action."

"That ass is mine." I pointed at it.

"Come get it." Aiden smirked and winked.

"Oh, hell yeah," I grinned and claimed what was mine for the second time tonight.

EPILOGUE

Aiden

Six months later...

CELEBRATING WITH MACIO IN THE OCTAGON AFTER A WIN NEVER got old. The feelings that came over me when he pulled me to him for a victory hug and a kiss for the world to witness were nearly indescribable. If forced to a pick a phrase, I'd go with deliriously happy.

I'd heard Macio referred to as an undisputed fighter many times since he first entered the ring, but he became so much more – a true champion. I watched him grow, not only as an athlete, but as a man who was proud of who he was and who he loved. Over the past few months, he became even more involved with LGBT shelters and charities. He was making lasting impacts on people's lives that would last for decades after he hung up his gloves and he did it because it felt right, not for any kind of notoriety. In fact, the spotlight made him very uncomfortable, which made the fact that he was being honored for Ringside's courage award quite hilarious.

"I can't believe I have to wear this monkey suit," Macio groused while trying to fix his bowtie. "Did you rig this award?" he asked for the tenth time. He wasn't the only one bitching that my boyfriend was receiving the honor. There were plenty of people who were upset that their preferred nominee didn't win and speculated that it was because of me that Macio won.

"You know that I didn't," I replied patiently, also for the tenth time. I went to him and pushed his fumbling hands away from the tie and fixed it myself while he poked fun of me for knowing how to properly tie a bowtie in the first place. That remark led into another one about my loafers. I ignored his comments and said, "You know I'd never put you in a position that made you uncomfortable."

Macio wrapped both arms around me and held me tight against him once I was finished. "All your talk about positions is making me horny," he growled before nipping my ear with his sharp teeth.

I snorted, then replied with, "You don't need an excuse to be horny, Champ. That's a constant thing." I stood back and ran my hands over his shoulders that looked a mile wild in the classic black tuxedo jacket. His beauty never failed to take my breath away. *Mine.* "Besides, I can't wait to strip you out of this tux." Hell, I'd been imagining it the moment he started to dress.

"I was hoping to save this tux for a special occasion," Macio said.

"What in the world could be more special than receiving this honor?" I asked him.

Macio reached inside his tuxedo jacket and pulled out a small box in a well-known shade of blue. "As special as tonight's award is, I was hoping to wear this tux on the night you permanently joined your life with mine."

"Macio…" I covered my mouth with my hands as tears stung the back of my eyes.

"So, I decided this tux would be the one I wore when I asked you to marry me instead. I'll buy a new one for our wedding." Macio lowered himself to one knee in front of me and opened the box to reveal two matching titanium rings. "Aiden James, will you marry me?"

"Yes!" I nodded vigorously to emphasize my words. Macio slid a ring on my finger and rose to his feet. I removed the one from the box that matched mine and slid it on the ring finger of his left hand. "They're beautiful," I said, looking at our hands.

"Titanium is strong, like our love," Macio explained.

The searing kiss we shared almost made us late for the award banquet. I sat proudly in my seat and listened to my fiancé give a speech that was filled with humor, humility, and compassion. I was in awe that he was going to be my husband.

Much later, after the banquet and celebration sex, I took off my ring to marvel over the beautiful, masculine cut and noticed the engraving on the inside. I tilted the ring toward the light so I could read it better.

Our love is undisputed.

THE END!

ACKNOWLEDGMENTS

Nicholas and Aimee would like to thank Heidi Ryan for working so hard to make the book shine. They'd also like to thank Jay Aheer and Stacey Blake for making the exterior and interior of the book look so beautiful.

As always, they wanted to thank their readers for all the love and support they've given them over the years. Without you, this collaboration wouldn't have happened.

ABOUT AIMEE NICOLE WALKER

I am a wife and mother to three kids, three dogs, and a cat. When I'm not dreaming up stories, I like to lose myself in a good book, cook or bake. I'm a girly tomboy who paints her fingernails while watching sports and yelling at the referees. I will always choose the book over the movie. I believe in happily-ever-after. Love inspires everything that I do. Music keeps me sane.

I'd love to hear from you.

You can reach me at:
Twitter - twitter.com/AimeeNWalker
Facebook – www.facebook.com/aimeenicole.walker
Blog – AimeeNicoleWalker.blogspot.com

ABOUT NICHOLAS BELLA

About me? Hmmm, I'm just a person with a wild imagination and a love for words who was sitting around the house one day and said, "Why hasn't anyone written a book like this before?". As with every storyteller, I wanted to share mine with the world. I like my erotica dark, gritty, sexy… and even a little raunchy. I'm not afraid to go there and I hope you aren't afraid to go there with me. When I'm not writing, I love watching movies and TV shows, clubbing, biking, and hanging out with family and friends. I love life.

I'd love to hear from you, feel free to send me a shout out!

You can reach me at:
Twitter – twitter.com/AuthorNickBella
Facebook – facebook.com/authornickbella
Website - www.nicholasbella.com